Janet Evanovich

BY JANET EVANOVICH

THE STEPHANIE PLUM NOVELS

One for the Money

Two for the Dough

Three to Get Deadly

Four to Score

High Five

Hot Six

Seven Up

Hard Eight

To the Nines

Ten Big Ones

Eleven on Top

Twelve Sharp

Lean Mean Thirteen

Fearless Fourteen

Finger Lickin' Fifteen

Sizzling Sixteen

Smokin' Seventeen

Explosive Eighteen

Notorious Nineteen

Takedown Twenty

THE FOX AND O'HARE NOVELS

with Lee Goldberg

The Heist

The Chase

THE BETWEEN THE NUMBERS NOVELS

Visions of Sugar Plums

Plum Lovin'

Plum Lucky

Plum Spooky

THE LIZZY AND DIESEL NOVELS

Wicked Appetite

Wicked Business

THE ALEXANDRA BARNABY NOVELS

Metro Girl

Motor Mouth

Trouble Maker (graphic novel)

NONFICTION

How I Write

TAKEDOWN TWENTY

TAKEDOWN TWENTY

A STEPHANIE PLUM NOVEL

Janet Evanovich

BANTAM BOOKS NEW YORK

Published in the United States by Bantam Books, an imprint of The Random House Publishing Group, a division of Random House LLC, a Penguin Random House Company, New York.

Bantam Books and the House colophon are registered trademarks of Random House LLC.

ISBN 978-0-345-54288-5
eBook ISBN 978-0-345-54290-8

Printed in the United States of America on acid-free paper

www.bantamdell.com

2 4 6 8 9 7 5 3 1

First Edition

TAKEDOWN TWENTY

ONE

IT WAS LATE at night and Lula and I had been staking out Salvatore Sunucchi, better known as Uncle Sunny, when Lula spotted Jimmy Spit. Spit had his prehistoric Cadillac Eldorado parked on the fringe of the Trenton public housing projects, half a block from Sunucchi's apartment, and he had the trunk lid up.

"Hold on here," Lula said. "Jimmy's open for business, and it looks to me like he got a trunk full of handbags. I might need one of them. A girl can never have too many handbags."

Minutes later, Lula was examining a purple Brahmin bag studded with what Spit claimed were Swarovski crystals. "Are you sure this is a authentic Brahmin bag?" Lula asked Spit. "I don't want no cheap-ass imitation."

"I have it on good authority these are the real deal," Spit

said. "And just for you I'm only charging ten bucks. How could you go wrong?"

Lula slung the bag over her shoulder to take it for a test drive, and a giraffe loped past us. It continued on down the road, turning at Sixteenth Street and disappearing into the darkness.

"I didn't see that," Lula said.

"I didn't see that neither," Spit said. "You want to buy this handbag or what?"

"That was a giraffe," I said. "It turned the corner at Sixteenth Street."

"Probably goin' the 7-Eleven," Spit said. "Get a Slurpee."

A black Cadillac Escalade with tinted windows and a satellite dish attached to the roof sped past us and hooked a left at Sixteenth. There was the sound of tires screeching to a stop, then gunfire and an ungodly shriek.

"Not only didn't I see that giraffe," Spit said, "but I also didn't see that car or hear that shit happening."

He grabbed the ten dollars from Lula, slammed the trunk lid shut, and took off.

"They better not have hurt that giraffe," Lula said. "I don't go with that stuff."

I looked over at her. "I thought you didn't see the giraffe."

"I was afraid it might have been the 'shrooms on my pizza last night what was making me see things. I mean it's not every day you see a giraffe running down the street."

My name is Stephanie Plum, and I work as a bond enforcement officer for Vincent Plum Bail Bonds. Lula is the office file clerk, but more often than not she's my wheelman. Lula is a couple inches shorter than I am, a bunch of pounds bigger, and her skin is a lot darker. She's a former streetwalker who gave up her corner but kept her wardrobe. She favors neon colors and animal prints, and she fearlessly tests the limits of spandex. Today her brown hair was streaked with shocking pink to match a tank top that barely contained the bounty God had bestowed on her. The tank top stopped a couple inches above her skintight, stretchy black skirt, and the skirt ended a couple inches below her ass. I'd look like an idiot if I dressed like Lula, but the whole neon pink and spandex thing worked for her.

"I gotta go see if the giraffe's okay," Lula said. "Those guys in the Escalade might have been big game poachers."

"This is Trenton, New Jersey!"

Lula was hands on hips. "So was that a giraffe, or what? You don't think it's big game?"

Since Lula was driving we pretty much went where Lula wanted to go, so we jumped into her red Firebird and followed the giraffe.

There was no Escalade or giraffe in sight when we turned the corner at Sixteenth, but a guy was lying facedown in the middle of the road, and he wasn't moving.

"That don't look good," Lula said, "but at least it's not the giraffe."

Lula stopped just short of the guy in the road, and we got out and took a look.

"I don't see no blood," Lula said. "Maybe he's just takin' a nap."

"Yeah, or maybe that thing implanted in his butt is a tranquilizer dart."

"I didn't see that at first, but you're right. That thing's big enough to take down a elephant." Lula toed the guy, but he still didn't move. "What do you suppose we should do with him?"

I punched 911 into my phone and told them about the guy in the road. They suggested I drag him to the curb so he didn't get run over, adding that they'd send someone out to scoop him up.

While we waited for the EMS to show, I rifled the guy's pockets and learned that his name was Ralph Rogers. He had a Hamilton Township address, and he was fifty-four years old. He had a MasterCard and seven dollars.

The EMS truck slid in without a lot of fanfare. Two guys got out and looked at Ralph, who was still on his stomach with the dart stuck in him.

"That's not something you see every day," the taller of the two guys said.

"The dart might have been meant for the giraffe," Lula told them. "Or maybe he's one of them shape-shifters, and he used to *be* the giraffe."

The two men went silent for a beat, probably trying to decide if they should get the butterfly net out for Lula.

"It's a full moon," the shorter one finally said.

The other guy nodded, and they loaded Ralph into the truck and drove off.

"Now what?" Lula asked me. "We going to look some more

for Uncle Sunny, or we going to have a different activity, like getting a pizza at Pino's?"

"I'm done. I'm going home. We'll pick up Sunny's trail tomorrow."

Truth is, I was going home to a bottle of champagne I had chilling in my fridge. It had been left on my kitchen counter a couple days before as partial payment for a job I'd done for my friend and sometime employer Ranger. The champagne had come with a note suggesting that Ranger needed a date. Okay, so Ranger is hot, and luscious, and magic in bed, but that didn't totally compensate for the fact that the last time I'd been Ranger's date I'd been poisoned. I'd been saving the champagne for a special occasion, and it seemed like seeing a giraffe running down the street qualified.

Lula drove me back to the bonds office, I picked up my car, and twenty minutes later I was in my apartment, leaning against the kitchen counter, guzzling champagne. I was watching my hamster, Rex, run on his wheel when Ranger walked in.

Ranger doesn't bother with trivial matters like knocking, and he isn't slowed down by a locked door. He owns an elite security firm that operates out of a seven-story stealth office building located in the center of Trenton. His body is perfect, his moral code is unique, his thoughts aren't usually shared. He's in his early thirties, like me, but his life experience adds up to way beyond his years. He's of Latino heritage. He's former Special Forces. He's sexy, smart, sometimes scary, and frequently overprotective of me. He was currently armed and wearing black fatigues with the Rangeman logo on his sleeve. That meant he was on patrol duty, most likely filling in for one of his men.

"Working tonight?" I asked him.

"Taking the night shift for Hal." He looked at my glass. "Are you drinking champagne out of a beer mug?"

"I don't have any champagne glasses."

"Babe."

"Babe" covers a lot of ground for Ranger. It can be the prelude to getting naked. It can be total exasperation. It can be a simple greeting. Or, as in this case, it can just mean I've amused him.

Ranger smiled ever so slightly and took a step closer to me.

"Stop," I said. "Don't come any closer. The answer is *no.*"

His brown eyes locked onto me. "I didn't ask a question."

"You were going to."

"True."

"Well, don't even think about it, because I'm not going to do it."

"I could change your mind," he said.

"I don't think so."

Okay, truth is Ranger *could* change my mind. Ranger can be very persuasive.

Ranger's cellphone buzzed, he checked the text message and moved to the door. "I have to go. Give me a call if you change your mind."

"About what?"

"About anything."

"Okay, wait a minute. I want to know the question."

"No time to explain it," Ranger said. "I'll pick you up tomorrow at seven o'clock. A little black dress would be good. Something moderately sexy."

And he was gone.

TWO

I DRAGGED MYSELF out of bed as the morning sun poured through the opening in my bedroom curtains. I showered, blasted my shoulder-length curly brown hair with the blow dryer, and pulled the whole mess back into a ponytail. I brushed my teeth, swiped some mascara onto my lashes, and went with cherry lip gloss.

Hunting down felons for my cousin Vinnie isn't a great-paying job, but I make my own hours and I wear what's comfy. A girly T-shirt, jeans, sneakers, handcuffs, and pepper spray, and I'm good to go.

I gave Rex fresh water and a Ritz cracker, grabbed the messenger bag I use as a purse, and took off for the office. I live in a second-floor one-bedroom, one-bath, no-frills apartment on the outskirts of Trenton. It's not a slum, but it's not high rent either. Mostly my apartment building is filled with seniors who take advantage of the early-bird special at the nearby diner and live for the moment they'll qualify for a handicap sticker on their car. They're all heavily armed, so the property is relatively safe, if you don't count shootings that are the result of mistaken identity due to cataracts and macular degeneration. My apartment overlooks the parking lot, which is fine by me because I can peek out once in a while to see if anyone's stolen my car.

It was a glorious Tuesday morning in the middle of summer, and traffic was light thanks to the absence of school buses. I parked in the small lot behind Vincent Plum Bail Bonds. There were four spaces, and three were already filled. My cousin Vinnie's Cadillac was there. Connie the office manager's Toyota was there. And Lula had her red Firebird there. I added my rusted-out mostly white Ford Taurus to the group and went inside.

"Uh-oh," Lula said when she saw me. "You got that look."

"What look?" I asked.

"That look like you didn't get any last night."

I went straight to the coffee machine. "I almost never get any. I'm used to it. Morelli is playing catch-up with his caseload."

Joe Morelli is a Trenton plainclothes cop working crimes-against-persons. I grew up with Morelli, lost my virginity to him, ran over him with my father's Buick in a fit of justifiable rage, and now years later he's my boyfriend. Go figure. He's a good cop. He's a terrific lover. And he's got a dog. He's six feet of hot Italian libido, with wavy black hair, a hard-toned body, and brown eyes that could set my pants on fire. He's been side-lined with a gunshot wound, but now he's back on the job, popping pain pills.

"So then how come you got that look this morning, like you need at least three donuts?" Lula asked.

"Ranger came by last night."

Lula leaned forward, eyes wide. "Say what?"

Connie looked up from her computer. "And?"

"He wanted a date."

"I'm havin' heart palpitations," Lula said. "That is one fine man. Fact is, that is the hottest man I ever saw. You did the nasty with him last night, right? I want to know everything."

"I didn't do anything with him. He wanted a date for tonight."

"Holy crap," Lula said.

"And?" Connie said.

"And I had a restless night thinking about it," I told them.

"I bet," Lula said. "If it was me I would have been burning out the motor on my intimate appliances."

I checked out the box of donuts on Connie's desk and chose a maple glazed. "Last time I agreed to be Ranger's date his friend blew himself up in my apartment."

"Yeah, but Ranger brought in a cleaning crew to get the brains and guts off the walls," Lula said. "That was real thoughtful."

"What's new?" I asked Connie. "Anything good come in for me?"

I don't get paid a salary. I make my money by retrieving

felons for Vinnie. When someone is accused of a crime they can sit in jail until trial or they can give the court a bucketload of money as a guarantee they'll return. If they don't have the money, they go to my cousin and he puts up a bond for a fee. If the bondee doesn't show for court, the court keeps Vinnie's money. This doesn't make Vinnie happy, so he sends me out to find the guy and drag him back to jail. Then I get a percentage of the money Vinnie gets back from the court.

"Nothing interesting," Connie said. "Just a couple low money bonds. Ziggy Radiewski didn't show up for court, and Mary Treetrunk didn't show up for court."

"What'd Ziggy do this time?" Lula asked.

"He relieved himself on Mrs. Bilson's dog," Connie said. "And then he mooned Mrs. Bilson. He said it was accidental, and he was a victim of temporary insanity due to alcohol poisoning."

"He probably got that right," Lula said.

"I don't care about any of those," Vinnie yelled from his inner office. "Why haven't you grabbed Uncle Sunny? He's a big bond. He killed a guy, for crissake. What the hell are you waiting for? Put the freakin' donut down and go to work. You think I pay you to sit around eating donuts?"

"You keep talking like that and I'm gonna come in your office and sit on you and squish you into nothing but a ugly grease spot," Lula said.

The door to Vinnie's office slammed closed and the bolt thunked into place.

"He's not having a good morning," Connie said. "We're running in the red, and Harry is unhappy."

Harry the Hammer owns the bonds office. He also happens to be Vinnie's father-in-law. Legend has it Harry got his name when he was a mob enforcer and persuaded customers to meet their financial obligations on time by hammering nails into their various body parts. I assume this was back in the days before pneumatic nail guns became the tool of choice for carpenters and wiseguys.

I took the two new files from Connie and stuffed them into my messenger bag.

"We did a four-hour stakeout on Uncle Sunny last night," I said to Connie. "The only thing that came of it was a new handbag for Lula."

"Jimmy Spit was selling Brahmins and he gave me a good price," Lula said to Connie. "I always wanted a Brahmin, and this is from their new designer Atelier line. This here's a pricey handbag."

Lula hung the handbag from her shoulder and modeled it for Connie.

"I've never seen a Brahmin bag with rhinestones," Connie said.

"That's on account of these are crystals and they're going in a new direction," Lula said. "You can tell it's a Brahmin by the little silver nameplate on it says 'Brahmin.'"

Connie looked at the nameplate. "It doesn't say 'Brahmin.' It says 'Brakmin.'"

"Hunh," Lula said, glancing down at the bag. "Must be a misspelling. Things like that happen, and it don't matter anyways, because it's a excellent bag, and it goes with my shoes."

"Maybe you need to talk to Uncle Sunny's neighbors," Connie said to me. "And his relatives. Isn't he related to Morelli?"

"He's Joe's godfather," I told her. "And he's Grandma Bella's nephew."

"Oops," Connie said. "That could be sticky."

Joe's Grandma Bella emigrated from Sicily a lot of years ago, but she still speaks with a heavy accent, she still dresses in black like an extra in *The Godfather,* and she puts curses on people who she feels have disrespected her. Probably the curses aren't real and people get boils and have their hair fall out purely by coincidence, still the woman scares the bejeezus out of me.

"It's not just Bella," I said. "Everyone loves Uncle Sunny. No one will rat on him."

"Worse than that," Lula said. "We asked at the Tip Top Deli if they knew where he was hiding, and they told us we should be ashamed to be going after Uncle Sunny. And then they wouldn't serve us lunch. And they told us never to come back. And that don't make me happy since I formerly considered their egg salad to be a important feature in my diet."

"I don't suppose you heard anything on the police band about a giraffe galloping down Sixteenth Street last night?" I asked Connie.

"No," she replied. "Was I supposed to?"

"We think we might have seen one," Lula said.

Connie raised an eyebrow.

"At least it seemed like it was a giraffe last night," Lula said. "But then when I woke up this morning I had doubts."

I chugged down my coffee, wolfed my donut, and turned to Lula. "I'm going back to Uncle Sunny's apartment building to talk to his neighbors. Are you riding along?"

"Only if I get to drive. Your radio is busted, and I need tunes."

THREE

UNCLE SUNNY LIVED on the second floor of a four-story brownstone walk-up on the corner of Fifteenth and Morgan. Mindy's Nail Salon occupied the first floor and served as a front for a variety of semi-illegal activities, such as loan sharking, flesh peddling, and bookmaking—at least in Trenton they were semi-illegal. When Uncle Sunny was in residence this laundry list of illicit activities expanded to include whacking and property owner's insurance enforcement. On the surface it might seem like Sunny lived in modest surroundings, but the truth was, he owned the building. In fact, Sunny owned the entire block. And his real estate holdings didn't stop there.

"I don't get it," Lula said, parking at the curb. "What's so special about this guy? Why's everybody love him?"

"He's charming," I said. "He's sixty-two years old, five-foot-six, and he sings Sinatra songs at weddings. He flirts with old ladies. He wears a red bow tie to funerals. On Thanksgiving and Christmas he helps out in the St. Ralph's soup kitchen. He's very generous with tips. And he's a member of the Sunucchi–Morelli family, which makes up half the Burg and sticks together no matter how much they hate one another."

And I'm pretty sure he also occasionally kills people, sets fire to businesses, and fornicates with other men's wives. None of this is especially noteworthy in Trenton, however, and it for sure can't compete with a red bow tie or the ability to croon Sinatra.

Sinatra is still big in the Burg, a working-class neighborhood in Trenton. I grew up in the Burg, and my parents, my sister and her family, and my grandmother still live there. The bonds office is just outside the Burg. St. Francis Hospital is located in the Burg. Plus there are four bakeries, twelve restaurants, five pizza parlors, a funeral home, three Italian social clubs, and there's a bar on every corner.

We stood on the sidewalk, looking up at the second-floor windows.

"I don't see nothing happening up there," Lula said.

Meantime, a balding, overweight, fiftyish man went into the nail salon and was shown into the back room.

"I bet he's gonna get the special," Lula said. "You come in before noon and you get a pedicure and a BJ for half price. Mindy wanted me to work for her back when I was a 'ho, but I declined. I didn't want to have to deal with the whole pedicure thing. I don't do feet. A girl's gotta draw a line somewhere, you see what I'm saying?"

I punched Sunny's number into my cellphone and listened to it ring. No answer. I marched into the building with Lula a step behind me. We took the stairs to the second floor and found Sunny's apartment. Easy to do since there were only two apartments on the floor. I knocked on the door and waited. Nothing. I knocked again.

"Maybe he's dead," Lula said. "He could be stretched out on the floor toes up. Probably we should go in and see."

I tried the door. Locked.

"I'd bust it in, but I got heels on," Lula said. "It wouldn't be ladylike."

I went across the hall and rang the bell. "Go away," someone yelled from inside the apartment.

"I want to talk to you," I yelled back.

The door was wrenched open, and a woman glared out at me. "What?"

"I'm looking for Uncle Sunny," I said.

"And?"

"I thought you might know where he is."

"What do I look like, his mother? Do I look like I keep track of Uncle Sunny? And anyways, what do you want with him? Are you the police?"

"Bond enforcement," I told her.

"Hey, Jake!" the woman yelled.

A big, slobbering black dog padded into view and stood behind the woman.

"Kill!" the woman said.

The dog lunged at us, Lula and I jumped back, and the dog clamped onto Lula's purse and ripped it from her shoulder.

"That's my new bag!" Lula said. "It's almost a Brahmin."

The dog shook the bag until it was dead, then he eyed Lula.

"Uh-oh," Lula said. "I don't like the way he's looking at me. I'd shoot him, but he got my gun." She cut her eyes to me. "You got a gun?"

I was slowly inching my way toward the stairs. "No," I whispered. "No gun." Not that it mattered, because I couldn't shoot a dog even if its eyes were glowing red and its head was rotating.

The dog made a move toward us, and Lula and I turned tail and ran. Lula missed a step, crashed into me, and we rolled ass over teakettle down the stairs, landing in a heap on the foyer floor.

"Lucky I ended on top of you, or I might have hurt myself," Lula said.

I hauled myself up and limped out the door. This wasn't the first time Lula and I had crash-landed at the bottom of a flight of stairs. A window opened on the second floor, Lula's purse sailed out, and the window slammed shut.

Lula retrieved the mangled bag. "At least I got my gun back," she said. "Now what are we going to do? You want to go for breakfast? I wouldn't mind having one of them breakfast sandwiches."

"Vinnie's going to hound me until I find Uncle Sunny."

"Yeah, but this looking for Uncle Sunny is making us unpopular, and I think I got a bruise from landing on you. I hear bacon is real good for healing a bruise."

I thumbed through Sunny's file. He'd been charged with second-degree murder for running over Stanley Dugan . . . twice. I suspected he'd done a lot worse to a lot of people over the years, but this time he'd been caught on video by a kid with an iPhone who'd posted it to YouTube. Since everyone who knew Stanley Dugan (including his ninety-year-old mother) hated him, the video only served to enhance Sunny's popularity.

Two men in their mid-fifties ambled out of the nail salon. They were balding, paunchy, wearing bowling shirts, pleated slacks, and pinky rings. One of the men had "Shorty" embroidered on his shirt above the breast pocket.

"Hey," Shorty said, eyeballing me. "We hear you been asking about Sunny."

"I work for his bail bonds agent," I told him. "Sunny is in violation of his bail agreement. He needs to reschedule a court date."

"Maybe he don't want to do that," Shorty said. "Maybe he got better things to do with his time."

"If he doesn't reschedule, he's considered a felon."

Shorty snickered. "Of course he's a fella. Everybody knows he's a fella. What are you, stupid or something?"

"Felon. Not fella. *Felon*. A fugitive from the law."

"Watch your mouth," Shorty said. "You don't go around calling good people like Sunny names that could tarnish his reputation. He could sue you for slandering him."

"So do you know where he is?" I asked.

"Sure. He's where he always is at this time of the day."

"And where would that be?"

"I'm not telling you. And you better back off, girlie, or I might have to get rough. I might have to shoot you or something."

"Blah, blah, blah," Lula said. "You and who else gonna do that, *Shorty*?"

"Me and him," Shorty said, gesturing to the guy next to him. "Me and Moe. Isn't that right, Moe?"

"Yeah," Moe said. "We don't like people trash-talking Sunny."

"And furthermore I don't like the way you said my name," Shorty said to Lula. "It was like you were implying I was short."

"You *are* short," Lula said. "You're short. You're going bald. And unless you just come from a bowling alley, you got no taste in clothes."

"Oh yeah? Well, you should talk," Shorty said. "You're *fat*."

Lula narrowed her eyes, rammed her fists onto her hips, and leaned forward so that she was almost nose to nose with Shorty. "Say what? Did I just hear that you think I'm fat? 'Cause that better not be the case on account of then I'd have to pound you into something looks like a hamburger pattie."

I glanced left and saw the giraffe gallop across the street a couple blocks away. "Holy cow," I said. "It's the giraffe."

Lula whipped her head around. "Where'd he go? I don't see no giraffe."

"He galloped across the street at Eighteenth."

"Gotta go," Lula said to Shorty. "Things to do."

We jumped into Lula's car, took off down the street, turned the corner at Eighteenth and cruised around, but we didn't see the giraffe.

"This is perplexing," Lula said. "It's not like he could get himself in a Subaru and drive away. I bet you couldn't even get him in a Escalade. He's a big sucker."

Morelli called on my cellphone. "Hey, Cupcake," he said. "What's doing?"

"Nothing's doing," I told him. "My boyfriend is a workaholic."

"I've got fifteen minutes free. Do you want to . . . you know?"

"Wow, fifteen whole minutes."

"Yeah, that's a minute for me and fourteen for you."

"Tempting, but I'm going to hold out for at least a half hour."

"I could throw lunch into the deal if you're up to multitasking."

"I'll meet you at Pino's for lunch, but you're going to have to take a rain check on the . . . you know."

"Better than nothing," Morelli said. "High noon."

· · ·

Morelli was already at Pino's when I walked in. He had a corner booth, and he was working his way through a bread basket. He was wearing jeans and an untucked black T-shirt that partially hid the Glock at his hip. His dark hair waved over his ears, and his brown eyes were sharp and assessing.

I slid into the booth across from him. "You have cop eyes," I said.

He pushed the bread basket my way. "That could change if you wanted to have lunch in the parking lot. Between the gunshot and the double shift I'm missing you . . . a lot."

"I miss you too."

I took a piece of bread and studied him. I've known Morelli for most of my life, and I was pretty good at reading his moods.

"There's more," I said.

Morelli nodded. "There's Ralph Rogers."

"The guy with the dart stuck in his butt. What about him?"

"He's dead."

"He was alive last time *I* saw him."

"He went into cardiac arrest at the hospital and they couldn't revive him. Apparently the dart contained some exotic kind of poison. And it contained *a lot* of it."

"Enough to take down a giraffe?"

"The toxicology report didn't cover that."

"Shocking."

"I know I'm going to regret asking, but why the interest in giraffes?"

"Lula and I were following a giraffe when we found Rogers lying in the road."

"This isn't a substance abuse issue, is it?"

"No. We really saw a giraffe. Lula was conducting some business with Jimmy Spit, and we saw a giraffe gallop past us and turn at Sixteenth Street. A black Cadillac Escalade with a satellite dish on its roof drove by seconds later, turned at Sixteenth, and there was gunfire. By the time we got to Sixteenth there was no giraffe and no Escalade. And Rogers was lying facedown in the middle of the road."

"Are you sure it was a giraffe?"

"Skinny legs with knobby knees, yellow with big brown spots, long neck. Yep, I'm pretty sure it was a giraffe. Hasn't anyone else reported seeing a giraffe in that neighborhood?"

"Not that I've heard. I'd ask dispatch, but I'd feel like an idiot."

"How's your leg? Are you in pain?"

"No pain at all. I'm loaded up with pain pills. I could set my hair on fire and I wouldn't feel it."

"Is it okay for you to be driving?"

"Yeah, they don't make me drowsy. They just make me nice and numb. Can't feel my leg. Can't feel my fingertips or my tongue."

"Good to know about your fingertips and your tongue. I'm glad we didn't waste time getting naked in the parking lot."

Morelli grinned. "I could have managed."

The waitress brought two meatball subs with extra coleslaw.

"I ordered for both of us when I got here," Morelli said. "Hope you don't mind. I'm on a tight schedule. Did Rogers say anything to you?"

I dug into my coleslaw. "No. He was stretched out with a dart in his butt. That's it."

"I don't suppose you got the license plate on the black SUV."

"Sorry, it flew past me, but how many Escalades have a satellite dish on the roof?"

"Was it a big dish, like for a news station?"

"It was a small dish, like for an idiot drug dealer or a tricked out rapper."

Morelli took a bite of his sub, and some red sauce leaked out of his mouth and ran down his chin.

"You might want to cut back on those pills," I told him.

He wiped up with his napkin. "Just in case you intend to spend the rest of your life with me, this is probably what I'm going to look like when I'm ninety."

"Is that a proposal?"

"No. I'm just saying." He stopped wiping and looked at me. "What if it *was* a proposal? Would you say yes?"

"Only one way to find out."

He smiled again. "I'm saving up for the ring."

That would have been a terrifying statement if I'd thought for a moment it was true. Morelli is just as unwilling to commit as I am.

"Something to look forward to," I said.

His smile widened.

We finished our lunch, Morelli got the check, and we slid out of the booth.

"Who's the unlucky person in your crosshairs today?" he asked.

"Uncle Sunny."

"You're kidding."

26

"He's in violation of his bond."

"Walk away from it. Let Vinnie give it to Ranger."

"Ranger doesn't do bond enforcement anymore."

Morelli wrapped his arm around me and ushered me out the door, into the sunshine. "No one is going to help you catch Sunny. And a lot of people are going to stand in your way. Some of them are vicious and crazy."

"Are you talking about your grandmother?"

"Yes. She's at the top of the list of vicious, crazy people."

I gave Morelli a sisterly kiss, got into my Taurus, and drove to my parents' house. It's not a fancy house, but it's home, and I feel safe and comfortable there.

FOUR

MY PARENTS' HOUSE is narrow, with three small bedrooms and a bath upstairs. Living room, dining room, and kitchen downstairs. The living room is filled to bursting with overstuffed furniture, end tables, ottomans, lamps, candy dishes, fake flower arrangements, and plastic bins filled with toys for my sister's kids. The sofa and all the chairs face the television. The rectangular dining room table is always set with a lace cloth and two candlesticks. The table seats eight but has been known to manage nine and a high chair. This leaves just enough space in the room for my niece to gallop around the table, pretending to be a horse. The kitchen is where all important decisions are made: what's for dinner, where should I go to college, should I have my gallbladder removed, should I go to Andy Melnik's viewing tonight or watch the Miss America pageant?

Grandma Mazur was at the door when I parked. Grandma moved in with my parents when my grandfather relocated his clogged arteries to a heavenly address. Her hair is steel gray and permed in a style that was fashionable in 1959. She stands straight as a broomstick. She likes a nip of whiskey before going to bed. And lately she's taken to wearing Pilates pants and tank tops that show the horrifying effects of gravity on slack skin. She's also a treasure trove of gossip, and she's my go-to source for underground information. She'd know things about Uncle Sunny that weren't on Connie's fact sheet.

"What a nice surprise," Grandma said. "I was hoping something interesting would come down the street. The cable is out and there's no television."

I followed Grandma to the kitchen, where my mother was making minestrone. My mother is the middle child caught between my grandmother and me. She wears her brown hair in a soft bob. Her wardrobe is conservative, heavy on slacks and cotton blouses. Her Catholic faith is strong.

"Have you eaten?" my mother asked. "We have lunch meat from Giovichinni."

"I'm good," I told her. "I had lunch with Morelli."

I set my messenger bag on the floor and pulled a chair up to the small kitchen table. Grandma brought the cookie jar over and sat opposite me. I lifted the lid and took out a Toll House cookie.

"Did you catch any bad guys today?" Grandma asked me. "Were you in any shootouts?"

"No and no."

I didn't look over at my mother for fear I'd see her rolling her eyes and reaching for the whiskey bottle. My mother isn't big on shootouts.

"I'm looking for Uncle Sunny," I said. "He skipped out on his bond."

"He's a slippery one," Grandma said. "Are you having any luck?"

"No. Lula and I staked out his apartment, but we didn't see any sign of him."

Grandma ate a cookie and helped herself to another. "I'd stake out the girlfriend."

"Sunny has a girlfriend?"

"He's been seeing Rita Raguzzi for ten years," Grandma said. "He's a real ladies' man, if you know what I mean, but word is he keeps his toothbrush at Rita's house. He was seeing Rita years before his wife died."

My mother and grandmother made the sign of the cross.

"His wife should rest in peace," my mother said. "She was a saint."

There were Raguzzis sprinkled all over the Burg. Emilio Raguzzi owned an auto body shop, and he and his wife lived across the street from Morelli's mom. His two sons also lived in the Burg. I didn't know Rita personally, but I'd heard she was living in Hamilton Township.

"I don't know why you can't get some other job," my mother said to me. "Why can't you get a job in a bank or a hair salon?

I heard there was an opening at the deli on Hamilton. You could learn to be a butcher."

My mouth dropped open and a piece of cookie fell out. I tried to stuff a chicken once and almost fainted. The thought of manhandling raw meat all day was enough to give me projectile vomiting.

"I hear butchers make good money," my mother said. "They work good hours and everybody likes them."

"And you'd get to be a real expert with a meat cleaver," Grandma said. "You never know when that could come in handy."

"I don't think I'm butcher material," I said. "And I sort of like my job. I meet interesting people."

"You meet *criminals*," my mother said. "And now you're going after the most popular man in the Burg. Already I'm getting phone calls that you should leave Uncle Sunny alone. Everyone *loves* him."

I took another cookie. "You just told me he was fooling around even when his wife was alive. That's not a nice guy. And besides, he kills people."

"He don't usually kill people anymore," Grandma said. "He's getting on in years. He's got peeps who do that now."

"What about Stanley Dugan? Sunny is accused of murdering Stanley Dugan."

"It could have been an accident," Grandma said.

"He ran over him twice! And then Sunny got out and choked Dugan. There was a witness who videoed it all on his iPhone."

"Well, Sunny shouldn't have run over Stanley," Grandma said, "but you gotta give him something for still being able to put in a day's work."

"I have a ham for tonight," my mother said to me. "You could invite Joseph for dinner."

I scraped my chair back. "That would be nice, but I'm working tonight."

"I bet you're chasing down a killer," Grandma said. "Am I right?"

"I don't very often chase down killers," I told her. *Unless you count Uncle Sunny.*

"Then what's up?" she asked. "Are you after a second-story guy? A car thief? A terrorist?"

"I have a date with Ranger, but I'm pretty sure it's work."

"I wouldn't mind that kind of work," Grandma said. "He's hot."

My mother pressed her lips together. Ranger wasn't marriage material. Ranger wasn't going to give her grandchildren . . . at least not legitimate ones.

"Gotta go," I told them. "Things to do."

· · ·

I called Connie from my car and asked her for a home address for Rita Raguzzi.

"I'll only give it to you if you come collect Lula," Connie said. "She's driving me nuts. We need to ration her coffee in the morning. She won't stop talking about giraffes."

I swung by the office and retrieved Lula.

"Here's the information you wanted," she said, handing me a computer printout and buckling herself in. "What's up with this Raguzzi?"

"Grandma says Uncle Sunny keeps his toothbrush at her house."

"Grandma knows everything. Did you ask her about the giraffe?"

"The giraffe didn't come up."

"How could the giraffe not come up? We got a giraffe in Trenton. It's practically a miracle. And it's not like he's some plain-ass horse or cow. A giraffe's special. It's the tallest animal. It's taller than a elephant. A giraffe can get to be nineteen feet tall. And his legs could be six foot. Did you know that?"

"No. I didn't know that."

"A giraffe could run thirty-five miles an hour, and they could weigh twenty-eight hundred pounds. And here's the good part: He got a tongue could measure twenty-one inches. Bet Mrs. Giraffe likes that one."

"That's a big tongue."

"Freakin' A. In the wild a giraffe lives about twenty-five years, but I think running around Trenton could shorten a giraffe lifespan. I'm worried about poor Kevin."

"Who's Kevin?"

"The giraffe. I named him Kevin."

I scanned the file on Rita. She was fifty-one years old, twice divorced, indeed living in Hamilton Township. She worked out of a downtown Trenton office as a realtor.

"I don't suppose you want to go look for the giraffe," Lula said.

"What would we do if we found him?"

"We could talk to him. He might be lonely. And we could make sure he's getting something to eat. There's not a whole lot of trees with nice juicy leaves in the neighborhood he picked out."

"Surely his owner has found him by now."

"Maybe his owner don't want him. Maybe he's an orphan giraffe. Like cats that go wandering around and don't have a home. What do you call them cats?"

"Feral."

"Yeah, this here could be a feral giraffe."

I looked at my watch. "We can take a fast drive down Morgan and scope out the side streets, but then I need to follow up on Rita Raguzzi."

"That works for me. I've just gotta make sure Kevin isn't laying in the road with a dart stuck in his butt like Ralph Rogers. Lucky for Ralph that was only a tranquilizer dart."

I nodded. "Lucky him," I said, thinking this probably wasn't a good time to tell Lula that Ralph Rogers was dead.

I took Hamilton to Olden and turned off at Morgan. Lula powered her window down so she could listen for giraffe noises, and I cruised up and down the streets.

"Hold on," Lula said. "What's that up ahead? Stop the car! I see giraffe poop."

I jerked to a stop, and we squinted at the mound of brown

stuff that was half on the sidewalk and half in the gutter about ten feet in front of us.

"How do you know it's giraffe poop?" I asked Lula.

"I saw a giraffe taking a poop on YouTube. Once you see giraffe poop, you don't forget it."

Lula got out, took a closer look, and returned to the car.

"It's pretty fresh," she said. "I bet it's only about a hour old."

"You know that by looking at it?"

"It's my professional opinion. We should get out of the car and look on foot. The little guy must be hiding somewhere."

"He's not a little guy, and there's nowhere he could hide here. You'd need a grain silo to hide a giraffe."

We were on Sixteenth Street. A door opened toward the end of the block, and Moe stepped out and lit up. He sucked in some tar and nicotine, looked our way, and gave his head a small disgusted shake, as if our presence was ruining his euphoric lung-destroying experience. He stubbed out his cigarette and sauntered over to my car.

"See, here's the thing," Moe said, looking in my window. "It's actually unhealthy for your health that you should be in this neighborhood."

"We were looking for the giraffe," Lula said.

"You shouldn't be looking for that, either," Moe said. "It's all detrimental to your well-being."

"Do you know the giraffe?" Lula asked.

"Not personally," Moe said.

"Move out of the way," I said to Moe. "We're looking for Sunny, and I think he's in that house."

"It happens he isn't in that house," Moe said. "And you're not looking there anyway." He pulled a gun and shot two rounds into my back door. "I'd hate to think that could be your head."

"You got a lot of nerve doing that to her car," Lula said. "You're gonna hear from her insurance company."

Moe stepped back and looked at the Taurus. "You got insurance on this?"

I blew out a sigh. "No."

"How about life insurance?" he asked me. "You got any of that?"

"No."

"Then you should be extra careful, girlie."

I put the car in gear and drove away.

"He got a attitude issue," Lula said. "If you ask me, he could use a personality adjustment."

"Do you think Sunny *is* in that house?"

"We could go around back and do some investigating."

I drove around the block and came back down the alley that ran behind the Sixteenth Street buildings. We counted off houses and stopped three from the end. I moved up a house and pulled in behind an Econoline van.

"We gonna be peeping Toms?" Lula asked.

"Yes."

A silver Toyota sedan drove past us and parked behind the house. A woman got out and took two brown grocery bags from the backseat. She was in her forties, clearly ate a lot of pasta, and needed a new hairdresser. The back door opened, and Moe came out and took the grocery bags. They both went into the house and closed the door.

"That's sweet," Lula said. "He came out to help with the bags. I bet that's Mrs. Moe."

So probably we'd found Moe's house, and chances weren't good that Sunny was holed up there.

"Let's check out Rita Raguzzi," I said to Lula.

I backtracked on Olden and headed for Hamilton Township. Rita Raguzzi lived in a residential neighborhood of single-family houses that had been developed in the seventies. Yards were large and lawns were green. Homes were comfortable but not luxurious. Raguzzi's house was a split-level with an attached garage. Convenient for sneaking a man in and out when he was someone else's husband. There was a black Mercedes in the driveway. It was the economy model, if there is such a thing.

"Looks to me like someone's home," Lula said. "Maybe Uncle Sunny's here, walking around in his underwear."

I thought that was doubtful but not impossible.

"You want me to sneak around and snoop while you ring the doorbell?" Lula asked.

"Sure."

I rang the doorbell, and Lula crept around the side of the house, walking tiptoed so her four-inch spike-heel Manolo knockoffs wouldn't sink into the grass.

A woman opened the door and looked out at me. "What?"

She was in her late forties to early fifties. Her complexion was Mediterranean and her hair was platinum, cut short with one side tucked behind her ear and the other side dramatically sweeping across her forehead and partially obscuring her eye. She was wearing red patent-leather stiletto heels and a little red dress that showed a lot of cleavage and a lot of leg, and had a lot of spandex in it.

"Rita Raguzzi?" I asked.

"Yeah, and unless you want to buy or sell a house I haven't got time. I'm late for a showing."

I gave her my card. "I'm looking for Sunny."

"Stephanie Plum. I thought I recognized you. Aren't you engaged to Joe Morelli?"

"Not exactly. Are you engaged to Sunny?"

"Not exactly."

"So we have something in common."

She did a fast scan of my jeans and sneakers and crappy car at the curb. "The only thing we have in common is an interest in Salvatore Sunucchi. And our interests aren't compatible. You want to lock him up, and I want to lock him down."

"Lock him down?"

"Marriage, stupid." Raguzzi narrowed her eyes at me. "I've got a ten-year investment in this goat, and *nothing* is going to stand between me and his offshore bank accounts and Trenton real estate. I'm a fraction of an inch away from a ring on my finger."

"Won't he want a pre-nup?"

38

"You get a pre-nup in case of divorce. I'm not planning on a divorce. I'm planning on being a widow."

"You mean because he's older than you?"

"I mean because he has a bad heart. I figure all I have to do is load him up with Viagra and invite a friend over for a three-some."

"I didn't know he had a bad heart."

"Yeah, he could go at any minute, so back off, because hanging out while Sunny sits in jail and maybe croaks isn't going to work for me."

"He's not going to sit in jail and croak. I'll take him in, he'll get bonded out again, and you can get married while he waits for his court date to come around."

"He was lucky to get bonded out the first time. The judge who set the bond is on vacation and, due to a large windfall of cash, might never come back, and Sunny might not have so much luck at getting another sympathetic judge."

"Hard to believe," I said.

She shrugged. "It's a crapshoot."

I looked over her shoulder, into the house. "I don't suppose he's here."

"No. And it's a good thing, because if he was here and you tried to apprehend him, I might panic over the home invasion and accidentally empty a clip into you."

"Then *you* would be in jail."

"Only if they found your body. And the probability would be slim to none."

I believed her. Sunny was good at making people disappear.

"Okey dokey," I said. "Good talk. You have my card. I get paid dead or alive, so if Sunny drops dead from whatever, I'd appreciate a call."

"Yeah, I'll be sure to do that. You'll be next in line, right after my dog groomer."

Lula was already in the car when I slid behind the wheel.

"Well?" she asked.

"I don't think she's going to be helpful."

"I looked in all the windows, and I didn't see no sign of Sunny. She got a nice house, though. Everything looked new and neat. I bet she got a cleaning lady."

I put the car in gear and headed for the office.

"I sure would like a cleaning lady," Lula said. "Wouldn't you like to have a cleaning lady?"

I have a small one-bedroom, one-bath apartment I share with a hamster. I have the bare minimum in furniture, one fry pan, one pot, and once a month I borrow my mother's vacuum cleaner. I suspect a cleaning lady would be overkill.

"You know what the first thing I'd have a cleaning lady do?" Lula said. "Baseboards. I hate doing baseboards. Most people would probably say they wanted the cleaning lady to do the toilet, but not me. It'd be baseboards."

I wasn't sure if my apartment even *had* baseboards. "I don't spend a lot of time in my apartment."

"Yeah, but when you're there you want it to be your favorite spot, right? It has to reflect your personality. Like, wall treatment is important. It gotta put you in a good mood. That's why my walls are orange. Orange is a good all-purpose color. It's the new neutral. And it goes good with my *favorite* color, which is leopard. I did a lot of accessorizing with leopard. I re-covered my most comfy chair in leopard, and I got a leopard bedspread. Now, if we want to talk about *your* apartment, it's pretty bare-ass. You might want me to help you redecorate someday being that it's one of my hobbies."

"I'll think about it."

"It could even be a bonding experience."

"You don't think we're bonded enough?"

"There's all kinds of bonding," Lula said. "This would be decorator bonding. We never done that before."

FIVE

CONNIE LOOKED UP from her computer when Lula and I walked into the bonds office. "How'd it go?"

"We got skunked for the day," Lula said. "We met the girl-friend, but we didn't see no Sunny."

"You should try later tonight," Connie said. "He has to be staying somewhere, and it obviously isn't in his apartment on Fifteenth Street."

"Stephanie got a hot date tonight," Lula said. "She can't be staking out Sunny. She gotta be concentrating on Ranger."

"It's not a date," I said. "It's work." I was almost certain of it.

A black shadow scuttled past the large plate glass window that faced the street, and we all sucked in air.

"What was that?" Lula asked. "That better not be what I'm thinking it was, because I'm thinking it was something scares the heck out of me."

The front door banged open, and Joe's Grandma Bella marched in. "I thought I would find you here," she said, glaring at me.

Her gray hair was pulled back into a bun. Her brows were thick and black. Her eyes were fierce, like the eyes of an eagle about to snatch up an unsuspecting rabbit and rip it to shreds.

"I put the eye on you!" Bella said, pointing her finger at me.

Connie ducked down behind her desk, and Lula jumped away and pressed herself against the wall.

"You're not supposed to be giving people the eye," I said to Bella. "I'm going to tell Joe's mother on you."

"Joe's mother give you good too," Bella said. "You no friend of this family. You hunt down Sunny."

"It's my job."

"*My* job to give you the eye. Stop you in your tracks." She scrunched up her face. "You ready?"

I blew out a sigh. "Yeah."

Bella pulled her lower eyelid down with her finger and stared at me.

"Okay," she said, releasing the lid. "I got you for sure. I give you a big one." She shook her finger at me. "You get new job."

She whirled around, marched out the door, and stalked down the street.

"I think I wet my pants," Lula said.

Connie came out from behind her desk. "That is one crazy old lady."

"So what did she do to you?" Lula asked me. "Do you feel any different?"

"No."

"Well, I don't see your teeth falling out yet. And you haven't grown a tail like a donkey," Lula said. "That's gotta be a good sign."

I hiked my messenger bag up onto my shoulder. "There's no such thing as the eye."

"Sure," Lula said. "We know that. But just in case, you might want to stop by the church and burn a candle or something."

. . .

It was a little after five when I got home. I hung my bag on a hook in the foyer and went into the kitchen. I said hello to Rex, asked him about his day, and gave him another Ritz cracker. Being that Rex lives in an aquarium and not much goes on, he didn't have a lot to say.

I looked around my kitchen and living room and had to admit there might be something to Lula's assessment of my decorating. I really hadn't done much to spruce things up after the last explosion when Ranger's friend blew himself up in my foyer. I added *Decorate apartment to make it a special place* to my mental to-do list, then tabled the project for a better time.

I wasn't sure if my Ranger date involved dinner, so I made myself a peanut butter and olive sandwich. I know this combination looks odd what with the lumps from the olives, but it contains major food groups, it doesn't involve cooking, and the olives keep the peanut butter from sticking to the roof of your mouth.

I took a shower and brushed my hair out into a bunch of soft curls that skimmed my shoulders. I went with an extra swipe of mascara, some smudgy liner, and shiny lip gloss. I had a closet full of jeans and T-shirts, but my choices for dresses were limited. I had a very sexy red dress with a swirly skirt, a professional-looking suit, a blue dress I wore to family functions, and a black dress that was moderately to pretty damn sexy.

I settled on the black dress, tugged it over my hips, zipped it up, and checked in the mirror to make sure my boobs weren't falling out too much. I shoved my feet into black spike-heel pumps and transferred essentials from my messenger bag to a small red evening clutch.

I was thinking if this was work-related I probably should take my gun, but the gun wouldn't fit in the clutch, and truth is, I didn't have any bullets anyway.

I felt a change in air pressure, got a hot flash, and Ranger knocked once and opened the door to my apartment. He was wearing a perfectly tailored black suit, and a black shirt open at the neck. He looked me up and down, and the corners of his mouth hinted at a smile. I assumed this meant he liked the dress.

We were silent in the hall and elevator, Ranger being only slightly more talkative than my hamster. We crossed the parking lot to his black Porsche 911 Turbo S, and he opened the door for me. It was a great car, but not the easiest to enter in a tight short skirt and heels. I grabbed my hem with both hands and managed to get in without my skirt riding up to my belly button. Not that it would matter entirely, since Ranger had already seen my belly button. Still, he hadn't seen it lately, and I thought it was a good idea to keep it that way.

"Where are we going?" I asked.

He drove out of the lot and turned left. "We're going to a viewing at the funeral home on Hamilton."

"Is that the whole date?"

"Yes. Unless you want it to be more."

"Why did you tell me to wear a sexy dress?"

"I wanted to have something to look at besides the deceased."

"So I'm just eye candy?"

"The eye candy is a bonus. This is a viewing for Melvina Gillian. Does the name mean anything to you?"

"She was murdered. Her body was found in a Dumpster a couple weeks ago."

"She was found ten days ago. She was kept on ice until now, pending the autopsy. Rangeman provides security for her son, Ruppert. He asked me to look into her death."

"Aren't the police investigating?"

"Yes, but Ruppert wanted a private investigation as well. I don't usually do this sort of thing, but Ruppert is an important client."

"Do you have any leads?"

"In the past eighteen months three women have been found in Dumpsters in Trenton. They were all robbed and strangled. They were all in their seventies. All lived alone, in different parts of the city. So far the police haven't identified any suspects."

"I knew one of the women. Lois Fratelli. She lived in the Burg a block over from my parents."

"Did you go to her funeral?"

"No, but I went to the viewing with Grandma."

"Anyone of interest there?"

"Not that I noticed. It was packed. There are a lot of Fratellis in Trenton, and there are always lots of people who come out for a murder."

"Like your grandmother?"

"Grandma comes out to *all* the viewings. She gets extra dressed up for a murder."

Ranger pulled into the small lot attached to the funeral home.

"You'll never get a spot here," I said. "This lot fills up at six o'clock for a murder."

He beeped his horn and a black Rangeman SUV pulled out of a space. Ranger parked in the space, and the SUV drove away.

"So it sounds to me like I could have sent you to this viewing with your grandmother," he said, cutting the engine, "and *I* could have taken a night off."

"Yes, but then you would have missed seeing me in this dress."

Ranger smiled. "True."

"Why do you want me at this viewing?"

"I'm looking for a common thread. You know most of the people here. They talk to you. I want you to move around and see if you can find a connection between Melvina and Lois. Mutual friends, shared interests, a stranger who suddenly entered their life."

I got out of the Porsche, tugged my dress down, and rearranged my breasts. "What will you be doing while I'm talking to people?"

"I'll be watching you."

The funeral home had originally been a large Victorian house with a wraparound porch. Over the years it had changed hands several times and extensions had been added. This evening, men were gathered in groups on the porch. The vestibule inside was filled with women milling around the tea and cookies, then quietly maneuvering their way into the crush of people already in the viewing room. The air was heavy with the smell of funeral flowers and too many overheated bodies.

"I'm two steps behind you," Ranger said. "Do your thing."

I wormed my way through the vestibule, talking to people, keeping my eyes open for murderers. I squeezed through the door to Slumber Room No. 2 and began to make my way forward toward the open casket. I spoke to Lily Kolakowski, Ann Rhinehart, Maureen Labbe, and Sheryl Stoley. Several moderately drunk men hit on me, none of them on the good side of ninety. None of them knew Melvina Gillian.

I worked the crowd to the first row of chairs facing the deceased and picked out Grandma Mazur.

"Well, for goodness sakes," she said, spotting me. "If I'd known you were coming I would have saved you a seat. I was here when they opened the doors, and I got a real good one. You sit up front like this and you don't miss a thing. I even filled my purse with cookies on the way through the lobby." She tapped her finger to her forehead. "Always thinking."

"Did you know Melvina?"

"No. Never met her, but she looks pretty good for having been thrown into a Dumpster. They do a real good job with makeup here. I was worried they might have a closed casket, and you know how I hate that, but they got her set up so she's almost lifelike."

I scanned the room for Ranger but couldn't find him.

"You should go take a look," Grandma said to me. "I especially like the shade of lipstick they got on her. I might need a lipstick like that."

Viewings weren't my favorite thing, and looking at dead people ranked even further down the list.

"I don't want to jump the line," I said.

"Nobody will mind. It's almost closing time and there's only stragglers left. All the people who really had their heart into it have gone through." Grandma got up and nudged me over to the casket. "This here's my granddaughter," she said to the man standing to one side. "She just wants to pay some fast respects."

I nodded to him, murmured my condolences, and stepped away. When Grandma and I turned back to her chair it was filled.

"Hey," Grandma said to the woman sitting in her chair. "That's my seat."

"You got up," the woman said.

"Don't matter," Grandma said. "I only got up to pay respects, and now I'm back, and I want my chair."

"You've been hogging this chair all night," the woman said. "It's my turn now."

"Oh yeah?" Grandma said. "How'd you like a punch in the nose?"

The woman glared at Grandma. "How'd you like to spend the night in jail on an assault charge?"

"I'm a poor, frail old lady," Grandma said. "Nobody's going to arrest me on *your* say-so. Besides, my niece here is almost engaged to a cop."

"Did you know Melvina?" I asked the woman.

"I saw her at Bingo sometimes. Every Wednesday I go to Bingo at the Senior Center, and Melvina would almost always be there. She was a nice person, but she was blind as a bat. She couldn't see a Bingo card if it was as big as a barn. Poor Lois Fratelli used to play Bingo there too. It's like one by one all the Bingo players are ending up in a Dumpster."

"The first one was Bitsy Muddle," Grandma said. "She played Bingo at the firehouse on Thursdays. I sat next to her a couple times. She was a Bingo demon. Nobody could keep up with her. I don't like to speak bad of the dead, but there were some who weren't unhappy to learn she wouldn't be at Bingo no more."

"Did Bitsy ever play at the Senior Center?" I asked the woman.

"Not that I can remember. I didn't know her."

"She would have stood out," Grandma said.

The lights dimmed, and bells softly chimed. The viewing was over. We filed out, and Grandma made a last stop at the cookie table.

"Do you need a ride home?" I asked her.

"No. I came with Eleanor Krautz. She was visiting Mort Kessler in Slumber Room No. 4. That's way at the end of the hall, and Eleanor don't move so fast since she had the hip replacement."

I felt a hand at my waist, and Ranger leaned in to me. "If I have to spend another ten minutes here I'll put a bullet in my brain."

"Don't you look nice in your suit," Grandma said to Ranger. "Black is a good color on you."

Eleanor Krautz pushed her way through the crowd and stage-whispered to Grandma, "Who's the hottie with your granddaughter?"

"That's Ranger," Grandma stage-whispered back at Eleanor. "I don't think Stephanie knows what to do with him."

"I'd know what to do with him," Eleanor said.

"Jeez Louise," I said. "We can hear this conversation."

Ranger looked down at me. "I could make suggestions if you're really in the dark."

I did a mental eye roll. "Your ten-minute countdown clock is ticking away," I said to Ranger.

We said goodbye to Grandma and Eleanor and slipped out

the side door that led to the parking lot. Three minutes later we were in the Porsche and headed for my apartment.

"Talk to me," Ranger said.

"I don't know if it means anything, but all of the murdered women played Bingo. Two regularly played at the Senior Center, and Bitsy Muddle played at the firehouse."

"Anything else?"

"I spoke to a lot of women while I was making my way through the lobby to the deceased, but I only spoke to one woman who knew all three. She knew them because she played Bingo five days a week. Tuesdays and Wednesdays at the Senior Center, and Thursdays and Fridays at the firehouse."

"What about Monday?" Ranger asked.

"Online Bingo."

"Did the three murder victims play online?"

"I don't know."

Ranger stopped for a light. "What about their social life? Mutual friends besides the Bingo addict?"

"The last time Melvina went to Bingo she told everyone she had a boyfriend, but no one knew his name or anything about him. It sounded like dating was unusual for her."

"Ruppert didn't mention a boyfriend," Ranger said.

"Did you go through Melvina's apartment?"

"Yes, but I didn't come up with anything. It's estimated that the time of death was around midnight. She was found early the next morning. The police sealed her apartment at ten A.M."

The thought that some creep was out there murdering

women and discarding them like garbage wasn't sitting great in my stomach.

"I'm feeling queasy," I said to Ranger. "Could you take it easy on the corners?"

"Are you sick?"

"It's been a long day, and I'm not good with the whole killing women and throwing them into Dumpsters thing."

"If it makes you feel any better, the women were all nicely wrapped in a sheet, and the killer left a note on the Dumpster each time so the women would be found."

"What did the note say?"

Ranger pulled into the parking lot to my apartment building. "'Body inside.'"

This was so completely lacking in remorse, and so impersonal, that it annoyed me more than if nothing had been left.

Ranger parked and turned to me. "How would you like to go to Bingo at the Senior Center tomorrow night?"

"Is this another date?"

"No. This is a Rangeman job with full compensation. I'd run through an active minefield before I'd *willingly* go to Bingo night at the Senior Center."

I was afraid to ask what was included in full compensation. I suspected it might be the realization of all my sexual fantasies. This was pretty darn tempting, but it wouldn't be smart.

Ranger walked me to my door. "What's the word on Bingo?"

I wasn't excited about Bingo. Been there, done that, and it wasn't wonderful. In fact, I sucked at Bingo. And the regulars were gonzo Bingo players, working thirty cards at a time. I was lucky if I could keep track of three.

"Sure," I said. "I'll go to Bingo."

It wasn't the paycheck or the promise of the doomsday orgasm that pushed me into the Bingo hall. It was the three dead women. The dead, discarded women nagged at me.

"You're doing a lot of sighing," Ranger said. "Is there a problem?"

"It's complicated."

Ranger unlocked my door, pulled me to him, and kissed me. The kiss started out gentle and finished with enough heat to raise the temperature in the hallway by ten degrees. Time stood still for a couple beats while we stared into each other's eyes and contemplated the next step.

Ranger's cellphone buzzed, he looked at the text message and punched in an answer. "That was from Tank," he said. "The control room picked up a police communication. They just found a fourth woman in a Dumpster. I'm going to check it out. The Dumpster is in the center of Trenton."

"Do you want me to go with you?"

"No. Not necessary. I'll let you know what I find."

SIX

I ROLLED OUT of bed at seven A.M., made coffee and took it into the shower with me. I got out of the shower, toweled off, and examined myself. No warts, no rash, no boils, no hemorrhoids. My hair hadn't all fallen out during the night. My teeth weren't rotting in my mouth. Not that I believed in Bella's ability to give people the eye, but still it was good to confirm that nothing hideous had happened to me while I was sleeping.

It was a little after eight when I got to the office. Lula and Connie were already there. Connie was busy on the computer, and Lula was reading *Star* magazine. They both looked up when I walked in.

"Well?" Lula asked. "Did you get any?"

I set my messenger bag on the floor and sat in one of the

uncomfortable orange plastic chairs in front of the desk. "That's confidential information."

"Hunh," Lula said to Connie. "She didn't get any."

I glanced over at Lula. "It was a business meeting."

"I wouldn't care if it was a business meeting or a meeting of aliens," Lula said. "That man is so hot I could butter him up and eat him like a ear of sweet corn."

Connie choked on her coffee, and I worked hard not to squirm in my seat.

"So where did you go on this business meeting?" Lula asked me.

"We went to the Gillian viewing. Ranger's been hired to investigate Melvina Gillian's death."

"They found another woman last night," Connie said. "Rose Walchek. Seventy-six years old. Widow. She lived in one of those little row houses on Stanton Street, by the button factory."

"Strangled?"

"It's not confirmed, but it sounds like it."

"It's bad enough that these women are murdered," I said, "but I hate that the killer throws them away."

"I know just what you mean," Lula said. "It's disrespectful. Least this guy could do is follow the mob's example and take these women out to the landfill for a proper burial."

The front door opened and Morelli limped in. He crooked his finger at me in one of those *come here* gestures. I followed him outside and around the corner of the building, where he stood hands on hips, staring at his shoes.

"And?" I said.

"Give me a minute. I'm waiting for the pain to go away. I'm off the pills, and walking is a bitch."

. "I'm sorry. Is there anything I can do to help?"

"Yeah, but we'd make a scene if we did it here."

"Anything other than that?"

"I had seven people call and tell me you were at the Gillian viewing with Ranger last night."

"Ranger's paying me to do some snooping for him. He's been asked by Ruppert Gillian to look into his mother's death."

"Ranger isn't a P.I."

"He's doing this as a favor for a good client."

"Butch Shiller is the primary on the Dumpster murders. He has no sense of humor, and he's got real bad acid reflux, so don't step on his toes."

"Good to know," I said. "Anything else?"

"Word on the street is that Sunny has a new pet project and isn't going to jail until he gets it up and running."

"What's the project?"

"No one's saying."

"Do you know where Sunny's hiding?" I asked.

"You want me to rat on my godfather?"

"Yeah."

"That'll cost you. That would be worth a night of sweaty gorilla sex."

Morelli pulled me to him and kissed me. The kiss was a mix of playful affection and libidinous desperation. It measured up to Ranger's kiss the night before, and it triggered a hot rush of guilt and desire. Getting kisses like this from two different men, both of whom carried guns, wasn't in anyone's best interest. Not to mention I suspected God didn't approve of this kind of stuff. Of course it wasn't as if I'd made the first move on either of the kisses, so maybe God would cut me some slack.

"So about Sunny?" I asked.

"Sorry, can't help you. Don't know where he is, but I know he's moving around. Are you working tonight?"

"I'm going to Bingo at the Senior Center. Turns out Bingo was a common interest for the murdered women."

Morelli grimaced. "Ranger should be giving you time and a half for hazardous duty. Those Bingo ladies are tough."

"Yeah, and that's not even as bad as it gets. Your grandmother put the eye on me."

"Bummer."

"That's it? Bummer?"

"There's no such thing as the eye."

"Are you sure?"

Morelli gave his head a small shake. "Actually, no."

"Then *do* something. Tell your grandmother to take the whammy off me."

"I'll talk to her."

I walked Morelli to his car. "Is there anything you can tell me about the Dumpster murders? Do you guys have a lead?"

"I'm not involved, and Butch isn't looking happy. Butch is looking like he's running down dead-end streets."

I watched Morelli drive away, and I went back inside the bonds office to collect Lula.

"Let's saddle up," I said. "We need to get serious about Sunny. I'm tired of being the bad guy. I want this behind me."

"I like your attitude," Lula said. "Get serious. Take charge. Kick ass. It's downright inspiring. Look at me. I'm on my feet and I'm ready to root that little crooner out of his hidey-hole."

Fifteen minutes later Lula turned onto Nottingham Way and meandered around Hamilton Township until she found Rita's house.

"Are you sure you want to do this?" Lula asked. "I know she's our number one candidate for harboring Mr. Bow Tie, but didn't she say she was going to shoot you?"

"Only if I broke into her house."

"That don't instill me with too much confidence. How do you want to do this? Do you want me to stay parked here at the end of the block so you can sneak around and look in her windows? Or do you want me to park in her driveway so you can go ring her bell while I sit in the car with the motor running?"

"I couldn't help notice both those options had you staying in the car."

"I figure I need to keep myself safe so I can call the paramedics when you get shot."

"It's good to know you're looking out for me."

"That wasn't sarcasm, was it? On account of I thought I detected some sarcasm."

I was talking to Lula but I was looking straight ahead,

watching a black Lincoln Town Car cruise down the street and swing into Rita's driveway.

"Timing is everything," I said to Lula.

"Well, shut up," Lula said, spotting the Lincoln. "You think they're doing a pickup or making a delivery?"

"I'm guessing pickup."

After several minutes the front door to Rita's house opened, Uncle Sunny appeared, the door closed behind him, and he got into the backseat of the Lincoln.

"Now what?" Lula asked, rummaging around in her Brakmin. "I got a gun in here somewhere. You want me to shoot out their tires?"

"No. I'm going to follow them and wait for a better place to make an apprehension."

"Like what better place are you hoping for?"

"A place without his henchmen."

The Lincoln eased out of the driveway and rolled down the street the same way it'd come. They didn't seem to have noticed us, or maybe they didn't care. I suspected they thought of me more as a nuisance than a genuine threat.

We followed at a distance, allowing a couple cars to come between us. The Lincoln took Nottingham Way past Hamilton Avenue and Greenwood and turned onto State Street. Sunny was going back to his home base at Morgan and Fifteenth Street.

The Lincoln stopped at the corner of Fifteenth and Freeman. Shorty, Moe, and Sunny got out of the car and walked into a three-story brownstone. A young guy ran out of the building and drove away with the car.

"Valet parking for the mafia staff car," Lula said.

"Sunny owns the building," I told Lula. "He rents it out to the Chestnut Social Club."

"I performed at the Chestnut Social Club when I was a 'ho," Lula said. "It was a bunch of old Italian geezers who liked talking about the good old days when they could get a boner. We figured the club was named after their shrunken privates, which were about the size of chestnuts."

"So you know the building?"

"Haven't been there in a bunch of years since I'm not a 'ho no more, but used to be the ground floor was where they played dominoes and cards on a couple cheap-ass card tables with folding chairs. There was a bar on the second floor and a kitchen, which I never saw them use because they got food delivered. They had a big TV there and some leather couches and a back room with a bed. I never got to the third floor. I figured they counted out the day's receipts up there."

"Not an ideal place to make a bust."

"It might not be so bad. It's someplace Sunny feels safe, so he could go upstairs to see what they took in last night, and Shorty and Moe might not feel like climbing all those stairs. Shorty and Moe are probably gonna watch the domino players and scarf down some cannoli."

"How would I get to Sunny if he's on the third floor?"

"Backstairs. Every floor got a little balcony with stairs

connecting them. It's an emergency exit they could use if they gotta sneak out. I know about it because it's the 'ho exit."

. . .

Lula parked and we walked around the corner and took stock of the back of the building.

"I only see a window at each balcony," I said. "No door."

"Yeah, you gotta climb through the window and you end up at an inside back stairwell that got a door to each floor. You could go up on the inside or you could go up on the outside. Problem is, if you go up on the inside you could run into one of the Chestnuts."

We were standing in a narrow alley that ran the length of the block. The alley was wide enough to accommodate a garbage truck and limited parking, but I didn't see any cars parked. There were similar two- and three-story row houses on the other side of the alley. People occupying those row houses would be able to see me climbing the outside stairs. Fortunately the two closest houses didn't look occupied. Their windows were boarded, and there was a construction Dumpster backed up to one of them.

I tucked handcuffs into the back pocket of my jeans, rammed a small canister of pepper spray into my front pocket, and clipped an illegal stun gun onto my waistband.

"You need a real gun," Lula said.

"I don't need a real gun. I'm not shooting anyone."

"Suppose they shoot at you first?"

"I wave my arms in the air, scream like a girl, and run away as fast as I can."

"Hunh," Lula said. "I suppose I should come with you then in case that don't work."

We climbed the stairs to the third floor and tried the window. Locked.

"Probably because nobody hardly ever goes out this window," Lula said.

We went down one level and tried that window. Also locked.

"Well, it's just a window, and accidents happen," Lula said.

She swung her Brakmin at the window, the glass shattered, and the security alarm went off.

"Oops," Lula said. "I wasn't counting on that."

We bolted down the stairs and hid behind the construction Dumpster. The back door to Sunny's building opened, and two overweight, out-of-shape guys stepped out and looked around. They peered up at the balconies but couldn't get motivated to climb the stairs.

One of them pointed to the broken window. "Must have been a bird," he said.

The other guy nodded, then they wheeled around and went inside.

"You should hurry up and go in before they turn the alarm back on," Lula said. "I'll stay here and be the lookout. I'll tell you if someone comes to fix the window."

"What if I need help getting Sunny out?"

"Call me and I'll be there in a flash."

I trudged up to the second floor, carefully stuck my hand through the broken window, and unlocked it. I opened the window, climbed in, and put my ear to the door. I could hear people talking, and noise from the television. I tiptoed up to the third floor and listened at that door. Silence. I eased the door open and found myself face to face with Uncle Sunny. He was sitting on a folding chair behind a long wood table, counting money. There was a monster safe on the far side of the room. The door to the safe was open, and a thin, balding, middle-aged guy was trying to stuff a large leather satchel into the safe.

For a long moment the two men looked at me in shocked surprise, mouths open.

"Did you order takeout?" the skinny guy asked Sunny.

"She's a bounty hunter," Sunny said. "And she's a pain in the ass."

The skinny guy turned and reached for the gun that had been placed on top of the safe, but I crossed the room and sent a couple million volts into him before he could wrap his finger around the trigger. Sunny scuffed his chair back and bolted for the door. I lunged and tackled him, taking us both to the floor. We rolled around, grunting and cussing. He paused to catch his breath, and I snapped a cuff on him. There was some more scrambling and wrestling, and I got the second cuff on. I scooted away, got to my feet, and pulled him up. He put his head down for a head butt and charged me. I stepped away, and he ran into the wall and knocked himself out.

I stared down at him in complete disbelief.

"Hey!" I said, nudging him with my toe, not getting a response.

I took a closer look to make sure he was breathing. I felt for a pulse.

"Ice cream," he murmured. "Chocolate."

The skinny guy was coming around. He was drooling, his eyes were open, and his fingers were twitching. I didn't want to zap him again, and I didn't have a second set of cuffs, so I took the cuffs off Sunny and used them to cuff one of the skinny guy's hands to the safe.

I dragged Sunny into the back stairwell, but I wasn't going to get him through the window or down the stairs without some help. I leaned out the window to yell for Lula and saw her at the end of the street, running after the giraffe. I dialed her cellphone and was told to leave a message. I closed my eyes and took a deep breath. Stay calm, I told myself. Murdering Lula wouldn't solve anything.

I was going to have to try to get Sunny down the inside staircase. I grabbed him under his armpits and backed my way down. I reached the second-floor landing and heard gunshots coming from the floor above me. Probably the skinny guy trying to get someone's attention. I'd kicked his gun out of reach, but I hadn't searched him.

Sunny opened his eyes. "Mom?"

"You bet," I said. "Don't worry. I'm going to take care of you."

I dragged him across the landing to the edge of the stairs. I stepped back, lost my balance, and slid the rest of the way on my back with Sunny on top of me. I shoved him off and lay there for a couple beats, trying to catch my breath, thinking the whole falling-down-stairs thing was getting old. In fact, I thought, I might not even be liking *any* of my job all that much. I heard men thundering down the stairs from the third-floor landing, and Sunny turned his head and focused on me. *"You!"*

Ignore the pain, I thought. *Get up and run!*

I had just hit Freeman Street when Sunny's goons burst out the door and spilled into the alley. I rounded the corner and saw Lula standing by her Firebird on Fifteenth.

"Hey," Lula called to me. "I saw Kevin!"

"Get in!" I yelled. "They're after me."

I reached the Firebird, grabbed at the door, and hurled myself into the car. "Go!" I told her.

Lula took off as a bullet zinged past us and shattered her side mirror.

"What the heck is the matter with those people?" she said, stomping on the gas pedal. "What did you do to get them so mad? Honestly, you have no way with people. And who's gonna pay for my mirror? Do you know which one of those morons did this?"

I slouched in my seat and closed my eyes. "Remember how you were going to be there in a flash to help me?"

"Yeah, but then Kevin galloped up. He stopped right in front of me and looked at me. He's got big brown eyes and movie star eyelashes that are about a foot long. And he talked to me and told me he appreciated that I was his friend."

"He talked to you?"

"It was one of them telepathic conversations." Lula looked at me. "You don't look good. You got a hole tore in your jeans, and your knee is bleeding. What happened to you?"

"I fell down the stairs."

"You gotta stop doing that," Lula said.

"I'm thinking about getting a new job."

"What would you do?"

"That's the problem."

Truth is, I was a college graduate with no skills. And after a bunch of years spent working as a bounty hunter I feared I was no longer especially smart.

"Where are we going now?" Lula asked.

"St. Francis Hospital. I think I broke my finger."

• • •

Two hours later Lula and I straggled into the bonds office. The middle finger on my right hand was in a splint and taped to my index finger.

"What happened?" Connie wanted to know.

"Broke my finger," I told her. "I don't want to talk about it."

"She fell down the stairs," Lula said. "Again."

"You ran off and left me," I said. *"Again."*

"Kevin came right up to me," Lula said to Connie. "I swear I was just inches from him. I was standing in the alley waiting for Stephanie, and I was checking my text messages, and next thing I see Kevin has sneaked up and is looking down at me.

And he's a lot bigger when he's that close. You'd get a crick in your neck from looking up at him."

"I don't understand how a giraffe could be running loose in that neighborhood," Connie said. "At the very least you'd think someone would have reported it to animal control. How is it eating? Where is it sleeping?"

"I don't know where it's sleeping, but there's not a lot of leaves left on any of the trees for about a four-block chunk of real estate," Lula said.

"So where did it come from?" Connie asked. "It's not like a giraffe just wanders into town. You'd see him if he was walking down Route 1. People would notice. He'd be on the evening news."

"Maybe Bella sent the giraffe as a distraction and it's a magic giraffe that only me and Stephanie can see," Lula said. "Probably Bella was the one who broke Stephanie's finger, too."

"Something to think about," Connie said.

I hiked my messenger bag up onto my shoulder. "The only thing I'm thinking about is lunch. I'm going to Giovichinni's."

"I'll go with you," Lula said. "I could use some of their chicken salad."

We walked the short distance and went straight to the deli counter in the back of the store. I ordered a turkey club, and Lula ordered a large container of chicken salad, a large container of potato salad, a medium container of coleslaw, and a large container of macaroni salad.

"That's a lot of food," I said to her. "I thought you were trying to lose weight?"

"Yeah, but I don't have bread like you. The bread goes right to your belly. And I'm having a diet soda. Plus I got three heads of lettuce for Kevin."

We were at the checkout with Loretta Giovichinni at the register when she looked past us, went pale, and made the sign of the cross.

"Holy Mother," Loretta whispered.

I turned and saw Bella heading in my direction. Her eyes were small and glittery, and her narrow lips were pressed tight together. Lula threw a handful of money at Loretta and ran out of the store with her food. Loretta ignored the money and ducked down behind the counter.

"Shame to you," Bella said to me. "I heard what you do to Sunny. You knock him out and throw him down the stairs. You go to hell. I make sure of it. I give you the eye to hell."

I heard Loretta suck in air behind the counter, and somewhere farther back in the store something clattered to the floor.

"That seems extreme," I said to Bella. "I was only trying to do my job, and I didn't throw him down the stairs. He fell down the stairs on top of me."

"Liar, liar, pants on fire," Bella said.

She put her finger to her eye, pulled down her lower lid, and glared at me. "Ha!" she said. She turned on her heel and walked, head held high, out the door.

Loretta popped up from behind the counter. She looked

down at my turkey club and waved me through. "It's on the house if you promise not to come back. That woman scares the crap out of me."

"Could be worse," I said. "At least I know the consequences of the curse."

"You're going to hell," Loretta said. "How could it be worse?"

SEVEN

LULA POLISHED OFF the last of her macaroni salad and chucked her empty food containers into the trash.

"I'm all refreshed now," she said. "I'm ready to go kick some more butt. What should we do next? You want to pick up the Sunny hunt?"

"No. I'm going to table Sunny until tonight."

I was starting to get a grip on Sunny's schedule. He spent the night with Rita and in the morning he went to the club to check on the previous night's business. I thought my best shot at Sunny was to break in on him when he was sleeping. I just had to figure out how to get around the *home invasion shooting me dead* thing.

"Then how about we drive over so I can give Kevin his lettuce?" Lula said.

"I was thinking we should look for Ziggy Radiewski," I told her. "He's probably in the bar next to the hardware store on State Street. That's his usual afternoon hangout."

"Yeah, but I got this lettuce for Kevin, and I don't want it to wilt."

"I think we should let things chill out in that neighborhood. Put Kevin's lettuce in the fridge and we'll take it over tomorrow."

"That don't work for me," Lula said.

"How about this, you can risk your life by going back to Sunny's turf to feed Kevin, and I'll pick up Ziggy."

"That don't work either," Lula said. "You shouldn't be driving with your injury."

I looked at my finger. "It's not a big deal."

"It's gonna be a big deal when everyone thinks you're flippin' them the bird and you get to be a victim of road rage," Lula said. "You're lucky you don't get shot driving with that finger sticking up like that. I'll make a deal. We do a real fast drive down Fifteenth Street, I leave Kevin's lettuce sitting out for him, and then we go snatch Ziggy."

Twenty minutes later Lula and I turned onto Fifteenth Street. She drove four blocks and tossed the lettuce onto the sidewalk at the corner of Fifteenth and Freeman.

"I got a plan," Lula said. "The lettuce is bait. I figure if I keep leaving lettuce here Kevin's gonna hang around the lettuce, and then I can trap him. I haven't got all the details worked out yet, but I'm thinking I could use a big net."

"He's *huge!*"

"Yeah, I'd need to get up real high and drop it over him. Like from a helicopter. Or you know what would be really good? Spider-Man. You know how he shoots those webs out from his fingers? He could wrap webs around Kevin."

"So all you have to do is get in touch with Spider-Man?"

"It's a shame he don't live here, right?"

"It's a shame he doesn't live *anywhere.*"

"Ranger's pretty close," Lula said, "except he can't do the web throwing thing, and so far as I know he don't wear spandex."

Lula cut through downtown and turned onto State Street. The hardware store and Ginty's Bar were on the outermost perimeter of the Burg. Ginty's was a dark hole-in-the-wall-type dive that drew regulars from the shantytown row houses that lined Post Street, and ran parallel with State. Ziggy owned one of the row houses, but he lived in Ginty's.

Lula parked in the small lot the bar shared with the hardware store, and we got out and walked to the bar's front door.

"How many times have we pulled Ziggy out of here?" Lula asked. "Must be a dozen. I swear I think he just likes to ride in my Firebird."

We stepped into the bar and took a moment to allow our eyes to adjust to the dark. The air was cold and damp, and the room smelled whiskey-soaked. There were three small round tables near the door, empty at this time of day. The highly polished mahogany bar stretched the length of the back of the room. Ziggy was one of three men at the bar.

"If he smells bad I'm putting him in the trunk," Lula said. "Last time we took him in I had to have my car detailed."

Ziggy was a fifty-six-year-old white male who was on a disability pension from the government and was working hard at destroying his liver. There was no Mrs. Ziggy, and no Rover or Kitty Ziggy. Just Ziggy in all his pickled glory.

The bartender waved to us and said something to Ziggy. Ziggy swiveled on his barstool and saluted us with his empty beer glass.

"Ladies," Ziggy said. "Long time no see."

"Are you ready to go for a ride?" I asked him.

"Barkeep," Ziggy said. "One for the road."

The bartender set a fresh beer in front of Ziggy, Ziggy chugged it, and fell off his barstool.

"You have this strange effect on men," Lula said to me. "They're always passing out on you. Guys get stuck with darts, and run into walls, and fall off barstools."

I hooked my hands under Ziggy's armpits. "Help me get him outside."

"I'll help you get him outside," Lula said, "but he's not going in my car. He just wet hisself."

We carted Ziggy outside, and I called a cab.

"I can't keep from thinking about Spider-Man," Lula said. "God made cats and dogs and cows and humans, but he only made superheroes in comic books. What the heck was he thinking?"

"I guess he was counting on us to do the job."

"You mean us personally? Because I'm a big woman, but I couldn't stop no speeding train single-handed."

"I was talking about human beings in general."

"Probably we're in a lot of trouble on that one, since most of the men I know can't even keep their pants up, much less save the world."

I waved the approaching cab to the curb and loaded Ziggy into the backseat.

"Follow us to the police station," I said to Lula. "I'll need a ride after I drop him off."

The driver looked over the seatback at Ziggy. "He isn't dead, is he?"

"He's sleeping."

. . .

I handed Connie the body receipt for Ziggy and she wrote a check out to me for the recovery.

"That looks like pizza money," Lula said. "If you don't get too many extra toppings you could get a soda with it."

"I have information on the latest Dumpster murder," Connie said. "Definitely strangled. And her bank account was cleaned out the day before."

"It's terrible that these old ladies are getting murdered," Lula said. "It gives me the creepy-crawlies."

Vinnie's door was open, and his office was empty.

"Where's Vinnie?" I asked Connie.

"The ponies are running."

"I thought Lucille signed him up with Gamblers Anonymous."

"He said his G.A. group is meeting at the track. Field trip."

75

"If Lucille's daddy finds out, he'll field trip Vinnie to the landfill," Lula said.

A text message buzzed on my phone. It was from Ranger. *Catch up with you after Bingo.*

Oh boy.

"Is something wrong?" Lula asked. "You just got that look."

"What look?" I asked her.

"Your *Oh boy* look."

"It was a message from Ranger reminding me about Bingo."

"Oh boy," Lula said.

I dropped my check into my messenger bag. "There's not a lot left of the afternoon. I'm going to take my broken finger home."

"That's a good idea," Lula said. "You could take a nap to get ready for *Bingo*. Do you want a ride to the Senior Center? I could come pick you up."

"Sure."

. I detoured to the supermarket on the way home and filled my shopping cart. Milk, eggs, bread, cereal, pickles, a variety of disposable aluminum pans, crackers, cheese, Marshmallow Fluff, olives, cracker crumbs, butter, ice cream, aluminum foil, garbage bags, paper napkins, canola oil, orange juice, potato chips, bags of frozen vegetables, ketchup, frozen chicken cutlets all breaded and ready for the oven, a *Cooking Light* magazine, several home decorator magazines, and a frozen banana cream pie. Am I a domestic goddess, or what?

I lugged everything up to my apartment, called Morelli, and invited him to dinner.

"Sure," Morelli said. "What do you want me to bring? Pizza? Chinese? Wings?"

"You don't have to bring anything," I said. "I'm cooking."

There was a long moment of silence.

"Cooking?" he asked.

"Yes. Cooking. Jeez, you'd think I never cooked."

"Cupcake, you only own one pot."

"I have to be at Bingo at seven, so we have to eat at five o'clock."

"Can't wait," Morelli said.

I hung up, opened the bag of chips, and gave one to Rex. "He has no confidence in me," I said to Rex. "Just because a girl doesn't have a toaster doesn't mean she can't cook, right?"

I pushed the clutter to one end of my dining room table and laid out two place settings. I stepped back, looked at the table, and made a mental note to buy two place mats, just in case I decided to ever do this again.

I took a shower with my broken finger encased in a plastic sandwich bag. Under the white gauze wrapping, the finger was swollen and throbbing. I felt like a wimp since there wasn't even any bone sticking out, but the finger didn't feel great. I dried off and applied a new super-sized adhesive bandage to my skinned knee. The knee would heal, but my jeans would never be the same.

It had been a long time since I'd used the oven, but I figured out how to turn it on. Just like riding a bike, I thought. You never forget. Call me Chef Stephanie. According to the box, the cutlets would take fifteen minutes. No need to even defrost the little suckers before roasting. So I had the oven going and the meal all planned out, now all I had to do was wait for Morelli and hope he'd bring something to drink, since I'd run out of money before I could get to the liquor store.

He showed up precisely at five with his big shaggy dog, Bob, who rushed in and galloped around my little apartment, returning to the kitchen with his tongue hanging out. I gave him a bowl of water, he slopped it all over the floor, and then he flopped down in my living room to take a nap.

Morelli put a six-pack of beer and a bottle of red wine on my kitchen counter. "Pick your poison," he said.

"I'm going with the wine. It's more romantic."

"That sounds hopeful. Are we getting romantic?"

"Maybe. Did you bring drugs?" I held my finger up for him to take a look. "Broken."

"Compound fracture?" he asked.

"No."

"Hardly worth worrying about."

"*It hurts!*"

Morelli grinned. "Did you invite me over here to score drugs off me?"

"Not originally. I thought I might want to be more domestic, but now that you're here I'm thinking drugs could be the way to go."

"Why do you want to be more domestic?"

"I don't know. It just came over me."

"Is it that time of the month?"

"No!"

"Lucky me," Morelli said.

I checked out the wine. Screw cap. The greatest invention since fire. I poured out two glasses and toasted the screw cap. Not easy to do with two fingers taped together and in a metal splint. I dumped the box of cutlets onto one of my new disposable broiler pans and shoved them into the hot oven.

"Easy-peasy," I said to Morelli. "They'll be perfect in fifteen minutes. The box wouldn't lie."

"I'm getting turned on by all this domesticity," Morelli said.

This wasn't an impressive admission. Morelli got turned on by lint.

I took the bag of vegetables out of the freezer and tossed them into my microwave. I figured I'd just cook the crap out of them until the chicken was done. I topped off my wine, and minutes later there was an explosion.

Morelli and I instinctively dropped to the ground.

"What the heck?" I yelled. "What was that?"

Morelli was on his back, laughing. "I think you exploded the vegetables!"

We got to our feet and looked in at the massacre inside the microwave.

Morelli was still grinning. "It's like a crime scene."

"It's not funny." A tear leaked out of my eye. "I'm a big stupid failure!"

Morelli wrapped an arm around me and hugged me into

him. "They were just vegetables," he said. "Vegetables are way overrated."

"I can't do anything right."

"Not true. You excel at many things."

"Such as?"

"You give a damn good happy-ending massage."

"That's it? Sex? That's my field of expertise?"

"It beats being able to cook a vegetable."

I did an eye roll so severe I almost lost my balance. "I want to be able to do both."

Morelli took another bag of vegetables out of my freezer and read the instructions. "Pierce the bag before microwaving."

"I didn't do that." I swiped at my nose. "I'm too dumb to even read directions."

"Anything else go wrong today?"

"I broke my finger."

"Besides that."

"I ripped my jeans when I fell down the stairs. Your grandmother said I was going to hell. A couple guys shot at me. I apprehended Ziggy Radiewski, and he peed himself."

"So it was a normal day," Morelli said.

I gave up a sigh.

"And you're going to Bingo tonight?"

I nodded. "That's why I need the drugs."

Morelli took the chicken out of the oven. "The chicken looks good. What else do you have to eat?"

"Potatoes in the form of chips."

"Works for me," Morelli said.

We ate the chicken and chips, and Bob came over and pushed against me.

"Don't feed him," Morelli said. "He's getting fat. I fed him before we got here."

"Tell me about the latest Dumpster victim."

"Not much to tell. She fit the profile. Seventy-six years old. Lived alone. Withdrew money from her bank account one day and dead the next. She was strangled and wrapped in a sheet. The details were consistent with the other victims."

"Do you know what was used to strangle her?"

"A Venetian blind cord. Just like always."

"You'd have to be pretty strong to strangle someone."

"Not necessarily. The women selected were frail," Morelli said. "And two of them had blunt force trauma to the back of their heads. They were knocked out and then strangled."

"Anything else?"

"We haven't made it public, but they all had a single sunflower somewhere in their home. Melvina had it in a jelly jar in her kitchen. Lois had one in a vase on her dining room table."

"A calling card?"

"Something like that."

I brought the banana cream pie and two forks to the table, and we dug in.

"You even defrosted it," Morelli said.

"I'm no slouch when it comes to pie."

We finished the pie and carried our dishes into the kitchen. Morelli gave the last chunk of pie crust to Rex, gave a small piece of chicken he'd been saving to Bob, and reached out for me, pulling me flat against him. "I haven't taken any pills today," he said. "I have full control over my tongue."

"No time," I told him. "Lula will be here any minute. Maybe we can test out your tongue after Bingo."

"Can't do it after Bingo. I promised my brother I'd go to the ball game with him." He looked at my splinted finger. "Do you really want drugs?"

"No. I'm feeling better now that I'm full of wine and pie."

Morelli moved to kiss me, and the doorbell rang.

"Don't answer it," he said. "Eventually she'll go away."

"She won't go away. She'll shoot the lock off the door. I'll have to pay for a new door."

"Hey!" Lula yelled. "I know you're in there. I can hear you breathing. What are you doing?"

I opened the door, and Lula looked past me and waved at Morelli.

"I saw your car in the lot," Lula said.

"I'll give you twenty bucks if you go away," Morelli said to Lula.

"I gotta take Stephanie and her granny to Bingo," Lula told him. "I bet we win the jackpot. I feel lucky. I got my lucky undies on."

Morelli snapped the leash onto Bob and gave me a fast kiss. "I can't compete with her lucky undies. I'll try to catch you tomorrow."

EIGHT

I'D BEEN TO the Senior Center before and it always smelled like eucalyptus, canned peas, and orange blossom air freshener. It was a single-story redbrick structure straddling the line between Trenton and Hamilton Township. Bingo was held in the largest of the meeting rooms. Rectangular folding tables were set out in rows that ran perpendicular to the small stage at one end. The caller sat at a little table on the stage, and an overhead flat-screen television flashed the numbers as they were called.

"This is a real professional setup," Lula said, taking a seat.

"It's pretty good, but it's not as good as some of the Bingo halls in Atlantic City," Grandma said. "Some of them are all electronic. You don't need cards or daubers or nothing."

I'd elected to play four cards. Grandma took twelve cards. And Lula bought thirty.

"Are you going to be able to keep track of all those cards?" Grandma asked Lula. "That's a lot of cards."

"Yeah, but the more cards you got, the more chances you got to win, right?"

"That's true," Grandma said. "Do you play Bingo a lot?"

Lula laid all her cards out in front of her. "I'm one of those intermittent players."

"Me too," Grandma said. "I don't know how these women have the time to do this every night. I got a schedule to keep. I gotta see *Dancing with the Stars* and *America's Got Talent.* I record my shows when I have to, but it's not like seeing them live."

We were sitting to the side and back of the room and I could see all the players. Most were women in their sixties and seventies. The demographic would be a lot younger when we went to Bingo at the firehouse. There were a few men mixed in with the women. I knew some of them. They were, for the most part, the core participants in the senior program. They went on the bus trips to Atlantic City, they played cards in the afternoon, they took a variety of classes that were available at the center, and they went to Bingo.

"I got my eyes open for the killer," Grandma said. "If I had to pick someone out in this room, it would be Willy Benson. I always thought he looked shifty."

"He's ninety-three years old!"

"Yeah, but he's crafty. And he gets around pretty good."

"I know Willy," Lula said. "He looks shifty on account of

his one eye don't look at you. It looks someplace else. You can't malign a man for a disability."

"It depends where the other eye's looking," Grandma said.

Marion Wenger was onstage twirling the cage containing the numbered Bingo balls. She selected one and called out B-10.

"I know I got a B-10 somewhere," Lula said. "Here's one. And here's another one. Am I off to a good start, or what?"

"I got one too," Grandma said, marking it off with her dauber.

"G-47," Marion called.

"Got it," Lula said. "Here, and here, and here . . ."

"N-40."

"Hold on," Lula said. "I'm not done looking for G-47."

"B-15."

"Say what?"

"You've got a bunch of B-15s," Grandma said to Lula. "I can see them from here."

"B-2."

"Hey!" Lula yelled to Marion. "You got some better place to go that you gotta rush us through our Bingo game?"

The game came to a screeching halt and everyone turned to look at us.

"Lula's new at this," Grandma announced to the room. "She hasn't got the hang of it yet."

Across the table and two chairs down, Mildred Frick narrowed her eyes at Lula. "Amateur," she said on a hiss of air.

Lula glared back. "Who you calling a amateur? You got a lot of nerve calling someone a amateur when you don't even know them."

"You have a lot of nerve sitting there with thirty cards when you're not capable of playing them," Mildred said to Lula. "Clearly you're too dumb to manage thirty cards. It's an insult to the rest of the room that you would even try. You're a *dumb bunny*."

"Well, you're a ugly old hag," Lula said. "And I find your choice of accessories to be a insult. You got a handbag hanging on the back of your chair that I wouldn't be caught dead in."

Mildred was at least eighty years old. She was five feet tall. And she had a spray tan that made her look mummified. She jumped to her feet and leaned across the table at Lula. "You take back what you said about my handbag."

"Will not," Lula said.

Mildred shook her blue-veined bony fist at Lula. "I'll *make* you take it back, you *dumb bunny*."

"Oh yeah?" Lula said. "You want a piece of me? Come get it."

Mildred got one foot up on her chair and launched herself across the table at Lula. Bingo cards went flying, the chair tipped over and crashed to the floor, and Mildred tried to claw her way to Lula while the women on either side of her grabbed hold of her feet and tried to haul her back.

"Holy bejeezus," Lula said.

Marion Wenger pulled her .45 out of her purse and fired one off at the ceiling. A big chunk of ceiling fell down and everyone looked over at her.

"Let's have some decorum here," Marion said. "This is a Bingo game, not a WWE match."

"Too bad," Grandma said. "I wouldn't mind being at a WWE match. I like when those big men get naked except for them little baggies over their privates."

"Boy," Lula said, "that Mildred is a scary old lady."

"Yep," Grandma said. "She's a nasty one."

"I heard that," Mildred said. "At least I'm not a slut."

Lula went indignant. "Are you implying that Granny is a slut?"

"I do get around a little bit," Grandma said to Lula.

"You should leave," Mildred said to Lula. "We don't want your kind here."

Lula leaned forward in rhino mode. "And just exactly what *is* my kind?"

"You're a *dumb bunny*," Mildred said.

"Well, I don't want to play no more anyways," Lula said. "And I want my money back, because this game isn't run right."

We left the Senior Center, piled into Lula's car, and sat there for a moment.

"I kind of like being a slut," Grandma said. "It beats the heck out of being an old lady."

"Now what?" Lula asked. "Are we going home now?"

"I'd like to check on Uncle Sunny," I said. "I want to see if he's in Hamilton Township."

"I'm on it," Lula said. "I'm in a mood to kick some butt."

"I wasn't thinking of kicking butt tonight," I said. "I mostly wanted to confirm that Sunny spends his nights with Rita. And that Tweedledum and Tweedledee don't stand watch."

Lula found Rita's street and drove by her house. Lights were on in the front room. No car in the driveway. No thugs hanging out on the front porch. Lula made a U-turn and parked across the street.

"Stay here," I said to Lula and Grandma. "I'm going to take a quick look around the house."

I crossed the street and quietly ran to the side of the house that was shadowed by a large maple tree. I crept up to a window and peeked in at the dining room. The room was dark, but I could see light spilling out of the living room and I could hear television noise. I worked my way around to the back of the house, looking in windows, mentally cataloging the interior. I turned a corner and saw Grandma and Lula with their noses pressed against Rita's kitchen window.

"I told you to stay in the car!" I stage-whispered.

"That wasn't no fun," Grandma said. "We're here watching Rita fix Sunny a grilled cheese sandwich."

"Uh-oh," Lula said. "I think they see us."

Lula and Grandma jumped away from the window, there was shouting inside the house, and the back door crashed open. Lula grabbed Grandma by the hand and yanked her at a flat-out run around the side of the house. Lula was in four-inch spike-heel 'ho boots, and Grandma was in red and white Vans, and all things considered they were making good progress at beating a retreat.

Sunny came through the door first with a gun in his hand. I tackled him from the side, knocking the gun away, taking us both to the ground.

"Step away or I'll shoot," Rita said.

"You can't shoot," I told her. "This isn't a home invasion. I'm in your yard."

"Easier to clean up the blood," Rita said.

I heard the ratchet of a shotgun, and I rolled away from Sunny. I scrambled to my feet and was about to take off when Sunny came at me. He barreled into me, there was a shotgun blast, and Sunny yelped and went down to one knee.

"You fucking idiot," he yelled at Rita. "You shot me!"

"You got in the way," Rita said. "Stay down."

I saw her shoulder the shotgun, and I ran around the corner. I was halfway across the street when Rita's front door burst open and she squeezed off her second shot. A bunch of pellets pinged against the Firebird, but I didn't get hit. I dove into the backseat, and Lula took off.

"Boy, that was something," Grandma said. "That was way better than Bingo."

NINE

I **WAS ON** the couch, in front of the television, enjoying a glass of wine, when Ranger knocked once and walked in. Every part of Ranger is perfectly hinged and in perfect proportion. When he walks into a room his stride is fluid and self-assured. His athleticism is unconscious. He relaxed back into the overstuffed chair opposite me.

"Pretty," he said.

"The wine?"

"You."

I was wearing a white T-shirt and striped pajama bottoms with a drawstring waist. My feet were bare and my hair was down and disorderly.

"This would be perfect if we were in my apartment and not yours, and you were spending the night," he said.

"I didn't know you were interested in that."

"I'm always interested in that," Ranger said. "I'm just not willing to pay the price right now."

I felt my eyes go wide. "Right now?"

"Probably never," Ranger said. "How did it go tonight?"

"We sort of got kicked out of Bingo."

"Babe."

"Lula got into a fight with Mildred Frick. You don't want to know the details."

"Did you learn anything helpful?" Ranger asked.

"I can honestly say I didn't see anyone there that I could suspect of murdering the women. Okay, maybe Mildred Frick, but she would be a long shot."

"Was there any talk of the murdered women?"

"Not that I heard. Bingo is serious stuff at the Senior Center. You get your cards set up, you hunker down and concentrate. There's not a lot of chitchat."

"Men?"

"I counted seven. None of them looked robust enough to heave a body into a Dumpster."

"Did any of them look robust enough to persuade a woman to empty her bank account?"

"Hard to say. You can't always tell with old people. You think they have one foot in the grave, and next thing they're ramming you with a shopping cart at Costco."

Ranger stood, crossed the room, and pulled me to my feet. He slid his hands under my T-shirt and leaned in to kiss me.

"Um," I said.

He stopped a fraction of an inch away from my mouth. "'Um'?"

"What about paying the price?"

"I wasn't going to pay the price."

"Okay, but you have to be careful of my finger. You noticed it, right?"

"You're carrying a tracking device in your messenger bag," Ranger said. "I called the hospital when you checked in."

"You planted a bug in my messenger bag?"

"Is that news?"

It wasn't news. Ranger tracked me all the time. Sometimes I was relieved to be rescued from a crazed killer, and sometimes it was an invasive annoyance.

"I guess it's not news," I told him.

"Would you like me to stop tracking you?"

"Would it do any good if I said yes?"

He smiled. "No." He took the remote from the coffee table and shut the television off. He closed the distance between us and kissed me.

"Wait!" I said, pulling back. "What's that sound?"

He stopped and listened. "Rain?"

"It's raining? How long has it been raining?"

"It started when I pulled into your lot."

"Is it just a shower?"

"It's supposed to rain for the rest of the night."

I jumped away and straightened my T-shirt. "You have to go. The game will be called."

"And?"

"Disaster!" I pushed him toward the door. "This is a sign," I told him. "An act of God. I swear I'm going to church tomorrow."

"That sounds extreme," Ranger said.

"Morelli wanted to see me tonight but he promised his brother he'd go to the ball game with him. And now it's raining!"

"Babe," Ranger said, "you need to make some decisions."

"I made decisions. I'm just having a hard time sticking to them."

• • •

Ten minutes after Ranger left, Morelli showed up with Bob and a box of hot dogs. He shucked his shoes and his soaking wet windbreaker in the foyer and handed the box to me. "It started raining and they put the hot dogs on sale."

I took the hot dogs into the kitchen, pulled the six-pack of beer from the fridge, and we stood at the sink and tore into hot dogs and beer. Morelli flipped a hot dog to Bob, who snatched it out of the air and ate it in one gulp.

"Catch any murderers tonight?" Morelli asked me.

"No. But Lula, Grandma, and I got kicked out of the Senior Center."

Morelli looked over his hot dog at me. "So the night wasn't a complete bust."

"True. It's not like I didn't accomplish *anything*. How was the game?"

"Short."

I debated telling him about Uncle Sunny getting an assful of buckshot, but decided against it. He'd find out soon enough, and he'd probably calm down by the time I saw him again.

Morelli polished off a third hot dog and slung an arm around my shoulders. "Do you know what I'd like now?"

"Ice cream?"

"Not even close." He kissed my neck.

"Remember I have a broken finger."

"I can work around it."

. . .

I woke up smelling coffee. I opened my eyes as Morelli was setting a mug on my bedside table.

"How's your finger?" he asked.

"Okay. How's your leg?"

"It's okay. I'm on my way out. I need to walk Bob and take him home. What's going on with you today? Anything I should know about?"

"Bingo at the firehouse tonight."

"Another chance to create chaos," Morelli said. "Go for it."

He kissed me on the top of my head, Bob gave me a slurp on the cheek, and they left.

I sipped my coffee and thought about my day. Probably it

wasn't going to be great. I took a shower, pulled my hair into a ponytail, and swiped on extra mascara to perk up my mood. I had a leftover hot dog for breakfast and headed for the office. I got the call just as I parked in the bonds office lot.

"Notice how calm I am," Morelli said. "I'm not yelling, right?"

"Right."

"You should know it's costing me. I can feel myself getting a double hernia from keeping it in."

"I'm supposing you heard something."

"*Everyone* heard. It's stopped just short of the morning news on CNN. What the heck happened?"

"What did you hear?" I asked him.

"I heard that you caught Sunny taking the garbage out for Rita, and you filled him with buckshot."

"Actually, Rita was the one who shot Sunny. She was trying to shoot me, but she got him by mistake."

"That doesn't even make me feel better," Morelli said.

"Lula, Grandma, and I were doing surveillance, and one thing led to another, and Sunny got a load of buckshot. How is he?"

"He'll live. My mother said he got a few pellets in his leg and his ass."

"Your mother said 'ass'?"

"She said 'buttock,' but I feel stupid saying 'buttock.' My crazy grandmother is going to be on the rampage."

"She already condemned me to hell. What's left?"

"She could send you there sooner rather than later, and I wouldn't be happy to have a dead girlfriend and a grandmother behind bars."

"Do you really think she'd shoot me?"

"No. She'd poison you. She's Sicilian. She'd get you with a meatball."

I said goodbye on that happy thought and walked myself into the office.

"I'm not driving you anymore," Lula said to me. "Every time I take you somewhere, people shoot at us."

"Not every time."

Vinnie stuck his head out of his office. "Way to go, cuz. I hear there's a contract out on you for shooting up Uncle Sunny."

"I didn't shoot Sunny. Rita shot Sunny."

"I don't give a rat's ass *who* shot Sunny," Vinnie said. "Bottom line is he's still out there, and I'm in the red for a *lot* of money. And you know what happens when this agency is in the red? Harry gets nervous. And you know what happens when Harry gets nervous? He smashes things . . . like fingers and knees and private parts I'm real fond of. So get on your horse and make a freaking capture. The guy's full of buckshot. He's not gonna be moving fast. How hard could it be to run him down?"

"He's never alone," I said to Vinnie. "He's got bodyguards. And no one will snitch on him."

"Not everyone likes him," Vinnie said. "A guy like Sunny makes enemies. Mostly they have a short life expectancy, but there's gotta be someone out there who wants him caught besides me. Be creative, for crissake!"

The front door to the bail bonds office crashed open and Bella took two steps in and pointed her finger at me.

"*You!*" she said. "Devil woman. You shoot my nephew. Now I shoot you."

She pulled an ancient six-shooter out of her purse, aimed, and fired off a shot that went wide. I rushed her before she could gather herself together and took her to the floor.

"*Cuffs!*" I yelled, wrestling the gun from Bella, holding her down. "Someone cuff her!"

Connie peeked out from behind her desk and tossed cuffs my way. I snapped them on Bella and got her up on her feet. Her lips were pressed tight together, and her eyes looked like steel bearing balls.

"What the hell?" Vinnie asked. "What's going on?"

I sat Bella in one of the cheap orange plastic chairs and called Morelli.

"You know your meatball theory?" I said to him. "You were wrong. Your grandmother is here with a revolver. You need to come get her."

"Was anyone hurt?"

"No one was hurt, but I think Vinnie messed his pants."

It took Morelli fifteen minutes to get across town. Bella still hadn't said a word. Vinnie was barricaded in his private office. Lula and Connie were hunkered down at the back of the room, where Bella couldn't see them to give them the eye.

Morelli looked at his handcuffed grandmother, the hole in the far wall, and the revolver on Connie's desk.

"You're right," he said to me, "That's no meatball."

"She the devil," Bella said. "She shoot your godfather, a good man. And she do this to a granny. She have no respect. Look how she treat a poor old lady."

Morelli blew out a sigh. "Where'd you get the gun?"

"I got lots. An old lady got to protect herself."

He unlocked her cuffs. "You can't go around shooting people. It's against the law, and it's not nice."

"I spit on the law," Bella said. "I do what's right."

Morelli took the six-shooter in one hand and held on to his grandmother with the other.

"Thanks for the phone call," he said to me. "Sorry she shot at you."

Bella flipped us the bird and marched out with Morelli.

Vinnie opened his door a crack. "Is she gone?"

Connie made the sign of the cross. "Maybe we should bring in a priest. Do an exorcism or something. I could call Father Lenny."

"Forget Father Lenny," I said. "I need donuts. Lots of them."

TEN

"I GOTTA GO feed Kevin," Lula said. "We could get the donuts on the way."

"Do you already have his lettuce?"

"Yup. I got a whole bag of it in the fridge in the back room."

Lula drove us to Tasty Pastry and we got half a dozen donuts. The donuts were gone by the time we got to Fifteenth Street. Lula was looking satisfied, and I was feeling queasy.

It was midmorning, and the weather was glorious. Blue sky, puffy clouds, mid-seventies. Not a lot of traffic at this time of day in this part of town. This was Sunny's neighborhood, so while it was lousy with wiseguys it was free of street gangs, and no one was loitering at corners or doorways.

Lula had her head out the window while she cruised a four-block grid. "Here, Kevin!" she called. "Come get your lettuce!"

We didn't see Kevin, and we didn't see Sunny or his goons.

"I hope nothing happened to Kevin," Lula said.

"Maybe he had a late night and he's sleeping," I said. "Why don't we leave the lettuce, and we can come back later."

Lula dumped the lettuce out at the corner of Fifteenth and Freeman, we took one last ride around, and Lula drove to the mall.

"I gotta see how much one of them genuine Brahmin bags costs," Lula said. "I like my Brakmin okay, but it's no Brahmin."

"I think a Brahmin bag might be pricey."

"I could save up for it. I could get a night job, if you know what I mean."

"I thought you didn't do that anymore."

"I've been doing it in the name of passion, so I don't see where it'd hurt to do it once or twice for the sake of being fashionable. I mean, I got a passion to get a Brahmin bag, so where's the difference, right?"

We passed by the store's shoe department without so much as a glance and found ladies' handbags. Lula went straight to the Brahmins.

"There's too many," she said. "How am I supposed to choose when they got all these colors? It's true that none of them got crystals like my Brakmin, but that's on account of these bags are real classy. These bags are *ladies'* bags."

"That might leave you out since you're planning on buying one by selling your wares on a street corner."

"There's no rules saying a lady can't do a BJ," Lula said. "And some of these bags aren't so expensive. I could have one of these bags in no time."

"You could also make money by helping me capture Sunny," I told her.

"That's true," Lula said. "I don't have much confidence in that happening, but I guess we could give it another try."

We drove back to Fifteenth and Morgan and sat there for a half hour.

"Nothing's happening," Lula said. "This is boring. I say we get out and walk around. Maybe we'll come across Kevin."

We walked three blocks down Fifteenth and turned onto Willard. We walked one block on Willard and turned onto Sixteenth.

"This is good," Lula said. "I bet we already walked off those donuts what with walking in the mall and walking here." She stopped and tipped her nose up and sniffed the air. "I think I might have just caught a whiff of giraffe."

I looked around. I sniffed. "I don't smell anything."

"That's because you aren't so finely tuned to Kevin as I am." She walked twenty paces down Sixteenth. "Yep, that's giraffe I'm smelling. He's up there in front of us. I bet he's heading for Freeman Street."

"Freeman and Fifteenth is ground zero for Uncle Sunny Land," I said. "I think we should stay away from that block."

"Yeah, but Kevin's going after his lettuce. He'll be real disappointed if he don't get to see who's been leaving him all that delicious food."

"He'll be even more disappointed if the food stops showing up because Sunny's goons drilled you full of bullet holes."

"Hey, *I* didn't shoot Uncle Sunny. I was just a innocent bystander. I'm pretty sure the goons got that figured out. *You're* the one they want to drill full of holes."

"I didn't shoot Sunny!"

"I know that and Uncle Sunny knows that and you know that," Lula said, "but the rest of the world don't know that."

"Well, I'm going to be careful until the rest of the world knows I didn't shoot Sunny."

"I'm not sure the rest of the world cares," Lula said. "I'm thinking they might want to shoot you anyway."

"This is ridiculous. I'm a nonviolent person. I hate the *Godfather* movies. I get nauseous when I see Bruce Willis bleeding. I never even carry a gun. Why do people want to shoot me?"

"Because you're a bounty hunter?"

"I need a new job."

"You say that all the time," Lula said, "but I don't see you *getting* a new job. And just because you got a new job don't mean people won't want to shoot you. For instance, you get a job as a chef or interior decorator, and I bet some people want to shoot you."

"I could sell shoes."

"Yeah, you'd get to spend time on your knees, looking up people's hoo-has. I can't see you doing that job neither. That'd be a job for Vinnie."

"Maybe we should split up. You go look for Kevin, and

I'll make my way back to the car. I'll meet you there in a half hour."

"That sounds like a plan. You want my gun?"

"No!" Even if I'd had a gun I didn't think I could shoot it with my two fingers splinted together.

"Yell if you need help," Lula said.

"I'll be fine," I told her.

I was happy with the plan. It was a beautiful day, and I didn't mind walking. You see things on foot that you miss in a car. You hear things. You meet people. Sunny owned properties here. He did business here. He had friends and also enemies here. And probably Vinnie was right. Sunny's enemies would be more helpful than his friends.

This block of Sixteenth was primarily residential. The conjoined redbrick houses had originally been single family but were now subdivided into flats. Most were nicely maintained. No gang graffiti. No burned-out crack houses. No rats scurrying around in the gutters. There also were no yards or porches. Each house had a front stoop that was three or four steps high. This allowed for small basement windows. A few of the houses had first-floor businesses. A bridal shop, a realtor, a tailor who was most likely a front for something.

I passed an older woman carrying a grocery bag, but that was it for foot traffic. Car traffic was almost as sparse. I reached the end of the block and crossed the street. I walked past two row houses, and a black SUV rolled down the street and parked in front of me. Two guys got out of the SUV and pulled guns.

I turned to run and saw the black Lincoln Town Car idling at the curb behind me. Shorty and Moe got out and walked toward me. Moe had his gun drawn. Shorty was holding a stun gun.

I didn't see any little businesses on this block. No open apartment building doors. No place to run for shelter. I could sprint across the street and start trying doors, but they'd be on me if the first door didn't open. I grabbed my cellphone, pressed the speed dial for Ranger, and took off. I was across the street, attempting to get into a house with my phone still in my hand, when I felt the stun gun charge rip through me. After that it was all mental confusion and scrambled muscle connections.

• • •

The fog started to clear and I found myself in total darkness. I had a vague memory of being carried. I was in a cramped position, unable to straighten my legs. My hands were cuffed behind my back. I lay perfectly still, trying to clear my head, fighting the panic that was burning in my chest. I could feel motion and bumps. I was in the trunk of a car. The Lincoln, I thought.

I could scream, but that wasn't going to do me any good while the car was moving. I was pressed against something hard and scratchy, and it was preventing me from maneuvering my legs into a position to kick anything.

The car came to a stop, and I started screaming. The lid to the trunk opened, and I saw daylight and Moe looking down at me.

"That screaming's annoying," Moe said. "If you don't stop I'm going to zap you again."

"Where are we?"

"We're on the bridge. You're going swimming."

Shorty and another guy came around and helped Moe wrangle me out of the trunk. The job was made more difficult by the fact that a cinderblock was attached to my ankle by a long rope.

"You've got to be kidding," I said, looking down at the cinderblock. "Mob guys don't actually do this."

"Turns out, we do," Moe said.

Cars were zipping by, drivers gawking. Some honked their horns and waved.

Moe waved back. "They think we're making a movie or something." He slammed the trunk closed. "We usually do this at night, but I got to go to an anniversary party for my in-laws."

The SUV was parked behind the Lincoln. One guy was behind the wheel and the other guy was standing next to Shorty, taking it all in.

"Okay, here we go," Moe said. "We'll alley-oop her over the guardrail."

"Why are you doing this?" I asked.

"That's one of those questions that got an obvious answer," Moe said. "You're a pain in the ass, and you won't go away. And you shot Sunny."

"I didn't shoot Sunny. Rita shot Sunny."

"I wouldn't find that hard to believe," Moe said, "but we got our orders."

The guy from the SUV gave a grunt and hefted the cinder-block.

"No! Help!" I yelled. *"Helllllllp!"*

"You just can't help yourself, can you?" Moe said to me. "Always the pain in the ass."

"Help!" I screamed. *"Somebody help me!"*

Some cars slowed to look, but no one stopped.

"For crissake," the SUV guy said. *"Move her!* I'm gonna pop a hemorrhoid holding this motherfucking cinderblock."

Moe had me by one arm, and Shorty had me by the other. I was struggling against them, kicking out with the foot not tied to the cinderblock, but I was losing ground. They got me to the guardrail, and I could see the Delaware River dark and deep, swirling away from the bridge abutments.

I was still screaming and kicking as I was lifted off my feet, and I felt the guardrail against my back.

"Shove her over," the SUV guy said.

"I'm fucking trying," Moe said. "We should have tied her other foot."

I connected with Shorty's crotch and heard him expel a *woof* of air. He released my arm and doubled over. The SUV guy dropped the cinderblock and grabbed me. There was a lot of swearing and grunting and struggling, and I went over the side. I dropped about ten feet, heard something go *thunk,* and I hung there, twirling around in the breeze.

"What the fuck?" Moe said.

"The goddamn block is stuck," the SUV guy said.

"Are you shitting me?"

"No. It got pulled into the guardrail when she went over, and it's caught there."

I heard more grunting and swearing and then a moment of silence.

"It's not coming loose," the SUV guy said.

"So cut the rope," Moe said.

"I haven't got a knife," the SUV guy said. "You got one?"

"Isn't there one in the car?"

"Why would we have a knife in the car? In case we want to cut salami? I don't use a knife. I'm a gun guy."

"Great. Then fucking *shoot* the rope," Moe said.

I heard someone leaning on a horn, more swearing, and the sound of men running. There was shouting and car noise, but I couldn't sort any of it out. I had my own problems. I was hanging upside down by one foot with my heart racing and the rope biting into my ankle.

I tilted my head to look up at the bridge and saw Ranger straddling the guardrail.

"Try to stay still," he said to me. "I'm going to pull you up, but you have to stop twirling. You're loosening the knot."

I instantly froze, but I was still gently swaying, and I felt the knot slip. A heartbeat later I was in free fall. I caught a glimpse of Ranger flying off the bridge after me. I curled into a cannonball position, and took a deep breath a split-second before I hit the water. I plunged below the surface and came out of my fetal position disoriented. I felt myself being pushed up, and in the longest moment of my life I struggled not to breathe and suck in river water. I surfaced sputtering and gasping for air. I went under briefly and was pushed up again. I could feel Ranger against my back, his arm wrapped around me.

"Relax!" he shouted. "I'm going to float with the current and tow you in."

I tried to tell him I could swim, but I was shaking and my teeth were chattering and I couldn't get any words formed. By the time we reached the bank there were four Rangeman guys in the water waiting to help us, and an EMS truck and a police car were idling a short distance away, lights flashing.

I was pulled out of the water and wrapped in a blanket. Someone removed the cuffs. Ranger held me tight against him, his cheek against mine.

"You're okay," he said. "You're safe."

I nodded, unable to speak.

He stepped back and looked at me. "Anything broken?"

I shook my head. "N-n-n-no."

"Do you need to get checked out by the EMS tech?"

"N-n-n-no."

"I need to take care of things here," he said. "I'm going to have Tank take you home. You can talk to the police after you've had a shower and gotten into dry clothes."

"It was M-m-moe and Shorty," I said. "Damn, I can't stop shaking."

"Adrenaline burn-off," Ranger said. "It's normal."

"Why aren't *you* sh-sh-shaking?"

"I'm not normal."

ELEVEN

TANK IS APPROPRIATELY named. He's big and indestructible. He's second in command at Rangeman, and he's the guy Ranger trusts to watch his back. A while back he dated Lula, but Lula was allergic to his cats, and Tank wasn't giving up his cats for love or money or Lula.

"Your messenger bag is on the backseat," Tank said. "We found it in the Lincoln. Good thing they threw it in with you, or we wouldn't have been able to track you down."

"Did you capture Moe and Shorty?"

"They took off in the SUV, and Hal and Gino and five police cars went after them."

I retrieved my bag from the backseat, found my cellphone, and dialed Lula.

"Where the heck are you?" Lula asked. "I've been standing here by the car, waiting for you."

"I sort of got kidnapped and thrown in the river, but I'm okay now. Tank is driving me home."

"Say what?"

"It wasn't a big deal. I'll tell you about it later. Did you find Kevin?"

"No, but there was some homeless guy eating Kevin's lettuce. I gave him five bucks for a bottle of wine and he left."

"Are you going to Bingo tonight?"

"I'm gonna pass. I got a date."

"Does your date involve standing on a corner?"

"Maybe for a moment."

I disconnected, and Tank looked over at me. "Seemed to me that it was a big deal."

I leaned back against the headrest and closed my eyes. "I'm trying to forget."

"Don't forget too much or it might happen again."

The very thought made me shudder.

A half hour later Tank walked me to my door.

"Would you like me to stay?" he asked.

"Not necessary. But thank you. I'm fine."

I closed and locked my door. I looked in at Rex and told him not to worry, because I was okay. And then I burst into tears. I cried all through my shower and halfway through drying my hair. I'd stopped sobbing, but my eyes were red and my nose was still leaking, when my cellphone rang.

"I'm at your door," Morelli said. "You're supposed to be in

there, according to Ranger, but I'm pounding on your door, and you're not answering."

"I didn't hear you. I had the hair dryer going."

I opened the door to Morelli, and he scooped me into him.

"You're crushing me," I said. "I can't breathe."

"Do you have any idea what it's like to find out the woman you love has just been thrown off a bridge? My heart stopped beating. Are you okay? Were you hurt?"

"I got some scratches and bruises, but nothing serious. Mostly I was terrified. I was so scared I don't even remember hitting the water."

His cellphone buzzed with a text message.

"I hate this thing," Morelli said, eyes on the message.

"It's okay if you have to go. All I want to do is sleep. Now that I'm warm and dry, I'm flat out done."

He kissed me on the forehead. "I'll call when I get a break."

I locked up after him, crawled into bed, put a pillow over my head, and instantly fell asleep.

• • •

I woke up when the pillow got lifted off and Ranger looked down at me.

"Babe."

"Getting dropped into the Delaware is exhausting."

Ranger was sitting on the side of the bed, and he was look-ing comfortably dry and perfectly groomed in Rangeman black fatigues. There was almost always a softness to his mouth that was sensuous and youthful, but his eyes were dark and serious and reflected his troubled history.

"How are you doing?" he asked.

"I'm doing great."

And that was true. Turns out I'm very resilient. All I need is some chattering teeth, about an hour of uncontrollable sobbing, some sleep, and I'm ready to face the world again. Plus I was pretty sure there was one last leftover hot dog in my fridge, and that would make everything just about perfect.

"I wish I could say the same," Ranger said. "I'm having a hard time erasing the vision of you falling from the bridge."

"Yes, but you jumped in and saved me. You're my hero."

"Being your hero is a full-time job. I worry that someday I'm not going to get to you in time."

"I didn't know you worried about *anything*."

"I worry about *everything*."

"What happened to Moe and Shorty and the two guys in the SUV? Were they captured?"

"They were captured and booked, and they're already out on bail."

"They tried to kill me! They were serious. How could they get released?"

"Sympathetic judge. Would you consider moving into Rangeman until we get this sorted out?"

"It's tempting, but no."

Rangeman was headquartered in an under-the-radar

office building on a quiet side street in the center of the city. There was secure underground parking and seven secure floors aboveground. Ranger's one-bedroom, one-bath private apartment, professionally decorated in earth tones with black accents, occupied the entire seventh floor. It was calm and cool and immaculate, thanks to the building's housekeeper, Ella. The problem was with the bed: Ranger slept in it.

Moving into the Rangeman building would protect me from everyone but Ranger. Not that I could compare sleeping with Ranger to being dead. And not that Ranger would force himself on me. My fear was more that *I'd* force myself on *Ranger* and screw my life up in a major way.

I looked at my watch. "*Damn.* It's almost seven o'clock! I'm late. I told Grandma I'd pick her up for Bingo at seven." I thunked my forehead with the heel of my hand. "My car is still parked at the bonds office."

"I had it picked up and brought here. It's parked in the lot."

. . .

The firehouse is on the fringe of the Burg. It has a large public-use room that holds Bingo games, wedding and baby showers, small wedding receptions, and pancake breakfasts that benefit a variety of causes. The floor is oak, the walls are painted a bilious green, and the lighting is fluorescent. The Bingo game setup is pretty much the same as at the Senior Center.

Grandma and I, the last to arrive, were relegated to the back of the room. This was perfect for me. I could see everyone playing. Twenty percent of the players were gonzo Bingo junkies who played Bingo every day and were also at the Senior Center. The remaining 80 percent were mostly from the Burg. A bunch of Grandma's cronies were there, plus some of my grade school and high school friends. At least half the room had been drinking, and they were feeling no pain.

"Your hair is different," I said to Grandma.

"Yeah. I went blond. The gray made me look too old."

Grandma's gray hair was just the tip of the iceberg. She was young at heart, but she had a body like a soup chicken and skin like an elephant.

"I went to the beauty salon today and got spruced up," Grandma said. "Ever since Mildred Frick called me a slut my phone hasn't stopped ringing. I got two dates for the weekend."

"It might not be such a good thing to have men calling you because they think you're a slut," I said. "They're only going to be after one thing."

"I hope that's true. I don't want to find out I went blond and bought them thongs for nothing."

"Did you happen to hear anything about me this afternoon?"

"Just how you got thrown off the bridge and Ranger jumped in to save you."

"Does Mom know?"

"Yeah. She ironed sheets for three hours, mumbling about how she wished you were more like your sister with all the kids and a lawyer for a husband, and how she couldn't understand you not wanting to be a butcher. And then she had a couple nips of booze while she was making supper, and some red wine when we sat down to eat, and she was pretty much in a nice stupor by the time I left."

My mother always irons when she's upset. If you walk into the house and see the ironing board up, it's usually a good idea to turn tail and leave. I guess that's cowardly, but Grandma and I are almost always the cause for the stress, and we've learned it's best to give my mother some space when she's freaked.

Grandma and I each had three Bingo cards. Every time a number was called I'd bang my splint onto the Formica table-top, trying to use my dauber.

"How long do you gotta wear that thing?" Grandma asked.

"A couple weeks."

"Maybe you want me to take over your cards so you don't break any more of your finger bone."

"That would be great. Thanks."

There were three men playing Bingo. All three had been at the Senior Center. Two were a gay couple who were probably in their seventies. It was hard to judge their exact age because they were Botoxed, exfoliated, and moisturized, and had skin like a baby's bottom.

Gordon Krutch was the third man. He was also in his seventies, but without the benefits of gaydom his face looked like a road map of Newark: lots of intersecting streets, plus a bunch of potholes, and skin the color and texture of concrete.

Grandma caught Gordon's eye and waved at him. Gordon waved back and blew Grandma a kiss.

"Isn't he something?" Grandma said to me. "We're going to the movies tomorrow. He still drives and everything. He's a real catch. He's kept himself in shape. He takes the fitness class for old people at the Senior Center."

I suppose it's relative, but Gordon didn't look to me like he was in great shape. He was about fifty pounds overweight, and he broke into a sweat from the exertion of walking. Plus there was the near-death pallor.

"Ever since his wife died he's been the hot ticket," Grandma said.

"Has he dated any of the women who were murdered?"

"Not that I know about."

I had a feeling the Bingo connection wasn't going to lead to a suspect. There had to be something else the murdered women had in common.

Morelli's ringtone sang out on my cellphone.

"I've only got a minute," Morelli said. "Double homicide in the projects. Not sure when I'll be done here."

"Bingo!" Grandma yelled. *"Stephanie got Bingo!"*

I looked over at my card, and I looked up at the screen. Bingo.

"What did I win?" I asked Grandma.

"One of them slow cookers."

"No money?"

"No. It wasn't a money game. It was a potluck game."

"I won a slow cooker at Bingo," I told Morelli.

"You're at Bingo?"

"Yeah, and I won!"

. . .

Two hours later I carefully stepped out of the firehouse and looked around. No big black cars with gun turrets. No thugs with Tasers. No scary Italian granny with an assault rifle. Good deal.

I dropped Grandma off at my parents' house and took my slow cooker home. I parked in the lot to my apartment building, and Ranger's 911 Turbo slid in next to me. I hauled the massive slow cooker box out of my car and saw Ranger's mouth twitch at the corners, suggesting the beginning of a smile.

"I won it," I told him.

"The perfect prize."

"Scoff all you want, but I might use it. I've been thinking about taking up cooking. I made dinner the other night."

"How'd that go?" Ranger asked.

"I exploded the vegetables in the microwave, but other than that it went pretty good."

"You never disappoint," Ranger said, taking the box from me.

He carried the box into my apartment and set it on my kitchen counter. Rex came out of his soup can to take a look, decided the box wasn't all that interesting, and went back into his soup can.

"I think the Bingo connection is dead in the water," I said

to Ranger. "The women must have had something else in common."

"Keep working at it. Do you need help with Sunucchi?"

"I might. He spends his nights with Rita Raguzzi. She has a house in Hamilton Township, and I think that's the best place to grab him. It's the only time Sunny isn't surrounded by his posse."

"This is shotgun Rita?"

"Yeah. It should be fun."

"Good," Ranger said. "I'm all about fun."

"Since when?"

He pulled me into him and kissed me. There was some highly skilled groping and use of tongue, and on a fun scale of 1 to 10 it was an 11.

"Call me when you're ready to do the takedown," Ranger said.

I locked the door after him, took the slow cooker out of the box, and set it on my kitchen counter. I had no clue what I was supposed to do with it. I thumbed through the instructions and did a quick scan of the little recipe book that came with the cooker. It sounded simple enough. Throw a bunch of stuff in the pot and turn it on.

TWELVE

LULA ROLLED INTO the office five minutes after I did. Her hair was a big orange frizzball, and she had bags under her eyes.

"How was the *date*?" Connie asked her. "You look like you got run over by a truck."

"First off, there were no good corners left. I've never seen so many hookers. They're all over the place. And then there's a real impact on the trade being that the economy is in the toilet."

"Did you make enough money for the Brahmin bag?"

"I didn't make nothing. I stood out there until the sun come up and the only bite I had all night was some fool wanted a hand job and was gonna pay me in food stamps. I'm telling you there's a lot of food stamps floating around out there. I mean, what the heck is this country coming to? Food stamps aren't gonna buy me no genuine Brahmin, you see what I'm saying?"

"Maybe you don't need a Brahmin," I said.

"Of course I need a Brahmin," Lula said. "You carry a Brahmin and everybody knows you got class and fashion flair. They got ads in *Vogue*."

"Mary Treetrunk is still in the wind," Connie said. "She's not a big ticket bond, but she'll get you pizza money."

"What did she do this time?" Lula wanted to know.

"She got raided for having a pot farm behind her double-wide. And then when they tried to take her in she kicked one of the cops in the nuts and offered to kiss it and make it a lot better."

"You see what I mean," Lula said. "Everybody's a 'ho these days. How's a professional supposed to compete in the market-place?"

I pulled Mary's file out of my messenger bag and paged through it. "It looks like she's still living in that patch of mud and scrub down by the river."

"So far as I know," Connie said. "She's probably there even as we speak, planting a new crop of cannabis."

"I'm not having her smell up my Firebird," Lula said to me. "If we do this we gotta take your P.O.S."

We'd busted Mary twice before, and neither time was pretty. She weighed upwards of two hundred pounds, she smelled like dead fish, and she was cranky about leaving her doublewide.

"Sure," I said. "Let's do it."

I took Hamilton to Broad and turned onto the narrow rutted road that led down to Mary Treetrunk's homestead. She owned a half acre of land that was part floodplain and part garbage heap. Her doublewide was rusted out and listing, propped up on cinderblocks. An electric line ran to the mobile home that was anything but mobile, and a satellite dish was precariously attached to the roof. A Ford Crown Vic was parked off to the side. A lot of years ago it had been a police car, but it was now a wreck. A pirate's skull-and-crossbones flag had been tied onto the antenna.

"This here's a mess," Lula said. "I'm glad I dressed down today and I'm not wearing my Louboutins."

Lula was wearing a shocking-pink tank top, a poison-green spandex skirt that came two inches below her ass, and gold sequined sneakers. If you put her in a room and turned the lights off, she'd glow in the dark.

"Are you still dressed from last night?" I asked her.

"Of course not. If I was dressed like this I wouldn't draw no attention. As it was I could have stayed home. Did I tell you I'm thinking about getting a cat?"

"You're allergic to cats."

"Yeah, but I saw one in the pet store that didn't have no hair, and they said it was a nonallergic cat."

Lula and I got out of my car, the door to the doublewide crashed open, and Mary looked out at us.

"The store's closed," Mary said. "I haven't got any damn merchandise. The damn police took it all. Get off my damn property."

"Sounds like Mary's not in a good mood," Lula whispered to me.

I pulled flexi-cuffs out of my bag and stuffed them into my

back pocket. Mary's wrists were too large for ordinary handcuffs. "Mary's never in a good mood."

"It's no wonder. I'm a big woman but I'm big in a beautiful way. This woman here is just plain too fat. She look like she got no muscle tone. She's all lumpy."

Mary squinted at me. "Do I know you?"

"It's Stephanie Plum," I yelled. "You need to get rebonded."

"I don't got time for that. It's supposed to rain later today. I gotta get my plants in before it rains."

"You aren't putting in more cannabis, are you?"

"What do I look, stupid?" Mary said. "You can't start a new crop outside at this time of the year. I got them little guys under grow lights in my doublewide. I'm setting out some cabbage."

"This will only take an hour or two, and you'll be released on bond again," I told her. "And we can stop and get a bag of breakfast sandwiches on the way."

"I could use a breakfast sandwich," Mary said.

"Me too," Lula said. "I wouldn't mind a breakfast sandwich myself. And if we go to Cluck-in-a-Bucket we could add some fried chicken for a extra boost of protein. And maybe some biscuits with the chicken."

"They got good gravy there," Mary said. "I'm partial to gravy."

I cuffed Mary's hands in front of her so she could eat, and we loaded her into my backseat.

"I don't mean to be rude or nothing," Lula said to Mary, "but you stink."

"I don't smell nothing," Mary said.

Lula powered her window down. "You smell like dead fish."

"That's because I'm one of them green people. I don't participate in fertilizing my plants with that phony nitrogen stuff. I wait until there's a fish kill in the river and then I go collect all the dead fish that wash up. I let them rot out, and I use them for plant food. It's why I grow such quality product. You get weed from Mary Treetrunk and you know it's good organic shit."

"Is there lots of fish kills?" Lula asked.

"Yep. There's dead fish laying around all the time. Some of them only got one eye, and a couple times I found fish with two heads."

I returned to Broad Street, drove to Cluck-in-a-Bucket, and loaded up at the drive-through. Mary was happy in the backseat with a bag filled with breakfast sandwiches, a bucket of chicken, and a side of biscuits and gravy. Lula had a super-sized diet cola, a single breakfast sandwich, and a medium box of chicken nuggets. No biscuits. No gravy. No apple pie for dessert. I assumed this relatively small portion for her was the result of listening to the car groan under Mary's weight and not wanting to go there. The other possibility was nausea from the fish stench.

I pulled out of the lot, onto the street, and a black Cadillac Escalade with a satellite dish on the roof passed me going in the opposite direction.

"That's the car!" Lula said. "That's the dart gun car."

I checked my rearview mirror and saw the Escalade make a U-turn. It zoomed up to my bumper and gave me a tap.

"What the heck?" Lula said. "I almost spilled my soda. I think they hit us on purpose."

"Can you see who's driving?"

Lula turned in her seat. "I can see him, but I don't know him."

There were cars stopped for a traffic light in front of me. I slowed for the light, and the Escalade tapped me again. The passenger side door on the Escalade opened, a guy got out, pulled a gun, and ran for my car. It was the cinderblock guy who had tried to throw me into the river.

I pulled out of the line of stopped traffic, jumped the curb, and drove across three front lawns. I hit the cross street hard, with the rear of the car scraping the cement curb. The muffler fell off with a loud *klunk,* and I roared away, fishtailing and leaving behind what meager tread had been left on my tires.

Lula had her foot braced on the dash, and Mary had her food clutched to her chest.

"*What the Sam Hill?*" Mary exclaimed.

I paused at the corner and looked back. The Escalade had followed me across the lawns but was now stopped in the middle of the road.

"What's going on?" I asked Lula.

"I don't know. They're stopped, and the one guy is out of the car again. Looks like he's trying to grab hold of something. I think they might have run over your muffler."

• • •

We brought Mary into the police station, and everyone took a step back from us.

"I'm gonna have to burn my clothes," Lula said. "I'm never getting this fish smell out, and this top was one of my favorites. I'm putting in to Connie for damages done on the job. Vinnie's gonna have to buy me a new outfit. We're gonna have to stop someplace on the way back to the office, because I'm not contaminating my Firebird with this smell. I'll have a pack of cats following me down the street."

I got my body receipt from the docket lieutenant and ran into Morelli on the way out.

"*Wow!*" he said. "Holy sweet Jesus. What's that smell?"

"I just brought Mary Treetrunk in," I told him.

"That would explain it."

"I don't suppose there's any breaking news on the Dumpster murders."

"Only that the chemistry hasn't been helpful. Butch got the latest report back from the state lab and it didn't show anything useful. The women were clean. Anything new happening in your life today?"

"My muffler fell off."

"Yeah, but it turned out to be a good thing," Lula said. "On account of the guy with the gun who was chasing us ran over the muffler, and it got stuck under his car. So you see, everything happens for a reason, right? All's well that ends well."

Morelli's face went blank for a moment. "Seriously?" he finally said.

"It was one of those random encounters," I told him.

"I can't stand here talking anymore," Lula said. "My eyes are burning. I got to de-fish myself."

I told Morelli I'd talk to him later, and Lula and I chugged off across town to T.J. Maxx on South Broad Street. After five minutes we pretty much had the store to ourselves. Lula went with a silver sequined tank top and a short fuchsia handkerchief skirt that looked like it should be worn by the Sugar Plum Fairy. I stuck with my fish jeans and T-shirt since I was going to have to find money for a new muffler.

I dropped Lula off at the office and drove to my parents' house. I could throw my clothes in the washer, mooch lunch, and grill Grandma on the dead women all at the same time. And hopefully it would go okay and my mother wouldn't be dragging the ironing board out when I left.

"Look who's here," Grandma said, opening the front door for me. "What a good surprise, but holy cow you smell like dead fish."

"Occupational hazard," I said. "Is my father here?"

"No. He's out with the cab. It's just me and your mother."

I stripped down to my undies and handed my jeans and T-shirt to Grandma. "I'm going upstairs to take a shower. Throw these in the washing machine for me."

I washed my hair twice and stood under the shower until the water turned cold.

"I left clothes for you on the bed in the spare room," Grandma yelled through the door. "Lucky I had some new underwear."

I toweled off and went in search of the clothes. There are three small bedrooms on the second floor of my parents' house. One for my mom and dad. Grandma Mazur slept in what used to be my sister's room. And the third used to be mine. It was left intact for a number of years after I moved out, but gradually it changed into the spare room and my things migrated to my apartment.

Grandma had laid out a bright yellow thong and matching yellow sports bra with the tags still attached. The mental picture of Grandma in the underwear wasn't good, but I liked that she felt comfortable buying it and wearing it. She was a little shorter than me, and our flesh was arranged differently, but the thong and the bra fit just fine. The lavender and white silky running suit she left for me was a whole other matter. Good enough to get me through lunch, but I was praying my own clothes would be dry before I was ready to leave the house.

My mother had the table set by the time I came down. "I have tomato soup and lunch meat for a sandwich," she said. "Or I can make you a grilled cheese."

"Tomato soup and grilled cheese would be great," I said.

"Me too," Grandma said. "I want extra cheese."

I sat at the table across from Grandma. "I need some help with the women who were murdered. When I discovered they all played Bingo I thought that might be the common interest that would lead me to the murderer, but I couldn't single out a suspect at either game. There has to be something else the women had in common that they would come into contact with the murderer."

"I didn't know Melvina," Grandma said. "I knew Bitsy Muddle, Lois Fratelli, and Rose Walchek. Poor Rose is going to be laid out tomorrow. I had to cancel a date so I could go. I heard you could see the cord marks on Rose's neck. I hope they don't get too covered up. I wouldn't mind seeing something like that."

"That's gruesome," my mother said.

"Maybe," Grandma said, "but I got a natural scientific curiosity about those things. I bet I could have been one of them forensic people like on television."

"Tell me about Rose," I said to Grandma. "How well did you know her?"

"I guess I knew her pretty well," Grandma said. "I saw her at Bingo, and I saw her at the beauty salon. And I saw her at the funeral parlor too. She liked to go to the afternoon viewings, because they weren't so crowded."

"Did she have a man friend?"

"She was seeing Barry Farver for a while, but he died. That's the problem with dating the old geezers. That's why I always say if you're going to invest in a man you got to go young."

"Gordon Krutch doesn't look all that young."

"Yeah, he's pretty old, but he's got a car. And Madelyn Krick went out with him, and she said he's hot."

My mother was at the stove, frying the grilled cheese. She wasn't facing me, but I could feel her eyes rolling around in her head.

"Did she play cards? Did she belong to a book club? Did she take tap dancing lessons?" I asked Grandma.

"She liked the Jumble. She always had one of them Jumble books when she was at the beauty salon."

"I knew Rose," my mother said, bringing the sandwiches to the table. "She liked to cook. She went to all the cooking demonstrations at the kitchen store next to the liquor store."

"That's right," Grandma said. "I forgot about that. Your mother and I go to some of them. They're real good. You should go with us next time."

I bit into my sandwich. "Are there men in the audience?"

"The times we were there it was almost half men," Grandma said. "The demonstrations are early Saturday morning, and it's a good location between the liquor store and the supermarket."

"Did any of the other victims attend the cooking demonstrations?"

"We don't go every week," Grandma said. "Bitsy was there once when they were doing crêpes Suzette. Bitsy liked her booze."

"What about Lois?" I asked. "Did she go to the cooking demonstrations?"

"I never saw her there," Grandma said. "But I saw her in the liquor store that was next to it. It's an excellent liquor store. Your mother and me get all our hooch there."

"Anything else about Lois?"

"She lived a block from here, but we didn't see her much," Grandma said. "Sometimes we'd see her at mass."

I finished my soup and sandwich and took my clothes out of the washing machine. They still smelled like fish, so I ran them through a second time and dumped in some bleach.

"I have to get back to work," I said. "I'll stop by later for my clothes."

"Come for dinner," my mother said. "I'm making stuffed shells, and there's chocolate cake for dessert."

"Sounds good." Hard to pass up stuffed shells and chocolate cake.

I rumbled off to my apartment, changed my clothes, and turned my laptop on. I plugged the four murdered women into a basic search program and printed out a page on each of them. Address, credit history, litigation, relatives, work history. Mostly I cared about the addresses and the relatives. I was sure I was duplicating police efforts, but Ranger wanted me to snoop, so I was snooping.

Melvina had lived in a garden apartment in Hamilton Township. She'd had a couple low-limit credit cards. No work history. No litigation. Besides her son, Ruppert, there was a daughter who lived in Chicago. Melvina had survived her husband and her two siblings.

Lois Fratelli had lived in the Burg. I knew the house. It was small and tidy. Single family. She'd had several credit cards. No litigation. She'd worked as office manager for the family plumbing business for thirty-two years. Nothing recent. She was survived by about a hundred and forty Fratellis, all of them living in the Burg.

Rose Walchek had a similar profile. Widowed. Lived in a small row house on Stanton Street. Worked at the button factory for fifteen years. Nothing recent. No children.

Bitsy Muddle had lived in a small retirement complex behind the strip mall containing the supermarket and liquor store. She'd worked as a bank teller for twenty-seven years, she'd operated a boxing machine at a sanitary products plant for eleven years, and she'd been a cashier at WalMart for five years. She'd never married.

I found none of this information inspiring. Truth is, I wasn't exactly an ace detective. I mostly found people through dumb luck and perseverance. Catching them was an even sketchier experience.

I looked out my living room window at the parking lot and didn't see any thugs lurking in shadows, or sitting behind the wheel of their big black cars, so I shoved the printouts into my messenger bag and headed out.

Lula was sitting at Connie's desk when I walked in. Connie was missing in action.

"Vinnie's at his Perverts Anonymous meeting," Lula said, "so Connie had to go downtown to write bond on some idiot."

"Do we know the idiot?"

Lula shook her head. "It's a new idiot."

"Did anything exciting happen while I was gone?"

"You mean like Sunny coming here and turning himself in?"

"Did he do that?"

"No."

"Too bad. I hate to say it out loud, but I'm spooked over Sunny. I kept waking up last night, thinking I was falling. Getting pitched off a bridge is freaking scary. And it wasn't any fun being locked in the trunk of the car, either."

"I hear you. Personally, I think those guys have been watching too much violence on television. They been seeing too many reruns of *The Sopranos*. Their behavior is disturbing. I'm even thinking twice about going over to check on Kevin. I haven't given him any lettuce today. 'Course I'm not sure he was the one eating the lettuce anyways. It might have just been the homeless fool. I mean, who eats lettuce like that? He didn't have no Thousand Island dressing or nothing."

"I've been thinking maybe I should talk to Joe's mother about Uncle Sunny."

"What? Are you nuts? She doesn't like you to begin with. And she's probably got Bella there. She'll send her out after you like a junkyard dog."

"Sunny kills people. How can they not understand that?"

"They probably think he only kills bad people. Like people who don't pay their protection money."

"That's wrong."

"Yeah, but that's *your* standards. You should live in *my* neighborhood. People get killed if they're wearing the wrong deodorant. Only thing good I can say is people in my 'hood don't drop people off a bridge. You know you're gonna get knifed or shot in my neighborhood."

"That must make you rest a lot easier."

"At least I don't have to worry about my hair looking like crap when I meet my maker."

I dropped the body receipt for Mary Treetrunk on Connie's desk. "Make sure Connie sees this. I'm going to do a drive-around and check out the dead women's neighborhoods. And then I'm going to my parents' house for dinner."

"No Bingo tonight?"

"I'm taking a night off from Bingo."

I was taking a night off from Bingo because I was going to get Ranger to help me snag Uncle Sunny.

THIRTEEN

BY THE TIME I got to my parents' house I had a raging head-ache from riding around in my mufflerless car.

"I knew you were here," Grandma said, opening the front door for me. "We could hear you coming a mile away."

"I'm going to have to borrow Uncle Sandor's car until I get mine fixed," I said. "I can't take the noise."

"No problem. It's in the garage. It's all filled up with gas and ready to go."

My Great Uncle Sandor handed his 1953 powder blue and white Buick Roadmaster over to my Grandma Mazur when he went into the nursing home. He's since died, and the monster car now lives at my parents' house, available for use as a loaner. It gets about three miles to a gallon. It drives like a refrigerator on wheels. And it does nothing for my self-esteem. On the plus side: It's free and it's invincible.

My father was in his chair in the living room, watching television. He's retired from the post office and now drives a cab part-time. He has a few regulars that he drives to the train station every morning and picks up every evening, and the rest of the day he drives the cab to his lodge and plays cards with "the boys." He used to keep a shotgun in the house for protection, but we had to get rid of it for fear he'd shoot Grandma in a gonzo moment of berserk frustration.

I passed through the dining room on my way to the kitchen and noticed that the table was set for five.

"Who's coming to dinner?" I asked. "There's an extra place setting."

The doorbell chimed and Grandma scurried off to get the door.

"Stephanie," my mother called. "Come get the shells. They're ready to go. And there's antipasto."

I draped my bag over the back of a kitchen chair and reached for the antipasto platter. "Who's coming to dinner?"

"No one special. Just someone I ran into today."

I stopped in the middle of the kitchen. "Who?"

"Randy Berger. And don't you dare go out the back door."

"Randy Berger the butcher?"

"He's not the butcher anymore. He owns the deli now. And he's still looking for someone to take over the meat counter. It could be a good job for you. You could get a regular paycheck, and no one would shoot at you or drop you off a bridge. And Randy is single. Who knows what could happen? He could turn out to be *the one.*"

"I found *the one*. I'm almost engaged to Morelli."

Problem was I hadn't just found *the one* . . . I'd found *the two*.

Grandma came into the kitchen with Randy Berger in tow. Berger was a giant. He was 6' 3" and built like someone who ate four double pork chops in a single sitting. He had thinning sandy blond hair and a face permanently flushed from freezer burn and peach schnapps.

"It's real nice of you to invite me to dinner," Randy said to my mother, handing her a large chunk of meat wrapped in white butcher's paper. "I brought you a little something."

"My goodness," my mother said, reading the label. "It's a tenderloin."

"I just got it in," Randy said. "It's corn-fed, and it's got real good marbling. I know everybody's always talking about grass-fed beef, but if you ask me it's shoe leather. Give me a cow that's been shoved into a pen with a thousand other cows and forced to eat grain, and I'll show you a darn good pot roast."

"I guess you know a lot about meat," Grandma said to Randy.

"It's been my life," Randy said. "Except now that I own the deli I have to expand my horizons."

My mother put the meat into the fridge, and pushed everyone into the dining room.

"Frank," she said to my father. "Come to the table. We're ready to eat. Did you meet Randy?"

My father took his seat and looked over at Randy. "You're the butcher."

"I am," Randy said. "And proud of it. Except now I'm also the store owner."

"No kidding? I guess you must have done okay as a butcher to be able to buy the store."

My mother passed the shells to my father. "You see, Stephanie," she said, "you can make good money as a butcher."

"I'm willing to pay top dollar to get the right person," Randy said.

"What's going on?" my father asked. "Is Stephanie taking a job as a butcher? Will we get a discount?"

"We already got a tenderloin from Randy," my mother said.

"Yeah, and it was a big one too," Grandma said.

My father shoveled shells onto his plate and passed the casserole dish to me. "I like tenderloin," he said, looking down the table for the red sauce.

My mother jumped on the red sauce and passed it with the antipasto to my father.

"There's a ricotta cheese filling in the shells," my mother said to Randy. "But there's good capicola and roast beef from your store with the antipasto."

"Glad to hear it," Randy said. "There should be meat with every meal. Without meat there's no meal, am I right?"

"I like this boy," my father said. "He's got a good head on his shoulders."

"How do you feel about bacon?" Grandma asked.

"Bacon makes everything better," Randy said. "Personally, I don't like my bacon too crispy. I like to see some pink in the meat and some nice white fat glistening up at me."

"Stephanie won a slow cooker at Bingo," Grandma said. "She's thinking about taking up cooking."

"If you stop by the meat counter I'll fix you up with just the right thing," Randy said to me. "Some nice beef cubes, or maybe some chicken thighs. And if you want to try it out we could put a butcher's apron on you and get you over to the carving station and let you butcher your own chicken."

"Would she get to use one of them big cleavers?" Grandma asked.

"Sure," Randy said. "She can use whatever she wants. If she comes to work for me she'll even have access to the meat grinders and the power saw for when we get the whole side of beef in. I got a power saw that makes slicing through a steer's thighbone child's play. And she can make blood sausage and chopped liver."

"It sounds like a real exciting job," Grandma said.

"I can't wait to get to work every day," Randy said. "It's always something new. One day you get sheep brains, and then the next day it's cow tongue." He turned to me. "Have you ever had tongue? It's a real delicacy. I like it when it's sliced thin, but I know some people stew it up."

I had half a shell in my mouth, and I didn't think I was going to be able to swallow it. I'd had a decent amount of tongue over the years, but I hadn't sliced or stewed any of it. I took a sip of wine and hoped the shell would slide down and not come back up.

"I'm not actually interested in the butcher job," I said to Randy. "I'm not good with meat and poultry."

He nodded. "It takes a special person. It's a calling."

"She's a darn good bounty hunter, though," Grandma said.

"And she's investigating about the murdered women who got thrown into Dumpsters."

Randy forked in some shells. "I knew all those women. They shopped at my deli."

"I would have thought they'd shop locally. Rose Walchek lived by the button factory on the other side of town. And Melvina lived in Hamilton Township."

"They all belonged to the Senior Discount Club," Randy said. "They got special deals at a handful of stores."

"What were the other stores?"

"The liquor store at the Woodley Mall. The gas station on the corner of Hamilton and Bryant. Morton's Bakery. There were some other stores, too, but I can't remember them all."

"How come I don't know about this?" Grandma said. "I'm a senior."

Randy spooned red sauce over his shells. "It's part of the wellness program at the Senior Center. You have to be signed up for the wellness program."

"I don't go to the Senior Center much," Grandma said. "I get depressed looking at all those old people."

Isn't it strange how life works? Here I was thinking I was paying a steep price for shells and chocolate cake, and then out of nowhere this nugget of information got dropped into my lap. All the women belonged to the Senior Discount Club. I knew there was a chance it'd be another dead end, but it *felt* meaningful. It was as if God had sent me Randy Berger. I smiled at him, and he broke out in a sweat.

We worked our way through the shells and moved on to

dessert. I was debating the wisdom of a second piece of cake when the doorbell rang, and Grandma jumped up and ran to the door.

"There he is," she said. "There's my honeypot."

Gordon Krutch was wheezing from the effort of walking into the dining room. He was wearing a collared three-button knit shirt that stretched tight across his big belly and was showing signs of sweat seeping through the material in the chest area. He had a roll of fat hanging over his belt, and his tan slacks had a lot of crotch wrinkles. The wrinkles came down almost to his knees because he had legs like a Hobbit. Gordon Krutch was 5' 4" on a good day.

"Howdy do," he said, smiling wide. "Looks like you're just finishing up. Sorry, I'm a little early. I like to be punctual. It comes from being a public servant for forty-five years."

"Gordon worked for the DMV," Grandma said. "He made sure everyone's form was filled out right, and he gave the eye test."

"You'd be surprised at how many people try to cheat on the eye test," Gordon said.

"I got perfect eyesight," Grandma said. "Except I gotta wear my glasses for the movies."

"Do you belong to the Senior Discount Club?" I asked Gordon.

"I sure do. It's a wonderful thing. All the best stores participate." He looked at Randy. "In fact, I shop at this young man's deli."

"Strip steak and my special meatloaf mix," Randy said.

"That's me," Gordon said. "Every week like clockwork."

"Did you know the women who were killed?" I asked him. "They were members of the Discount Club too."

"They sure were. I knew all of them. Lovely ladies. Just a terrible shame."

"We're going to the movies," Grandma said. "We're going to see that film where everybody gets eaten by bugs."

My father looked over at Gordon. "I'll give you fifty bucks if you take her to Vegas and marry her."

"Your son-in-law is a great kidder," Gordon said to Grandma.

"He isn't kidding," Grandma said. "You could probably get him up to a couple hundred."

Okay, so Gordon Krutch is short, fifty pounds overweight, and can't breathe without an inhaler. And I can't see him, gasping and wheezing, choking the life out of even the frailest old lady. And I'm pretty sure Grandma could beat the snot out of him. Still, he made me uncomfortable. He knew all the women, and he was icky.

"Call me on my cellphone when you get home," I said to Grandma. "I want to hear about the movie."

FOURTEEN

I HELPED MY mother straighten the kitchen, retrieved my jeans and T-shirt, swapped out my Taurus for the Buick, and went home. Usually I go home with a bag of leftovers, but Randy'd eaten them. The shells, the cake, the antipasto . . . all gone. He said anytime I wanted to butcher some meat I should give him a call. I told him he'd be the first person I'd think of if I got the urge.

I drove around the parking lot, and didn't see any menacing cars. I parked, hustled inside, and locked myself in my apartment. It was almost nine. Too early to roust Sunny out of Rita's bed, but not too early to call Ranger.

"Hey, sexy guy," I said to him. "Guess who?"

"Have you been drinking?"

"Maybe a little."

"I can get to your apartment in five minutes."

"No, no, no. That's not why I'm calling. I thought we could snag Sunny tonight. Maybe around ten o'clock."

"Will you still be awake?"

"I'll be waiting for you in the lobby."

"Babe," Ranger said. And he hung up.

I did some television surfing but couldn't find anything wonderful, so I parked Rex in the slow cooker and cleaned out his cage. I was waiting in the lobby at ten o'clock. A new black Porsche Cayenne glided to a stop in front of the lobby door and blinked its lights. I was pretty sure it was Ranger, but not entirely, so I called him on his cell.

"Is this you?" I asked.

The lights blinked again.

I disconnected and got into the SUV. "A girl can't be too careful," I said, buckling up.

Ranger glanced over at me for a beat and moved the Porsche out of the lot. I suspected the glance was the Ranger equivalent of an eye roll.

Ten minutes later we were in front of Rita's house. Lights were on in the front room. Drapes were drawn. No car in the driveway. Ranger and I got out and walked to the house. We looked in the dining room window and the kitchen window. We saw Rita but no Sunny. The light went out in the living room, Rita walked through the house, and the light went on in the back bedroom. We had a clear view of the room for a moment before she drew the drapes. No Sunny.

"Call him," Ranger said. "Let's see if we hear a phone ringing somewhere in the house."

We didn't hear any ringing, but Sunny picked up.

"Hey, handsome," I said. "Do you need a date?"

"Yeah. Do you need to die?"

I disconnected.

"He knew it was me," I said to Ranger.

"Do you have an alternate address for this guy?"

"I have several."

Ranger drove to Sunny's apartment building at the corner of Fifteenth and Morgan. We parked across the street, stood on the sidewalk, and looked up into Sunny's windows. All dark.

"Either he's asleep or he's not home," I said.

Ranger stepped off the curb. "Let's find out."

"Finding out" with Ranger is a whole different deal than finding out with Lula. Lula and I are Lucy Ricardo and Ethel Mertz. Ranger is Batman. I tagged after him into the building and up the stairs to 2B. He knocked twice, bumped the lock, and opened the door with his gun drawn. He paused for a moment, taking the measure of the room, listening for sounds of clothes rustling or a man sleeping. He quietly closed the apartment door behind him and flicked the beam from his Maglite around the room. I followed after him as he moved into the short hallway and the bedroom and looked in the closet and the bathroom. We moved on to the kitchen. He flipped the flashlight off and we exited the apartment, left the building, and returned to the Cayenne.

"He's not spending much time there, if any," Ranger said. "No food in the refrigerator, hardly any clothes in his closet, no razor in the bathroom."

"He owns the entire block plus scattered properties in the area, but this was the address he listed as his residence. He rents out a three-story brownstone on Freeman next to the Chestnut Social Club. He uses the third floor as a counting room. It's got a big safe in it. I know he spends time there, but I can't see him making it home."

Ranger looked down the street. "Let's take a walk."

We ambled along, looking in windows and doorways, listening to sounds of television and conversation that escaped from the buildings. We turned the corner, walked half a block, and entered the alley. It was dark and narrow, a place where trashcans and recycling bins were kept. Some of the houses had parking spaces, and some had outdoor backstairs. Windows overlooking the alley were small, and the lights behind them were dim.

I stopped and pointed to a redbrick building. "This is the back of the Chestnut Social Club. I broke my finger falling down these stairs." Lights were shining from every window. "The light you see is from an interior rear stairwell."

"Stay here in the shadows," Ranger said. "I'll look inside."

"There might be an alarm," I told him, as I moved under the outside stairs and pressed myself against the brick wall. Ranger bumped the lock on the back door, slipped inside, and the door clicked closed. No alarm rang out.

After what seemed like hours, Ranger reappeared and motioned me away from the building. "Sunny isn't in there," he said. "Do you have any other possibilities?"

"I have *too many* possibilities. There are all these row houses, plus he's related to half the Burg."

"Your call," Ranger said. "Where do we go from here?"

"How about a beer and onion rings?"

"I like it."

He was very close. I saw his eyes focus on my mouth, and I knew he was going to kiss me. I leaned into him, and his attention went from my mouth to something at the end of the block.

"I just saw a giraffe," Ranger said. "He was walking down Freeman."

"That's Kevin."

Ranger grinned. "You know him?"

"I've seen him around."

There was shouting from the front side of the building, and car doors slamming. An engine caught and tires chirped. Kevin skittered around the corner at full gallop, charged past us, and disappeared into the darkness. A black SUV with tinted windows rounded the corner, obviously chasing Kevin. It blew past us, screeching to a stop at the cross street.

"They've lost him," I said.

"Hard to believe you could lose a giraffe."

"Kevin is wily. And the guys in the SUV might not be exceptionally smart."

The SUV moved into the intersection and made a U-turn.

"Smart enough to come back to run over us," Ranger said.

He grabbed my hand, tugging me through the back door and into the social club's back stairwell. We ran flat-out through the club, past four old men playing cards. One of the men was Joe's Uncle Chooch.

"Hey, Stephanie," Uncle Chooch said. "Long time no see."

I looked over at him and stumbled, crashing into a rickety table holding a cappuccino machine. The machine fell off the table, and coffee and cups went flying in all directions.

Ranger grabbed me and shoved me out the front door. We sprinted to the Porsche, jumped in, and Ranger drove off. I turned in my seat in time to see several men standing in front of the social club with guns drawn. Hard to identify them in the dark, but I imagined they were the usual players. Maybe Uncle Chooch.

"So that went pretty smooth," I said to Ranger.

He glanced over at me. "If you ever tell anyone about this, I'll have to kill you."

I was almost positive he was kidding.

"You could buy me off with the onion rings," I told him.

"Deal."

• • •

We went to a downtown pub that was so dark we were almost invisible to each other as we slid into a corner booth. We ordered cheese fries, onion rings, and beer.

147

"Are you actually going to eat cheese fries and onion rings?" I asked him.

"That was my plan."

"What about the healthy food thing? Wouldn't you rather have a salad? Tree bark? A chunk of salmon?"

"I didn't see tree bark on the menu. Have you made any progress with the Gillian murder?"

"Melvina Gillian belonged to a senior discount club. All the murdered women belonged. So they all shopped at the same grocery store, liquor store, and bakery, because they were given a discount. I thought I'd get a list of the stores tomorrow and check them out. Also, Rose Walchek is being buried on Sunday, and there's going to be a viewing for her tomorrow night. I thought you would want to attend one or both."

"You thought wrong. I'll pay you double if you go without me."

"I'll go to the viewing, but I'm not going to the funeral. I get emotional at funerals."

"Good enough."

I checked my phone and found I had a message from Grandma. She said she was home and going to bed, and she'd talk to me tomorrow.

FIFTEEN

THE BONDS OFFICE is open for half a day on Saturday, but the truth is the bonds office never really shuts down. People need to get bonded out on Saturday night and Sunday afternoon, and Vinnie and Connie take the calls on their cellphones. My job is even more unstructured. I get paid when I catch someone, so I'm always looking. The day of the week doesn't matter to me.

I parked at the curb just as Connie was unlocking the front door. We went inside, and I got coffee brewing.

"Ranger and I went looking for Sunny last night, but we couldn't find him," I told Connie. "He wasn't with Rita."

"He just took a load of buckshot. He's probably sitting on a rubber donut somewhere, eating comfort food. Find a nurturing relative."

"Anything new come in for me?"

"Billie Jean Bailey skipped out. I called her mom, and she said Billie Jean followed her boyfriend to Florida. It was a shoplifting charge and not worth a trip south. You can keep it in your bag for when Billie Jean has a fight with the boyfriend and comes home. And the other one to come in is a bad one. Armed robbery and assault with a deadly weapon. Nineteen years old. His file photo shows gang tattoos. He gave Stark Street as his address, but it's an apartment in someone else's name. Probably this kid shuffles around."

I took both files and shoved them into my messenger bag. "I'm going to mooch breakfast from my mom. Have Lula call me when she comes in."

I left the office and drove the short distance to my parents' house. I parked in the driveway, got out of the car, and almost had an orgasm from the aroma of bacon frying. The smell was positively oozing out of the house.

"We got bacon and pancakes going this morning," Grandma said, opening the door for me. "Your mother got a new griddle, and we had to test it out. You're just in time."

I took a seat at the kitchen table and set my bag on the floor. "Where's Dad?"

"He's off to help your sister unplug a toilet," Grandma said.

My mother gave me a plate heaped with pancakes and bacon, and my grandmother brought a mug and the coffeepot to the table. I added butter and syrup and dug in.

"How'd the date go?" I asked Grandma. "Sorry I missed your message."

"It went real good. We went to the movies and then we stopped at the diner for pie. He even paid for it. And he told me all about when he was in the Army, and how his gallbladder almost burst last year, and how he only has four toes on one foot. Can you imagine?"

At the risk of being politically incorrect and an insensitive idiot, I thought four toes on one foot when coupled with the flab belly, wheezing and sweating, and zombie complexion might significantly lower his hotness rating for me.

"Gee," I said. "That's different."

"Yeah," Grandma said. "Good thing he has a car. It makes up for a lot of deformity."

"There's going to be a viewing tonight for Rose Walchek," I said to Grandma. "Do you want to go with me?"

"I already promised Gordon I'd go with him. He's picking me up early, so we get a seat with a view of the casket. And then we're going out after. They're having a wine tasting at the liquor store. You get to try all the wines for free."

"You shouldn't be drinking with him," my mother said. "I don't trust him."

"He was a perfect gentleman last night," Grandma said. "He didn't cuss or pass gas or nothing."

"How about you?" I asked Grandma. "Did you do any of those things?"

"I might have slipped one out in the movie," Grandma said, "but I don't think anyone noticed."

I was on my last piece of bacon when Lula called.

"I'm at the office," she said. "Do we have anything to do today?"

"We could track down a gang guy wanted for armed robbery and assault."

"That sounds like a lot of fun, but I might have to pass on account of I don't want to die right now."

"We could visit some of Sunny's relatives and ask if he's staying with them."

"Ditto for the above reason."

"We could do some leg work for Ranger on the Dumpster murders."

"I might be willing to help you with that if you bring me some bacon from your mama's kitchen."

"Too late. I ate it all."

"That's harsh."

. . .

Five minutes later I picked Lula up, and we drove to the Senior Center to get a complete list of businesses involved in the Senior Discount Club.

"We only give this list out to members," the woman in the small administrative office said.

She had short brown hair, narrow lips, military posture, and eyebrows that looked like they'd been drawn on with a brown crayon. She was in her mid-fifties to early sixties, and she was taking her Saturday job seriously.

"I realize that," I said, "but my granny is thinking about becoming more active at the Senior Center and she's interested in this program. I thought it would be helpful if I got some information for her."

"If she's thinking of becoming more active she should start now and pick our program brochure up for herself," the woman said.

"Good point," I said. "But this is a busy day for her, so I'm helping out."

"The rules say the list only goes to members," the woman said. "Your grandmother will have to become a member, and then she'll get the list."

"Fine. I'll sign her up to be a member."

"Impossible," the woman said. "She has to do that in person. How would we know whom we were signing up? It could be anyone. It could be a twelve-year-old."

"What's with this?" Lula said. "You could vote in this state with less fuss. Nobody cares how old you are or if you're dead. All's gotta happen is someone signs your name and they can vote. And here you are saying we can't get a list of stores for her granny. It's because *I'm* here, isn't it? You're doing racial profiling. You don't want no big and beautiful black woman to have the list. I'm gonna call people. I'm calling the newspaper and Oprah. I'm gonna organize and get some signs made. I got posterboard and Magic Markers in my trunk."

"Rules are rules," the woman said.

"Well, I'm not leaving without the list," Lula said. "I'm gonna sit here in this stupid little sad-ass office until I get it."

"I can have you removed," the woman said. "I can call the police and have you arrested."

"Oh yeah, I like that," Lula said. "I got my iPhone all ready to record. Prune-face volunteer in old people's home has big and beautiful black woman arrested for wanting to help her friend's granny. That's going viral on YouTube. I bet I get famous. I could get a model contract from that."

"Oh, honestly," the woman said. "Here! Take the list and get out of here."

I took the list from her, told her we appreciated her help, and we scurried out of the building.

"I can't believe you played the race card in there," I said to Lula.

"I didn't just play the *race* card," Lula said. "I played the race card *and* the fat card. *BAM!* My thinking is you gotta use what you got. God didn't make me a big beautiful black woman for nothing. I got cards to play. You see what I'm saying? And take you, for instance. You got no cards."

"I'm at a disadvantage," I said.

"Fuckin' A," Lula said.

I plugged the key into the ignition and we rumbled out of the lot. "I thought we'd check out all of the businesses on the list and see if anything strikes us as odd."

"You mean like some fool standing behind the counter, counting out his newfound money, holding a Venetian blind cord?"

154

"Yeah," I said. "Like that."

"Okay, then," Lula said. "I'm on it."

I didn't stop at the gas station, as most of the dead women hadn't had cars. And I didn't bother stopping at Randy's deli. Been there, done that. Plus I was afraid he'd make me slice up a pig brain or monkey gonads.

Morton's Bakery on Third Street was part bakery and part convenience store. By now it was midmorning and the store was packed with people buying bagels, donuts, babkas, and cannoli, plus the odd emergency carton of milk, jar of peanut butter, or roll of toilet paper.

I was familiar with this bakery, but I didn't often shop here. Tasty Pastry was a short walk from the bonds office on Hamilton, and it was my bakery of choice. There were three women working the counter at Morton's, and a swarthy mustached guy was at the register. I didn't know any of them. I would have liked to ask about the murdered women, but the store was too busy. Lula bought a bagel with veggie cream cheese and we left.

Next on the list was the liquor store. There were several people milling around debating the virtues of Grey Goose and Ketel One, pondering the price of Macallan single malt scotch, and filling their carts with cheap gin. I recognized the man at the checkout. He'd been my high school algebra teacher.

"Mr. Newcomb," I said. "I didn't know you worked here."

"It's a part-time job. Friday nights and all day Saturday. It's a nice break to sell legal addictive depressants to adults after five days of staring into the blank faces of illegally anesthetized juveniles."

"I guess I could see that," I said, and I introduced him to Lula.

"Mr. Newcomb was my high school algebra teacher," I said. "He gave me a C."

"It was a gift," Mr. Newcomb said.

"I didn't have algebra when I went to school," Lula said. "I studied beauty culture."

"Did you get a job as a cosmetician when you graduated?" Mr. Newcomb asked.

"No. I went to work as a 'ho. It was one of them tradition things. All the women in my family's 'hos. Except I'm not a 'ho no more. Well, actually I tried some 'hoing the other night, but I didn't have no luck at it. The industry just isn't what it used to be."

"I understand this liquor store is part of the Senior Discount Club program," I said to Mr. Newcomb.

"Some of our best customers belong to that program. They go to the cooking demonstrations next door, and then they come in here and load up on booze."

"Did you know Rose Walchek?"

"She was just murdered, right? I didn't know her, but she shopped here. I saw her picture in the paper, and I recognized her. She used to come in after the Saturday demonstration."

"There were three other women murdered. Did they shop here too?"

"You're talking about the women who were found in the Dumpsters? I've seen them here. Lois Fratelli was a regular.

She mostly bought wine. Bitsy Muddle was another regular. She bought wine and an occasional bottle of gin."

"What about Melvina Gillian?"

"She came in just before she was killed. She asked for help. She was having a dinner guest, and she didn't know what to serve."

"Do you remember what she got?"

"I suggested a pinot noir. It's my go-to wine for beginners."

"I bet she served that wine to the killer," Lula said. "What kind of man comes and drinks your pinot noir, and then throws you in a Dumpster? This man has no manners."

Mr. Newcomb and I agreed. The killer had no manners.

"Were the women alone? Or did they usually shop with a friend?" I asked Mr. Newcomb.

"Rose was alone, that I remember. And the Gillian woman was alone. I couldn't really say for the others."

Victory Hardware was next on the list. It was a hole-in-the-wall store that was crammed with lightbulbs, boxes of nails, shelf paper, claw hammers, electric screwdrivers, flashlights, Elmer's Glue, birdseed, tape measures, batteries, cans of Raid, bait boxes, trash bags, toasters, sandpaper, Buck knives, various toilet parts, umbrellas, DustBusters, plungers, bags of charcoal, and replacement cords for Venetian blinds. The store was owned and run by Victor Birch. Victor was as old and cracked as the linoleum on the floor. Both Victor and the linoleum looked like they'd been around for two hundred years, but probably it was more like eighty. Victor had been on the job seven days a week for as long as I could remember, chain smoking and hacking and ranting about the way the world was going to hell in a handbasket. The store reeked of cigarette smoke, and yellow streaks of tar stained the walls and Victor's fingers and teeth. Victor was both horrible and amazing. He was a living testament to the ravages of tobacco and the determination of the body and soul to survive under ugly conditions.

I knew the store by heart, but this was Lula's first time inside.

"Whoa," she said. "This is like walking into the lung cancer ride at the theme park from hell. Does anyone actually shop here?"

"Everyone shops here. Victor has washing machine parts that went out of stock twenty years ago. He's got shower heads without water savers, incandescent lightbulbs, cheap rat poison, a machine that will duplicate keys that say do not duplicate, and he's got a bottle of homemade hooch under the counter that he'll share with you for free or sell to you for four dollars."

"Does anyone work here besides him?"

"Various relatives and homeless sorts. There's a guy named Snoot who's been with Victor for a bunch of years. He's not the sharpest tack on the corkboard, but he manages to get the garbage out on time."

"Would Snoot kill old ladies?"

"Probably. If he could find them."

Footsteps shuffled toward us, and Victor popped out from behind one of the floor-to-ceiling racks of organized junk.

"What can I do for you girls?" he asked, cigarette stuck to his lower lip.

"I need a flashlight," I told him.

"Big or little?"

"Medium."

"Is this a fashion accessory, or do you want to be able to see something with it? I got some pretty red and blue ones, but they aren't worth snot."

"I'm thinking Maglite."

"That's serious flashlighting."

We followed him to the back of the store and waited while he sorted through bins and boxes.

"Did you know Lois Fratelli?" I asked him.

"Sure. Her whole family shops here. She was in just before she was murdered. She was looking for a shower curtain liner."

"That's pretty good that you'd remember that," Lula said.

Victor dragged on his cigarette. "Girlie, I got a mind like a steel trap."

"You shouldn't be smoking," Lula said. "It's bad for you. What's your doctor say about your smoking?"

Victor moved a box to get to another box. "My doctor's dead."

"How about the other women who were murdered?" I asked him. "Did they shop here too?"

"I expect so. We give a discount." He opened a box and pulled out a Maglite. "How's this?"

"It's perfect," I told him.

"What are you going to do with it? Hit someone over the head?"

"If I have to."

Victor gave a bark of laughter that brought on a fit of coughing and wheezing.

"Twelve bucks," he finally said. "Special price for you."

I paid him in cash. "Do you sell a lot of Venetian blind cord?"

"Yep. A fair amount. There's a lot of Venetian blinds out there."

"All those women were strangled with Venetian blind cord," I told him.

"I heard that." He shook his head. "Terrible. Just terrible."

"Do you think the cord could have been bought here?"

"I thought about it, but I couldn't see it."

"Good to know," I said. "Thanks for finding me the right flashlight."

"Anytime," Victor said. "Always a pleasure to have a pretty young lady in the store."

"He's charming," Lula said, buckling herself into the Buick. "It's a shame he's all yellow and wrinkled. Now where we going?"

"Gene's Pharmacy," I said. "It's at the corner of Broad and Mayweather."

SIXTEEN

I PARKED IN the small lot, and Lula and I walked through the drugstore to the counter where prescriptions were filled. There was a time when Gene himself was back there counting out pills, but that time was long gone. Now Gene was living the good life in a retirement community in Scottsdale, and his daughter Sue was running the pharmacy. I'd gone to school with Sue's little sister, and I'd briefly dated her brother.

"Hey, look who's here," Sue said. "Haven't seen you in a while. How's it going? How's Joe doing?"

"Joe's managing," I said. "He's trying to stay away from the pain pills. He said he couldn't feel his fingertips or his tongue."

Sue nodded. "He was prescribed some heavy-duty stuff." She put a label on a little plastic vial and looked back at me. "What can I do for you?"

"I'm doing some legwork for a friend, looking into the Dumpster murders. I'm guessing the women all shopped here."

"You guess right."

"Do you have any thoughts on this?"

"Obviously they came here because we were part of the discount program. Even if their meds were paid for by insurance they still used the discount for other stuff. Cosmetics, magazines, over-the-counter drugs."

"Did you know any of them? Did they come in alone? Were they always here on a certain day?"

"I knew Lois Fratelli. She lived a short distance from my parents' house. The others were faces in a crowd. When something as horrific as a murder happens you look back and realize the victim was a customer, but beyond that I don't have anything." She went to her computer. "Let me check something."

Lula wandered off to look at magazines, and I waited for Sue.

"Here it is," Sue said. "Saturday. With the exception of Lois Fratelli, they all came in on a Saturday. I guess they could have come in on other days too, but they always filled their prescriptions on a Saturday."

"Thanks," I said. "I appreciate the help."

Lula came back to the Buick with a copy of *People* magazine and some new lip gloss. "I'm thinking this investigating and detecting business is better than the bounty hunting business," she said. "So far no one's shot at us today. And we're talking to people that don't hate us."

"True, but the day isn't over."

"So what else is on the list?"

Cluck-in-a-Bucket was on the discount list, but I knew it would be a waste of time. The staff was transient and there was no room for personal contact beyond the thirty seconds it took to order a Clucky Burger and fries. The multiplex was on the list. Another waste of time. Ironically, the funeral home on Hamilton was also on the list.

"We're done," I said to Lula.

"Just as well," Lula said. "It's almost lunchtime, and I only work half day on Saturday unless there's something special going on. I got an appointment with Jolene for a manicure, and then I'm changing my hair color, being that pink was yesterday."

"What's tomorrow?"

"I'm feeling sparkly. I gotta talk to Latisha about it. She's my colorist."

I looked in the rearview mirror at my hair. It was brown.

"I like to coordinate my hair and my nails," Lula said. "I think of them as accessories, and you know how I feel about the importance of correctly accessorizing."

I dropped Lula off at the bonds office and continued down the street to Giovichinni's. The businesses we'd just visited were relatively convenient for Lois Fratelli, but the other women had to go out of their way to get to them, which was even more difficult for them because none of them had a car. So maybe this was why the women seemed to run their errands on Saturday.

They relied on others to take them shopping, and those others could only help out on Saturday.

Tina Giovichinni was working the deli counter, her white butcher's apron smudged with mustard and ketchup and other unidentifiable stains. "What's up?" she said. "You want your usual turkey club?"

"No. I'm going with ham and cheese on rye and a side of the homemade coleslaw."

"You got it."

"Are you going to the viewing tonight?"

"You mean for Rose Walchek? No, but my mother's going. She knew Rose from Bingo."

"Did Rose ever shop here?"

Tina shook her head. "Not that I can remember." She wrapped my sandwich and put it into a white paper bag. "I'm surprised you're not walking around in a disguise. I hear the whole Sunucchi family is looking for you."

"I didn't shoot him."

"Too bad. I would have thrown in the coleslaw for free."

I felt my eyebrows go up an inch. I leaned forward and lowered my voice. "You're not in love with Uncle Sunny?"

"He wasn't nice to my brother, Gino. He's not nice to a lot of people."

"I don't suppose you know where he's hiding."

"When Sunny shops here he buys blood sausage and fresh fusilli. We carry the blood sausage just for him. No one else wants it. Yesterday Bella came in and bought blood sausage and fresh fusilli."

Bella mostly lived with Joe's mom. When Joe's mom needed a break she shipped Bella off to one of the other relatives, but Bella always came back.

"Thanks," I said to Tina.

"Don't thank me," Tina said. "I didn't tell you anything."

I parked on a side street around the corner from the Morelli house and ate my lunch. If Sunny was holing up there, he was effectively off-limits to me. I was never Joe's mom's first choice for a daughter-in-law. If I barreled into her house with guns drawn and took down her houseguest, I could kiss any future with Joe goodbye. And I couldn't begin to guess what Bella would do. I suspected it would involve conjuring zombies and evil spirits, and shooting handheld missiles into my living room.

I called Morelli.

"What?" Morelli said.

"Are you in a bad mood?"

"I'm not in a good mood."

"Because?"

"Bob horked up last night's dinner on the rug."

"What did you feed him?"

"Hot dogs."

"Duh. Anything else?"

"My television isn't working."

"And?"

"That's it."

"That's not much. I bet I can put you in a *really* bad mood."

"Don't do me any favors."

"I think there's a good possibility your mom is hiding Uncle Sunny."

"Hiding?"

"In her house."

"Are you kidding me?"

"No. I'm serious. I think he's sitting there on a rubber donut, scarfing down blood sausage and pasta, watching *Ghost Hunters* episodes with Bella."

"That's ridiculous."

"Have you been there lately?"

"No. Not since I was shot."

"Maybe you should go over and check it out."

"No way. I don't want to know. This conversation never happened. If I found him at my mother's house I'd have to accuse her of harboring a fugitive."

"That would be awkward. Do you think I should go in and root him out?"

"No! I think you should go to the beach. Get some frozen custard."

"Do you want to come with me?"

"I can't. The cable company is supposed to come fix my television. If you're not here when they come they never come again."

"There's only a one percent chance that they'll show up anyway."

Morelli mumbled something about God and vengeance and the cable company, and hung up.

I couldn't see his mother's house from where I was parked, but I could see cars coming and going down the street. I was sitting there thinking the beach would be a terrific idea if I had a car that got more than three miles to a gallon when Ranger pulled up behind me in his 911 Turbo. He got out and walked over.

"Either you ran out of gas or else you're trying to execute a stakeout in this blue elephant," Ranger said.

"I think Sunny might be holed up with Joe's mom and Grandma Bella."

"That would be awkward."

"My exact words! Did you come to rescue me again?"

"Among other things. I kept waking up last night thinking about the giraffe. Why is there a giraffe running loose on Fifteenth Street?"

"I don't know. The first time Lula and I saw him there was a black SUV chasing him. They both turned the corner, there was gunfire, and when Lula and I went to investigate there was a guy lying in the road with a dart stuck in him. The guy died at the hospital."

"And the giraffe is still hanging out?"

"Yep."

"And there's been no mention in the media?"

"Nope."

"Nothing on the police scanners?"

"Nope."

"Have you told anyone about this?"

"A couple people."

"You don't seem to be very disturbed by it all."

"I have people trying to kill me. A giraffe is low on my list of disturbances."

"That's where we differ," Ranger said. "I'm used to people trying to kill me, but it's not every day I'm almost run over by a giraffe."

"So I'm guessing you want to go big game hunting?"

• • •

Ranger slowly drove his Porsche down Fifteenth Street as we looked for signs of Kevin. We'd been at it for about an hour, systematically following a grid that included alleys and cross streets. I'd done the drill with Lula and had turned up zip, but I didn't mind doing it again with Ranger. I loved the intimacy and the power of the Porsche, and in the confined space, Ranger smelled great. He smelled like the Bulgari shower gel his house-keeper bought for him. When I use his shower gel the scent disappears almost immediately, but Ranger carries it all day.

Plus there was the added benefit that we might run across Sunny. Instinct told me he was with Bella, but other parts of my brain knew he could just as easily be in one of the buildings on Fifteenth Street.

Ranger stopped at the corner of Fifteenth and Freeman. "No giraffe," he said.

"Yeah, it's a real bummer, isn't it? Whenever you go looking for him you can't find him, and then when you least expect it he gallops down the street."

"I can't believe I'm this hung up on a giraffe."

"That's just the way it is with some people."

Ranger looked at me. "Not you."

"Nope. Not me. But Lula is obsessed with him."

"That's not a comforting thought."

I burst out laughing, because it's not often I see the human side of Ranger. Most of the time Ranger is chill.

"We're done here, right?" I asked him.

"Right."

Ranger drove me back to my car, but my car wasn't there. A black Honda CR-V was parked at the curb.

"I replaced the Buick with one of my fleet cars," Ranger said. "You're too easily recognized in the Buick."

"Where's the Buick?"

"In your parents' driveway. Did you turn up anything interesting this morning on the murders?"

"The women shopped where they got the senior discount even though some store locations were inconvenient. Melvina, Bitsy, and Rose shopped on Saturday. Lois didn't completely fit that profile. I'm sure it's because Lois had her own car and wasn't relying on someone to chauffeur her around. I'm going to make some phone calls and try to find out who took the women shopping. Maybe you could have someone ask Ruppert for me."

The black Lincoln rolled past us and parked in front of the

Morelli house. Moe got out of the front passenger seat and carried a duffel bag into the house. He left a little later without the bag, got into the Lincoln, and the car disappeared down the street.

"He's in there," I said to Ranger. "What on earth is wrong with Joe's mom that she'd allow Sunny to hide out in her house?"

"He's family," Ranger said.

"That's no excuse."

"It is in the Sunucchi–Morelli family culture."

"How am I supposed to get him out of there? I can't just break down the door. We're talking about Joe's mom and crazy Grandma Bella."

"Do you want me to go in?"

"Would you do that for me?"

"We could make a deal."

"Oh boy."

"Think about it," Ranger said. "I'll catch up with you after the viewing."

I left Ranger and drove my loaner CR-V home to my apartment building. I'd watched Ranger's eyes go from brown to black when he suggested a deal. I knew what it meant when his pupils dilated like that. It meant Ranger was feeling friendly. And when Ranger was friendly it was hard not to want to be friendly back.

I pulled the files on the dead women out of my bag and took them to the dining room table. Besides former addresses and work histories, the files also listed relatives. Bitsy Muddle was survived by a younger brother who was living in Ewing. I called his phone, and he picked up on the second ring.

"I'm helping the police investigate your sister's death," I told him. "I have just a quick question."

"Sure, but I already told them all I knew."

"She usually ran her errands on Saturdays. Did you ever drive her around?"

"No. We would meet at the diner for lunch sometimes, but I didn't see a lot of her after she moved to that retirement place. She was always on the go. I figured she was being bused around by the retirement people."

I thanked him for his help and called the retirement community office.

"Most of our residents are very independent," the manager told me. "Some have cars, and others have friends and relatives who take them shopping. We have a wing for assisted living, but Miss Muddle wasn't housed there. She was living in what is simply an apartment complex for senior citizens."

"Would it be possible to speak to some of her neighbors?"

"Of course. We always try to cooperate with the police. Most of her neighbors have already been questioned. Some were questioned several times, so I can't guarantee a happy interview."

"Understood."

I wasn't in the mood to drive over to Golden Years Retirement Village and go door to door, grilling Bitsy's neighbors. I'd wait to see what Ranger got for me, and I could talk to Rose Walchek's relatives at the viewing.

Saturday was usually my designated clean-the-apartment day, so I squirted some toxic goop into the toilet and swished it around with the toilet brush. Then I took a bunch of toxic liquid-saturated wipes from the pop-up container and wiped down all the bathroom surfaces. I changed out the towels and made my bed with fresh linens. I ran over the kitchen and bathroom floors with the Swiffer contraption that uses the wet pads, and I considered the wall-to-wall carpet in the rest of the apartment. Usually I borrowed my mother's vacuum cleaner, but I'd forgotten to stop on my way home. Probably now that I had a slow cooker and was going to be Susie Homemaker I should get my own vacuum cleaner.

I wrote "Buy vacuum cleaner" on the notepad in the kitchen. I made myself a peanut butter and olive sandwich for dinner and gave a small chunk to Rex. He scurried out of his soup can, stuffed the chunk of bread into his cheek pouch, blinked his eyes at me, and scurried back into his can. I took the eye blink as a thank-you. Hamsters have limited communication skills.

I changed into skinny black slacks and a silky white blouse for the viewing. I still had my hair pulled up into a ponytail, and I slashed on some extra mascara since it was an evening affair.

I arrived a little after seven, which was a big mistake for the viewing of a high-profile murder victim. The lot was filled, and parking on the street was nonexistent. There was a huge crush of people on the front porch, and the crush spilled over onto the steps. It had to be total insanity inside. I drove around the block and pulled into the driveway to the funeral home garages. Unless they had to pull a hearse out to make an emergency dead guy pickup, I figured I'd go unnoticed.

I sneaked through the back door, walked past the small hostess kitchen and the funeral director's office, and came out into the packed lobby. The noise was a smidgeon below rock concert, the temperature had to be in the nineties, and the entire place smelled like carnations and deodorant failure.

I was standing by the table with the coffee and tea and cookies, and I had to somehow get to Rose. She was laid out in Slumber Room No. 1. This was the largest of the slumber rooms, the premier spot. It was reserved for murder victims and the grandmasters of various lodges and social clubs.

I pushed my way through the crowd to the room entrance and worked my way forward. Two men and a woman were standing at the head of the casket. Obviously relatives. They were my target. Grandma and Gordon had seats in the second row. I picked out Mama Giovichinni, my parents' neighbor Mrs. Ciak, a few women from Bingo, and a bunch of other people from the Burg. The line of mourners inching up to the casket ran the length of the room and out the door. If I tried to cut the line I'd be attacked and ejected. My only hope was to wait until the viewing was ending and everyone stampeded out to the lobby to get last-minute cookies.

Grandma turned and saw me and waved.

"Over here," she shouted. "We saved you a seat."

The seat was between Grandma and Randy Berger. I hadn't noticed it at first because Berger was occupying two seats. It wasn't that he was excessively fat, it was more that he was just *so big*. I made a *no thanks* gesture, but Grandma was having none of it. Berger managed to pull most of himself off the seat and I squished myself into it.

"I was hoping you'd be here," Berger said. "Have you thought about the job offer?"

"I'm sure it's a great job," I said, "but it's not for me. And I like being a bond enforcement agent."

"You could try butchering part-time."

"No."

"Okay, then how about dinner?"

"No."

"I'd bring a nice pork tenderloin."

"No."

"I heard that," Grandma said to me. "I bet it would be a pip of a pork tenderloin. Remember that boyfriend you had who could cook those pork chops? I never tasted a pork chop like that since."

"He was a killer!"

"Yeah, but he sure could cook pork chops."

"He probably brined them," Berger said. "You've got to brine pork to get it tender. I always brine my pork."

So now I had a dilemma. I wanted to run screaming out of the funeral home, but I needed to stay and talk to Rose's relatives.

"I'm going back for cookies," I said to Grandma and Randy.

"I'll go with you," Randy said.

"No! You have to stay here and save my seat."

"She's right," Grandma said. "I'll never be able to hold two seats in this location. These people get vicious when it comes to a good seat."

I made my way out of the room and back to the lobby, talking to people as I worked my way through the crowd. I was looking for information on male friends, new friends, shopping friends. I was hanging out at the cookie table when I started a conversation with a woman who lived on Stanton Street and was Rose's neighbor.

"Were you and Rose good friends?" I asked her.

"Truth is, I hardly knew her. I saw her all the time, because I lived right across the street, and my windows looked out at her house. We would say hello when we were both out, but other than that she kept to herself. She was quiet. She mostly went to the Senior Center. The little bus would come pick her up."

"That bus just picks up and drops off at the Senior Center," I said. "It must have been hard for Rose to go grocery shopping."

"Her daughter used to take her shopping every Saturday, but then a couple weeks before she was murdered there was a different car. I imagine it was some other relative."

"Was it an SUV?"

"No. It was a regular car. Gray. It looked like a man driving, so it might have been the son-in-law. I didn't know him."

"Are there any other neighbors here?"

The woman looked around. "I haven't seen any. It's hard to see anybody in this mob."

At eight-thirty I started maneuvering myself back into the viewing room. The tide was already turning and people were beginning to move out. I joined the line filing past the deceased, managing to get up to the casket just as the lights dimmed. I murmured the standard polite condolences and told Rose's family I was part of the team investigating the murders.

They introduced themselves as Rose's daughter, son-in-law, and younger brother. I asked if Rose had mentioned any new friends or activities in the weeks before she died.

Her daughter shook her head. "No. She had a set routine. She wasn't very adventuresome in her later years."

"What about the Saturday shopping trip?" I asked.

"We used to always shop together on Saturday," the daughter said, "but I had foot surgery, and couldn't drive."

I looked down at her foot, encased in a big black orthopedic walking boot.

"Fortunately one of Mom's friends from the Senior Center volunteered to take her shopping until I was driving again," she said.

"Did you know this friend?"

"No. I never met him, but Mom had known this person for some time. Apparently he was one of those good souls who help out when rides are needed."

"I don't suppose you know his name?"

"I believe it was Gordon."

I saw my whole day go up in smoke. It was Gordon.

The Jolly Hobbit. The guy with the car. Mr. Popularity. The guy who would have to strangle a woman with one hand so he could use his bronchial inhaler with the other. Even as I stood there I could hear him wheezing, trying to keep up with Grandma, who was hellbent for the cookie table. Problem was, Gordon could have an accomplice. Gordon could be luring old ladies off into the bushes with the promise of a ride to the butcher shop, and his evil twin, nutso cousin, or whackjob roommate could be strangling them and tossing them into the Dumpster.

I followed Grandma, Gordon, and Randy Berger out of the viewing room into the lobby.

"I'm going to head out," I told Grandma. "And I told Mom I'd give you a ride home."

"Thanks," she said, "but Gordon and I are going for a nightcap after we score some cookies."

"I don't think that's a good idea," I told Grandma. "I promised Mom I'd bring you home."

"Don't worry," Gordon said. "I'll take good care of her. And I won't keep her out too late."

"I'm holding you responsible for her welfare," I said to him.

"You can count on me," he said.

SEVENTEEN

I WENT OUT the funeral home's front door, walked through the parking lot, and bushwhacked my way through a hedge to get to the garages. I emerged from the hedge and experienced a moment of disorientation when I looked around and didn't see Ranger's CR-V. I walked to the middle of the drive court and did a 360-degree scan. No car.

I called Ranger. "The strangest thing just happened," I said. "I came out of the viewing, and your car is gone."

There was silence on his end, and I assumed he was checking with the control room. All his fleet cars had tracking devices.

"It's in the police impound lot," Ranger said.

"I guess I sort of parked illegally, but there weren't any parking places. I don't suppose you'd want to give me a ride home?"

"Babe," Ranger said. And the line went dead.

Ten minutes later Ranger picked me up at the funeral home.

"I thought I had a good lead on the murders, but it evaporated," I told him. "Did you find out who was taking Melvina shopping?"

"A man named Gordon Krutch. He seems to be the senior citizen go-to guy when someone needs a ride."

I blew out a sigh.

"Not liking that information?" Ranger asked.

"No. He seems entirely incapable. And he's with my grandmother."

"Are you giving up on Bingo?"

"Not entirely. I got a slow cooker out of it."

"Have you used it?"

"I put Rex in it when I cleaned his cage."

He had one hand resting on the steering wheel and the other on the back of my seat. His finger traced a line down the nape of my neck. "What's next? Am I taking you home?"

Okay, I have to admit I was tempted to strip my shirt off and straddle him. I'd actually done this once in his Porsche 911, and it was a complicated undertaking. He was driving his SUV tonight so it would be easier, but the consequences would be the same. Mind-blowing gratification followed by Catholic guilt and the munchies. I could probably handle the Catholic guilt, but I couldn't handle the three extra pounds the munchies would produce.

"Well?" Ranger said.

"Let's see if we can flush out Uncle Sunny."

Ranger put the Cayenne in gear and drove the short distance to Joe's mother's house. He parked across the street and one house down, and we sat silently watching the neighborhood. No activity. Lights on in all the houses. No Lincoln Town Car parked at the curb.

We got out and stood for a moment in front of the house. Upstairs windows were dark. Lights were on downstairs in the kitchen and living room. Shades hadn't been drawn. We moved closer, keeping in the shadows. Joe's mom and Grandma Bella were on the couch. Joe's mom was watching television. Bella was head down, snoozing. No sign of Sunny.

"Maybe he's asleep in an upstairs bedroom," I said.

Ranger stepped out of the shadows and went to the front door. "Let's find out."

Joe's mom answered on the second knock. She looked at Ranger and then at me standing by his side.

"We're looking for Sunny," Ranger said.

"He's not here."

I looked into the living room and saw Bella's head snap up with a snort. Her raptor eyes focused on me, and she sprang off the couch and rushed over to us.

"You!" she said, pointing her finger at me. "You devil."

"I thought we discussed this," Joe's mom said to Bella. "Stephanie is *not* the devil."

"She come to get my nephew. She's no good. And she's stupid. She come too late. Sunny's already gone. I spit on her."

"We don't spit on people," Joe's mom said to Bella. "And we especially don't spit on people when they're in my house."

"How about the porch?" Bella asked her.

Joe's mom looked like she was getting a migraine. "Are we done here?" she asked Ranger.

Ranger looked at me. "Would you like to search the house?"

"Not necessary," I told him. "If Joe's mom says Sunny isn't here, then he isn't here."

We retreated to the car, and sat there for a moment.

"Any ideas?" I asked Ranger.

"Babe."

"Any ideas about finding Sunny?"

"If he's as frustrated as I am, he'll be at Rita's," Ranger said.

Twenty minutes later we were parked across from Rita's house. Lights were on. Shades were drawn. No car in the driveway.

"Let's talk to her," Ranger said, getting out of the SUV.

I scrambled to catch up to him. "Just like that? No snooping first?"

"If I'm going to sneak around in the bushes with you, I'm not wasting time looking in Rita Raguzzi's windows."

"Okay then. Good to know. Snooping first is tedious anyway. Let's just knock on her door."

Ranger rapped a couple times and Rita answered. She looked at me, and she looked at Ranger. She did a slow whole-body scan of Ranger, head to toe, and she smiled.

"At least you came with a present this time," she said to me.

181

"We're looking for Sunny."

"He's not here, but tall, dark, and handsome is welcome to come in for a drink."

"Tall, dark, and handsome is going to pass on that offer," I told her, "but keep me in mind if Sunny drops dead in your bed and you want to get rid of him."

We left Rita and headed out of her neighborhood.

"Is it likely Sunny will drop dead in Rita's bed?" Ranger asked.

"He has a bad heart."

I was out of ideas for finding Sunny, so I had Ranger take me home. He walked me to my door, and waited while I unlocked it.

"Would you like to come in?" I asked him.

"Is this invitation out of passion or pity?"

"Do you care?"

Ranger smiled. "No."

The truth is, I felt inviting him in was the least I could do after declining Rita's invitation on his behalf. I mean I'd be a really terrible person if I didn't compensate him for that, right? At least give him a glass of wine. Tell him how appreciative I was for all he did for me.

I hung my bag on the hook in the foyer and went into the kitchen.

"Would you like a glass of wine?" I asked him.

"No."

"Pretzels? I went food shopping. I have crackers and cheese."

He shook his head, closed in on me, and I felt the first stab of panic.

"Um," I said.

Ranger pulled back and looked at me. "Really?"

I sucked in some air. "I can't do this. I'm almost engaged."

And the hideous part was that I *really* wanted to do it. I wanted to do it *bad*.

He brushed a kiss across my lips. "You know where to find me. In the meantime you can drive my car."

"The 911 Turbo?"

"My *fleet* car. I'll have one dropped off."

EIGHTEEN

I WENT TO nine o'clock mass. The last time I'd gone to mass was Easter, and my mother had made me go. I heard people gasp when I walked into the church. I'm sure they were wondering what horrible thing I'd done that had driven me to attend mass. Fortunately or *un*fortunately, however you were looking at it, the horrible thing was all in my mind. I'd thrashed around all night in a sweat over Ranger. On the one hand I felt good that I'd done right by Morelli and sent Ranger home. It was the *other* hand that was giving me problems. The *other* hand wanted to wrap itself around Ranger's most perfect body part and not let go.

I stopped in at my parents' house after mass. My grandmother was at the kitchen table doing a Jumble, and my mother was ironing.

"Now what?" I asked my mother. "Why are you ironing?"

"Since when can't a person iron?" my mother said.

"You iron on Thursdays after you do the laundry. Ironing on Sunday is mental health ironing. You probably ironed this same shirt ten times."

"It's breast cancer, isn't it? You found a lump. It's from those sports bras you wear."

"I don't have breast cancer."

"Then why did you go to church? Harriet Chumsky called and said she saw you at mass."

"I just felt like going to mass."

"Omigosh," my mother said. "You're pregnant."

"I'm not pregnant."

"There's something," my mother said. "You don't just go to mass. Are you sure it's not cancer?"

"It's not cancer!" I helped myself to a cup of coffee and added cream. "How did the date go last night?" I asked Grandma.

"It was pretty good. We went to the diner for rice pudding, only thing is he had car troubles when we came out, and he had to call his nephew to come get the engine started. He said he's thinking about buying a new car. I wouldn't mind that on account of his car right now is gray. If I'm going out with a guy who's shorter than me and has asthma, I think he should at least have a red car."

"I don't trust him," my mother said. "He's too happy. And he's not from the Burg. What do we know about him? Where does he live?"

"He's got an apartment in one of those buildings by the

185

DMV," Grandma said. "I haven't been there yet. It turns out he isn't as hot as people said."

"Melvina Gillian was talking about a new boyfriend just before she was killed," I said to Grandma. "Do you know if any of the other women had boyfriends?"

"Not that I heard."

"How about your friends now? Is there anyone talking about having a new boyfriend?"

"You mean besides me?"

"Yes."

"I haven't heard anything," Grandma said. "It's hard to get a boyfriend when you're a certain age. All the good ones are dead. Do you think there's some Don Juan going around sweet-talking the ladies and then throwing them into a Dumpster?"

I took a cookie out of the cookie jar and dunked it in my coffee. "It's possible."

And if you wanted to stretch your imagination the Don Juan could be Gordon, I thought. Or maybe Gordon and an accomplice.

"Wouldn't that be something," Grandma said. "Sometimes life is like a television show. I wouldn't mind seeing this Don Juan. I bet he's got a red car. Or maybe it's not some Don Juan. Maybe it's some mob guy. It came to me last night that these women could have owed the wrong people money. What if they were gambling, and they couldn't pay up?"

"What kind of gambling?" I asked her. "Off-track betting? Late-night poker?"

"Online Bingo," Grandma said.

"What makes you think they were gambling online?" I asked Grandma.

"I tried playing a couple times. It's real cutthroat Bingo. You got to pay to play, and you could sink a lot of money into it if you keep playing and don't win anything."

"Did all the murdered women play?"

"I don't know about all of them, but I know Bitsy Muddle was on all the time. And I was playing once when Lois was playing. I knew it was them because I knew their handles. Bitsy was 'Little Bit,' and Lois was 'Hotsy Totsie.'"

"When did they play?"

"Just about every night, but usually not until after nine o'clock," Grandma said. "There's other things to do up to nine o'clock. Television shows and real-life Bingo."

My mother had stopped ironing. "This is the first I heard about this."

"That's because you don't play Bingo, and you sleep at night," Grandma said. "When you get older you nod off all day long, and then you don't need to go to bed so early."

"I find it hard to believe those women were running up gambling debts," my mother said.

"That's just one of my theories," Grandma said. "It could also have been aliens from some other galaxy that got them. And the aliens needed money but they didn't need any old ladies."

"If I wanted to drop in and watch the Bingo games, how would I do it?" I asked Grandma.

"I can give you the website. There's lots of online gambling sites, but mostly I only hear talk about this one that comes off an island in the Caribbean."

I got the information from Grandma, finished my coffee, and stood to leave.

"You can stop ironing," I said to my mother. "I don't have cancer. I'm not pregnant. And Grandma isn't gambling her Social Security checks away playing online Bingo."

"There's always tomorrow," my mother said.

· · ·

I left my parents' house and drove past Joe's mother's house. It was only a few blocks away so it wasn't a huge effort. I idled for a moment and moved on. There was no indication that Sunny had returned, and I wasn't about to knock on the door without good reason.

My real destination was Victory Hardware. I was going to buy a vacuum cleaner. I had no idea if Victor carried them, but it seemed like a good place to start.

Snoot ambled up to me when I walked in. Snoot wasn't nearly as old as Victor, but he had the same deeply lined dead-skin look of a lifelong heavy smoker. If I had to guess I would say he was in his forties. He was about six feet tall, and lanky, walking slouched and loose-jointed. His thinning brown hair was pulled back into a low ponytail.

"Yuh?" he asked me.

"Is Victor here?"

"He stepped out to get us eats."

"I'm looking for a vacuum cleaner."

"We don't have none of those. We had a couple of 'em years ago, but they took up too much space, so Victor never got any more in. If you want a vacuum cleaner you should go to the Hoover store two blocks down. You can't go wrong with a Hoover."

"There's a Hoover store?"

"It's part of the tattoo parlor. They sell Hoovers and sewing machines, and you can get a tattoo. I've seen some fine tattoos come out of there."

"Did you know any of the women who were murdered and left in Dumpsters?"

"You mean like Mrs. Fratelli? She came in here all the time."

"Did you know any of the others?"

"Nope. Don't think so."

"You didn't kill them, did you?"

"Not that I remember."

I drove two blocks and parked in front of Fancy Dan's Tattoo Parlor. The front of the store had a vacuum cleaner display, and the back was given over to the tattoo business.

A heavily tattooed guy approached me and introduced himself as Fancy Dan. "I bet you'd like a rose tattooed on your shoulder," he said to me. "I'm pretty good at knowing these things."

"Not today," I told him. "I want a vacuum cleaner."

"Usually my wife sells the vacuum cleaners," he said, "but she had to take the dog to the vet for his annual. Do you have carpet or wood floors?"

"Carpet." I looked at the lineup of display vacuum cleaners and found one that was exactly like my mother's. "I'll take that one," I said.

Ten minutes later I was on the road with my new vacuum. I took it home, plugged it in, and cleaned my apartment, wishing I could have the same success at cleaning up my life. My life was a mess. I had a crappy job, no car of my own, and too many men in my bed . . . at least mentally.

"I'm going to fix it," I said to Rex. "I'm going to start with Morelli. I'm going over to his house and talk to him about our relationship. And then I'm going to apprehend the gang guy Connie just gave me, so I have money to buy a car." I dropped a peanut into Rex's cage. "I don't know what the heck I'm going to do about getting a better job. It's not like I have a bunch of amazing qualifications."

By the time I got to Morelli's house I had my speech all worked out. I had a slow cooker and a vacuum cleaner, and I had plans to get some throw pillows for the couch. I was ready to make a commitment. I didn't want to be *almost* engaged. I wanted to be *really* engaged. I might even want to set a date. After all, I wasn't getting any younger. If we were going to have a family we should get started. Probably Morelli would be relieved to have me force the issue. Probably he was sitting in his house all alone, nursing his gunshot wound. Poor guy. Just Bob and him.

I parked on the street, behind his green SUV. I rang the bell and let myself in. The television was blaring, and Kenny and Leo, two of Morelli's cop buddies, were on the couch. There were beer bottles and chips on the coffee table.

"He's in the kitchen," Leo said. "He's making up his famous wings."

Bob was in the kitchen with Morelli, watching him carefully, hoping for a wing to drop on the floor.

"What's going on?" I asked him.

"Ball game. The Mets are playing."

I looked at the platter of wings he was holding. "Leo said you were making up your famous wings. I didn't know you made wings."

"I buy them at Costco. When I want to get fancy, I put them on a plate."

"I wanted to talk to you."

"Go ahead," Morelli said. "We can talk while I make my famous blue cheese dressing for the wings."

He took a bottle of blue cheese salad dressing out of the fridge and dumped it into a bowl. I heard the front door crash open and lots of screaming and little feet pounding their way to the kitchen.

"That's Anthony," Morelli said. "He's got the kids today."

Little Anthony, Angelina, and Bobby ran in and jumped up and down, yelling.

"Uncle Joe! Uncle Joe! Uncle Joe!"

Morelli took a big bag of M&M's off the counter and threw it into the living room. "Fetch."

The kids ran out, and Morelli handed me the platter of wings. "Take this out to the guys."

"I didn't mean to barge in."

"You're not barging."

I set the platter on the coffee table, and Morelli's sister and two more kids arrived.

"Your sister is here," I said to Morelli.

"Yeah, she's a big Mets fan."

"Does this happen a lot?"

"What?"

"The party."

"It's not a party. It's game day." He pulled two more bags of chips out of a cupboard.

"Why wasn't I invited?"

"No one was invited. People just show up. I can't get them to stop. Anyway, you don't want to be here."

"Of course I do. You're my boyfriend. In fact, that's what I wanted to talk to you about."

"Sure," Morelli said, putting a bottle of beer in my hand. "Go ahead. Talk."

"I've been thinking about our relationship and how it's sort of in a holding pattern."

A pack of kids ran in, grabbed the bags of chips, and ran out. Bob ran after them. A moment later there was a lot of shrieking and screaming.

"Omigod," I said. "What happened?"

"Bob got the chips," Morelli said. "It happens all the time. Go ahead. What were you saying?"

"Maybe this isn't a good time."

Bob galloped through the kitchen with the bag of chips in his mouth and crashed through the screen door. The kids followed him into the backyard and chased him around in circles.

"I'm listening," Morelli said. "You wanted to talk about our relationship."

"Yes. The thing is . . . I bought a vacuum cleaner today."

Morelli was hands on hips. "A vacuum cleaner."

"Yep. And I already used it. And you know I have that slow cooker I won at Bingo."

Angelina was at the back door. "Uncle Joe, Bobby rolled in dog poop."

"Again? Don't let him in the house," Morelli said. "Anthony," he yelled. "Your kid rolled in dog poop."

"Again?" Anthony said. "Why don't you clean up your damn yard?"

Anthony walked into the kitchen, and Joe handed him a plastic garbage bag, a roll of paper towels, and dish detergent.

"What's he going to do?" I asked Morelli.

"Turn the hose on him." He grabbed a six-pack from the fridge and handed it to me. "Take this to Leo and you'll miss most of the screaming."

I took the six-pack into the living room, handed it to Leo, and the front door opened and Bella walked in. She was carrying a casserole and wearing a Mets ball cap. I turned on my heel and hustled back to the kitchen.

"Bella's here!" I said to Morelli.

"Did she bring the casserole? Is she wearing her lucky hat?"

"Yes! What is she doing here?"

"She's a big Mets fan. I know she's crazy, but she's our lucky granny. If she isn't here with her casserole, she could jinx the Mets."

Bobby ran in from the backyard and streaked naked through the kitchen, heading for the living room.

"Where is she?" Bella screeched. "I saw demon woman."

"She's coming to get me!" I said to Morelli.

"I'll talk to her," Morelli said.

"No way. I'm out of here."

"The conversation . . ."

I gave him a fast kiss. "Later."

He grabbed me and kissed me, and his kiss had a lot more passion than mine. "Promise?"

"Yes. Probably. Maybe."

I bolted out the door, jumped the hedge to his neighbor's yard, and sneaked through the narrow alley back to my car. I drove around the block, where I would be out of Bella's voodoo range, and took a moment to pull myself together.

Okay, I thought, so that didn't go exactly as expected. No problem. I'd just back-burner the commitment speech until Morelli's house emptied out. In fact, now that I'd had time to think about it, I might have been rushing things. Maybe my self-improvement project should start with the new car and new job, and then I could ease into the family scene. And if I was going to be brutally honest I'd have to admit I liked kids but might not be ready for the toddler-rolling-in-dog-poop experience. And an even more painful truth was that I couldn't wash away my Ranger lust and expect my hormones to be suddenly regulated by an engagement ring. I was going to have to get a grip on the hormones all by myself. And I would have to do it before I made the big commitment speech.

Without any effort at all on my part, my car somehow drove itself to Rangeman. I idled across the street from the neat seven-story brownstone and stared into the reflective impact-proof windows. I sat there comparing the men in my life, weighing my options, and not having a lot of luck at seeing my future. My future was murky. The crystal ball was hazy.

Ranger called on my cellphone.

"You've been sitting in front of the building for twenty minutes. Is there a problem?"

"Yes. It's my future. It's murky."

"Solving murky futures isn't my strong suit," Ranger said.

"It has to do with this physical attraction I feel for you. I was thinking you might want to come over tonight, and you could help me figure some things out."

"Babe," Ranger said. And he disconnected.

I assumed that was a yes, but it was hard to tell with Ranger.

I pulled the new file out of my bag and paged through it. Antwan Brown. AKA "Ants." Nineteen. Wanted for armed robbery and assault with a deadly weapon. Listed his mother as Shoshanna Brown with a New Orleans address. No father. No place of employment. No phone number. Secured his bail bond with a Rolex and a diamond ring. Stolen, no doubt. I studied his photo. The booking mugshot showed two teardrop tattoos on his cheek. That meant he'd killed two people. The full-length candid Vinnie'd taken when he wrote the bond showed a lean guy with some muscle: 5' 7" and 180 pounds.

I checked my bag for goodies. Self-defense spray. Illegal stun gun. Cuffs. Maglite in case I had to break his knees. I was good to go.

I drove to Stark Street and counted off blocks. The address Ants had given was in the dead zone: a block of burned-out buildings inhabited by crazies and crackheads. It was unlikely he was living in anything on this block. And if he was living here he would go undisturbed because I had no intention of stopping here, much less going in.

I made a U-turn and drove back to the first block of Stark where I felt it was safe to park. I read through the entire file one more time, but I couldn't find anything helpful. I had no starting point. No relatives. No friends. No work address. I called Morelli and could barely hear him answer over the background noise.

"Hold on," he shouted into the phone. "I'm going outside."

A couple beats later the noise went away. "What's up?" Morelli asked. "Do you want to come back? You didn't get any wings."

"I'm working, and I need some help."

"Anything."

"Really? Anything?"

"Almost anything," Morelli said.

"I'm looking for Antwan Brown, and I have nothing on him. No relatives. No friends. No address."

"Good. Walk away from it. He's a really bad guy. If you let him hang out long enough one of his friends will kill him, and you can collect the body."

"I don't have time for that."

"The thought of you going after Ants Brown gives me a cramp in my ass."

"I'll be careful. I just want to *find* him, and then I'll get help with the apprehension."

"He's a Stone Dead gang member. He'll be hanging with other Deads, and the Deads own the fifth block of Stark. Their color is purple. Their name is significant. These losers are dead inside. They've grown up with so much violence it's normal to them. They're like zombies. They feel no remorse. *You do not want to go up against one of them.* If you find this guy I want you to call me, and I'll send out the SWAT team."

NINETEEN

THE BUILDINGS ON the fifth block of Stark were covered with gang graffiti. It was Sunday, and most of the street-level businesses were closed and shuttered. A convenience store was open and a bar was open. It was a beautiful warm day, but no one was out. No stoop sitters. No strollers. A couple sullen teenagers stood smoking outside the convenience store. Neither of them looked like Ants. Maybe all the gangsta gangbangers were watching the Mets. Maybe they were all inside sharpening their knives and cleaning their guns for a fun night on the town.

I cruised up and down a few side streets in the area, but I didn't see anyone wearing purple, and I didn't see Ants Brown. I returned to my parking place on the first block of Stark, and I called Lula.

"I'm on Stark Street, looking for Antwan Brown," I told her. "I know he's a Stone Deader, and I know they own the fifth block of Stark, but it's like a ghost town here. No one's out on the street. Do you have any idea where these Dead idiots live? They can't all live on the fifth block."

"They're all over the place. Most of them live with their mamas. My friend Shirlene would know. She works a corner on the fourth block, and her little brother is one of those Deaders. At least he used to be. He got shot in the back and got paralyzed. The only thing he can move without help is his tongue. He's in a county hospital somewhere."

"How awful."

"Yeah, it's been hard on Shirlene. She's a real nice person too."

"Is she out working now?"

"We can go see. I'm bored anyways. I was supposed to have a date, but he got arrested. Where are you?"

"I'm parked on the first block of Stark. I'm in front of the used-appliance store."

"I'll be there in a couple minutes."

I checked my phone for email messages. I called my sister to say hello. I looked in my rearview mirror and saw Lula parking behind me.

"Why did he get arrested?" I asked Lula as she settled herself into my passenger seat.

"Who?"

"Your date."

"Don't know. Don't care. All I know is I got stood up. And then he had the nerve to ask me to bail him out."

"Did you?"

"Hell no. I'm not throwing my money away on some loser who gets himself arrested. Been there, done that."

I drove to Shirlene's corner, but there was no Shirlene.

"She's usually out here," Lula said. "She might be doing business somewhere. We could ride around and come back in a couple minutes. It don't usually take Shirlene long to do business. She gives people their money's worth, but she don't waste time."

I motored up and down Stark, and on the third pass we saw Shirlene get out of a car. She tugged at a hot-pink spandex skirt that barely covered her ass, adjusted her boobs, and sashayed over to her corner. I pulled up to the curb, and Lula stuck her head out the window.

"Hey, girl," Lula said. "How's business?"

"Business sucks," Shirlene said. "What's going on?"

"We want to talk to you."

"It'll cost you if you want to talk now. This is premium time. Women go to Bible study on Sunday afternoon, and men find Jesus with Shirlene."

"We don't want to find Jesus," Lula said, "but we'll spot you a pizza."

"Done deal," Shirlene said. "What are we talking about?"

"Antwan Brown," Lula said.

"That's unhealthy talking," Shirlene said. "That talking could get you set on fire."

"Let's talk in general then," Lula said. "Do you happen to know where any nineteen-year-old baggy-pants homeless killers live?"

"That covers a lot of ground," Shirlene said. "And if they're homeless then they don't got a home where you could find them."

"What do these kids do all day?" I asked Shirlene.

"The usual kid stuff. Smoke dope, play videogames, watch SpongeBob and cage fighting on television. The ones who want to get somewhere push drugs. Or if they can read they make drugs. Making drugs is better 'cause you eliminate the middleman. Otherwise they sit around working themselves up over who's dissin' them. And they tweet. They do a lot of tweeting."

"How would I hook up with them?"

"Same way you hook up with anyone," Shirlene said. "Twitter. Or you could walk down the fifth block wearing red, and then they'd show up and shoot you."

"Anything else?" Lula asked.

"I hear some of them play basketball on the city courts across from the projects."

"Do you know when they play?" I asked.

"They don't play in the morning."

I gave Shirlene twenty dollars, and Lula and I drove to the basketball courts by the projects. There were kids playing basketball, and some of them looked like killers, but none of them looked like Antwan.

"I don't know why Vinnie wrote a bond on this loser," Lula said. "It's no wonder we can't find him. We don't have any information. Who writes a bond on someone without an address or a single relative?"

"The bond was completely secured. Vinnie doesn't care if we find him."

"Then why are we looking?"

"*I* need to find him. I need the recovery money for a new car. Or at least a new muffler."

"I don't know why you're going there. You'll be rolling in dough when you capture Uncle Sunny."

"I'm making zero progress with the Sunny capture. I broke my finger, I've been condemned to hell, dropped off a bridge, and shot at."

"Yeah, but you can't expect everything to go perfect all the time. You just had a few bumps in the road."

"I need a new job."

"I don't think so. What about me if you get a new job? What am I going to do?"

"You'd be the office bounty hunter."

"That sounds pretty good. That's an important promotion. I like the way that sounds. Only wait a minute, then I'm gonna be the one getting dropped off the bridge. I'd hate that. It'd ruin my hair. And what happens to my Via Spigas when I go off the bridge?"

I drove through the projects, and then because we were close to Fifteenth I drove through Sunny's neighborhood. We didn't see Sunny. We didn't see Kevin. We didn't see Antwan. I drove back to the basketball court and the court was empty. I made one last pass down Stark Street and dropped Lula off at her car.

"This was a pretty good day," Lula said. "We didn't get shot at even once."

. . .

I let myself into my apartment, slumped into my bedroom, flopped onto the bed, and pulled the pillow over my face. I wallowed in self-pity for a couple minutes, did a couple minutes of berating myself, but ultimately it wasn't working for me. I got up, had a beer and a peanut butter sandwich, and felt pretty good. It's hard to feel bad after drinking some beer and eating some worthless white bread and peanut butter.

I went to the computer and logged on to Antwan's Twitter page. There was a lot of tweeting about music. Some chest beating about how tough he was. He had ham and cheese for lunch. Blah, blah, blah. He trash-talked about a girl he'd messed up. His brain-dead friends tweeted back supportive messages. More blah, blah, blah. He hung out with Big Al after basketball.

Eureka. This was exactly what I was looking for. He played basketball. He wasn't there yesterday, but he was there some-times. I kept reading, and there was another mention of his usual noontime basketball game. So maybe I knew where to find Antwan. Now I just had to figure out how to capture him. I wondered if Morelli was serious about the SWAT team.

At nine o'clock I followed Grandma's instructions and signed on to play Bingo. I read the rules and used my credit card to deposit fifty dollars in my Bingo account. I was able to buy cards with this account, and winnings would be deposited in it. I could withdraw my money at any time so it seemed okay. I gave "Luvbaby" as my screen name, and I bought three Bingo cards. It took three minutes for me to lose. I bought three more cards. Lost. Bought more cards. Won a small jackpot.

Morelli called a little before ten o'clock, and I told him I couldn't talk. I got back to the game and played until midnight, when I had to quit because I'd maxed out my credit card.

I crashed into bed, chanting *Stupid, stupid, stupid* to myself. The phone rang after I'd thrashed around for fifteen minutes.

"Babe," Ranger said, "I'm not going to get to you tonight. I have a client with a major security breach and a missing fifteen-hundred-pound safe."

"No problem," I said. "I have my own issues."

TWENTY

I LOOKED AT my reflection in the bathroom mirror at eight A.M. and couldn't believe what I saw. A Bingo addict was holding my toothbrush. I'd maxed out my credit card playing a game I didn't even like. What the heck was I thinking?

I rolled into the office a little before nine. Vinnie's car wasn't parked behind the office, and his door was closed. Connie was busy on her computer. Lula's car was parked outside, but she wasn't in the office.

"Where is everyone?" I asked.

"First thing this morning Vinnie got a threatening message from Harry about Sunucchi," Connie told me. "Harry's accountant was going over the books, and he wasn't happy. So Vinnie took a mental health day and went underground."

"Where's Lula?"

"She's taking inventory in the storeroom."

"Have you ever played Bingo online?"

"No, but I know lots of people who do. I'm more into poker."

"What happens if you gamble more money than you have?" I asked Connie. "Would the site put you into collection?"

"I guess they could, but I don't think that happens. Your credit card would just get declined."

I called Morelli at work.

"The women who were murdered and tossed into the Dumpsters," I said to Morelli. "Their bank accounts were cleaned out, right?"

"Right."

"Are we talking about a lot of money?"

"It ranged from fifteen hundred dollars to just under thirty thousand."

"Do you suppose they could have been paying off gambling debts?"

"Why were they killed if they were paying off debts? Usually you get killed if you *don't* pay off."

"I haven't got that part figured out."

"Do you want to do something tonight?" Morelli asked.

"What did you have in mind?"

"Depends. Do we need to have the aborted relationship discussion?"

"No. I had the discussion all by myself and got it all straight."

"Did you reach any conclusions I should know about?"

"Nope. It's all good."

"So I should stop at the drugstore on the way over?"

"Sure, and pick up some ice cream."

"Should I also pick up dinner?"

"Wouldn't hurt."

I hung up, took a deep breath, and told myself it would all work out. Somewhere, out there in the cosmos, there was a plan for me. Someday I'd get my life under control. My fear was that it might not be someday soon.

Lula came out of the storeroom. "Did I hear you talking to Morelli? Are you seeing him tonight? Because I was hoping we could go out under cover of darkness tonight and look for Kevin."

"Maybe Connie will go out with you."

"Pass," Connie said. "I'm taking my mother to a baby shower for Ann Marie Scarelli."

Connie comes from a big Italian family that has a baby shower or wedding shower every week. And on the odd occasion that there's not a wedding shower or baby shower, there's a jewelry party, makeup party, Botox party, or potluck dinner.

"I'm worried about Kevin," Lula said. "What if he's laying in the middle of the road starving? I haven't been leaving him lettuce."

"I think someone would notice a giraffe in the middle of the road," I said.

"Yeah, but what if he's a magic giraffe, and we're the only ones can see him?"

I didn't want to consider that possibility. That might indicate insanity. Fortunately Ranger had also seen Kevin, so I would at least have a boyfriend in the loony bin with me.

"We can look for Kevin this morning," I said to Lula. "I should do a drive-by on Sunny's properties anyway."

"I thought you didn't want to be seen someplace where people wanted to shoot you?"

"That was yesterday."

"Maybe we should go in disguise," Lula said. "I was just taking inventory, and we got some wigs back there from when Vinnie bonded out that drag queen what was robbing banks. He's doing ten to twenty and he never came back for his wigs. The wigs are pretty good, and we sprayed them for cooties when they came in, so they're even sanitary."

"It's not a bad idea," Connie said. "It wouldn't hurt to look at them."

Lula went to the storeroom and came back with a box filled with wigs. Blond wigs, red wigs, pink wigs, black wigs, brown wigs. Some were curly, and some were straight, in a variety of lengths.

"I even know which one I want already," Lula said. "I'm taking the Marilyn wig. It's just like her hair in *The Seven Year Itch*. Remember when the air from the subway grate blew her skirt up? It's what you call a iconic wig."

I went with a short red wig that had spiky curls and bangs. I tucked my ponytail under the wig and looked at myself in the bathroom mirror. I was kind of cute.

"You don't look like yourself at all," Lula said to me. "You look like you'd be a lot of fun."

I cut across town, and stopped at a light on Fifteenth.

"Have you noticed people are looking at us?" Lula said. "I wouldn't think we be attracting this much attention in this little SUV. It's a normal car compared to my red Firebird or your big blue Buick."

"I'm going out on a limb here and suggesting they're looking at the black woman in the platinum Marilyn wig."

"Do you think?" Lula flipped the visor down and looked at herself in the mirror. "I *am* spectacular. I guess I'd have to take a second look at me too. Probably people are wondering if I'm a supermodel or movie star."

I drove two more blocks and parked at the corner of Fifteenth and Freeman.

"I thought we were riding around," Lula said. "How come we're parked?"

"We can see more on foot. And I maxed out my credit card, so I'm watching my gas consumption."

"How about your life-or-death consumption? I bet you don't even have a gun."

"Wrong. I have my gun with me."

"Do you have bullets in it?"

"No. I haven't gotten around to buying bullets. It would be a lot easier if more places sold bullets."

"You mean like 7-Eleven and Cluck-in-a-Bucket? And why do you have your gun if you don't have bullets in it?"

"I could scare someone with it. Or I could hit someone over the head. And when Ranger asks me if I'm carrying a gun I can say yes."

"That all makes sense to me. Which way you want to walk first?"

"Let's go down Fifteenth."

We walked past the Chestnut Social Club, past Sunny's apartment building, and past the building on the next block that they were renovating. We didn't see Sunny, Moe, Shorty, or Kevin, and we didn't get kidnapped or shot at, but we did have two opportunities to make some spare change.

"I don't get it," Lula said. "I stood out on the corner all night, and business was terrible. And here I am looking respectable, trying to do a job, and we get two fools asking about our services. And they were cash customers. They didn't even offer food stamps. I think it must be you in that wig. I think you look like a loose woman."

Lula was wearing a sequined spandex skirt that came an inch below her doo-dah and a tank top that looked like it had shrunk in the wash. When you put it together with the Marilyn wig she might as well have had LOVE FOR SALE tattooed onto her forehead.

"What do you suppose they're doing to that building they're renovating?" I asked Lula. "You don't see a lot of renovating going on in this neighborhood. At least not on that scale. It looks like they're gutting the first two floors."

"Must be some business going in. Like another fake tailor."

"It's two floors, and it looks like they're also working in the basement."

"Maybe it's another social club."

"Nobody puts money into a social club. A social club in Trenton is like a senior center for the mob."

"Then maybe they're setting up to do Bingo."

"Three floors of Bingo?"

"I got a nervous stomach on account of I haven't seen any trace of Kevin," Lula said. "We didn't see piles of poop or anything. I'm worried something happened to him. Like he could have wandered away, and now he could be walking down the Garden State Parkway, looking for tender green leaves, on his way to Atlantic City. He could get hit. It's not like people driving that road are looking out for giraffes."

I didn't see anything good coming from spending more time on Fifteenth Street, so I steered Lula back to the car, and we headed for the basketball court. It wasn't raining yet, but rain was predicted and the sky was overcast. I parked across the street from the court, and pulled binoculars out of the glove box.

"What are we going to do if we find this guy?" Lula asked. "You busting in with your gun blazing? Oh, hold on a minute, your gun don't blaze."

"I thought we'd watch him, and wait for him to go his own way. We can't do anything when he's with his friends."

"So we just gonna hang with him?"

"Yeah."

"And then?"

"I don't know."

"Sounds like a plan."

The basketball court was surrounded by chain link fence. It backed up to an empty lot on one side, and ran along the sidewalk on another. A big kid lumbered around on the court, all by himself. He'd dribble the ball and shoot a basket. He'd shuffle after the ball and do more dribbling and shooting. It was like watching a dancing bear.

After ten minutes, two more kids strutted in. And a couple minutes later three more showed up. I was pretty sure one of them was Antwan. I trained the binoculars on him and made a positive ID.

"That's our idiot," I said to Lula.

They played basketball for almost an hour, and it started to rain. Nothing serious. Just an annoying drizzle. The dancing bear took his basketball and left. Antwan left with him. They walked down the street and disappeared into a six-story redbrick graffiti-riddled apartment building.

"Now what?" Lula asked. "We gonna be Girl Scouts selling cookies?"

I looked at my watch. "Let's give them a half hour, and see if they come out. If they don't come out we'll go in and quietly snoop around a little."

A half hour passed, and the rain picked up.

"You're going to have to get closer if we're going in that building," Lula said. "I don't want to ruin my Marilyn hair. And I don't know what rain's gonna do to my sequins."

There weren't a lot of cars parked on the street. Probably because anything parked longer than ten minutes got stolen. I pulled up to the front of the building, and Lula and I dashed across the sidewalk and into the small, dark foyer. Twelve mailboxes were set in the wall. None had names. No elevator. No pine-scented air freshener plugged into an outlet. Two apartments on the ground floor. We stood and listened. No sound coming from either apartment. We crept up the stairs to the second floor. Kids were shrieking in one of the apartments. It was happy shrieking. They were playing. The apartment across the hall was oozing cooking smells. Curry. Probably not Antwan or Dancing Bear. The third floor was quiet.

The fourth floor had a wall pockmarked with bullet holes. I took this as a good sign. We listened at the door of 4A and heard what sounded like Grand Theft Auto. Jackpot. I put my ear to the door across the hall and heard nothing.

Lula was rooting through her Brakmin. "Uh-oh," she said. "I might not have my gun. It might be in my other purse."

The door to 4A opened and Antwan looked out at us. "What's going on out here?"

"We're party girls looking for Jimbo," Lula said.

"There's no Jimbo here," Antwan said.

"Well, then, who are you? You want to party?"

"Hell no," Antwan said. "I don't party with old bitches like you."

Lula narrowed her eyes. "Excuse me? 'Old bitches'? Did you call me a old bitch?"

"Yeah," Antwan said. "You a fat old bitch. And you got on a 'ho wig. I don't party with bitches what wear wigs."

"This here's a Marilyn wig," Lula said. "You know nothing. You're nothing but a skank-ass, pencil-dick hemorrhoid. And you smell like anal leakage."

"Say what?"

"Anal leakage. It's when your anal leaks. And it don't smell good."

The bear shuffled over. "Am I missing something?"

"You ever heard of anal leakage?" Antwan asked him.

"I think it's when you squeeze a dog's butt and juice shoots out."

"This fat old 'ho told me I smelled like anal leakage," Antwan said.

The big guy looked down at him. "I never noticed."

"You need to stop calling me old and fat," Lula said. "It could get me mad, and then I'd have to put you in a lot of pain."

Antwan pulled a massive gun out of his baggy pants. It was nickel-plated and had a snake inscribed on the barrel. "Maybe I'll put *you* in a lot of *dead*."

"What the heck is that?" Lula said, staring at the gun. "It looks like something you got in the claw machine at Seaside Heights."

"I don't like people insulting my gun," Antwan said.

He fired off a round and got Lula in the Brakmin.

"You shot my Brakmin!" Lula yelped. "What the heck's the matter with you? This here bag's almost a Brahmin. And look what you did to one of my Swarovski crystals. You're gonna have to pay for this."

He raised the gun to fire again, and Lula clocked him on the side of his head with her bag. His eyes sort of rolled around in their sockets, he dropped to his knees, and the huge silver gun slipped from his fingers.

I had cuffs in one hand and my stun gun in the other.

"Hey," Bear said. "What's going on?"

"Fugitive apprehension," Lula said, taking the cuffs from me and clamping them onto Antwan. "Stand back."

"No way," Bear said.

He swiped at Lula and knocked her on her butt. I lunged at him with my stun gun, pressed the prongs into his arm, and hit the GO button. Nothing. No reaction.

"That tingles," Bear said. "I like it."

Antwan's eyes came into focus, and he realized he was cuffed. "Fuck."

"That's a bad word," Lula said. "You shouldn't say that in the presence of ladies."

"Gimme the key," Bear said.

I reached for the gun lying on the floor, and Bear grabbed me by my ankles and held me upside down.

"For a big man you're deceptively fast," Lula said to Bear. "And I gotta say I'm impressed with how strong you are."

I wriggled, trying to get loose, and Bear gave me a shake. "Stop wriggling. I want the key."

"She hasn't got the key," Lula said. "I've got the key, and you can't catch me." Lula waggled her butt and waved her arms. "You can't catch me. You can't catch me."

Bear tossed me aside and went after Lula, chasing her into the apartment and around and around the couch. The gun was still lying on the floor, leaving me to reach the conclusion that Bear might be big and strong but he definitely wasn't smart.

I scooped the gun up and held it with two hands. Awkward because of the splint on my broken finger. "Stop!"

"No way," Bear said, still running circles around the couch after Lula.

"Get the fucking gun from her," Antwan said to Bear.

Bear stopped and looked at me in surprise, like this was the first he saw that I had the gun. "How am I gonna do that?" Bear asked. "She'll shoot me."

Antwan was on his feet, hands still cuffed. "She's not gonna shoot you. She's just a dumb bitch. Look at her. She don't even know how to *hold* a gun."

Bear lunged at me and I fired off a shot. The gun kicked back and smacked me in the face. I saw stars and tasted blood, and my brain fogged for a beat.

Through the fog I heard Antwan yelling. "She shot off my ear! The fucking bitch shot off my ear!"

I'd intended the shot to go wide as a warning shot, but Antwan had moved at the wrong time and the round had obviously caught him on the side of the head. My face was throbbing, and blood was dripping off my nose onto my shirt. Lula was dancing in place, shrieking. Bear stood frozen, mouth open, eyes wide.

"Don't just stand there," Antwan said to Bear. "Get me to a fucking doctor."

Bear slung Antwan over his shoulder, ran past me, and I heard him thundering down the stairs. I heard the front door open and slam shut. I was still holding the gun, and Lula was still shrieking.

"You can stop shrieking," I said to Lula.

"Sorry," Lula said. "I freaked when you shot off that cannon and everyone started gushing blood."

"We need to get out of here before Antwan sends in someone with a brain and a gun."

"Your nose don't look good," Lula said. "It's swollen up already, and it's making a right-hand turn." She searched her purse and came up with a tissue. "You could stick this tissue up it for the time being. And you know what? Here's my gun! I had my gun in here all the time. It must be what stopped the bullet when he shot up my purse, and it's what gave him a good clunk on the head."

I gave Antwan's gun to Lula and took the tissue. I retrieved my messenger bag, and we crept down the blood-splotched stairs. We left the building and stood on the sidewalk in the pouring rain. No car.

"I don't know what it's coming to when people go around stealing cars in the rain," Lula said. "Some people just don't think what a inconvenience it is to other people when they steal a car in the rain."

I walked, head down, to the corner and called Ranger.

"Someone stole your car," I told him.

"We're on it. Do you need a ride?"

"Definitely. And Lula's with me."

Ten minutes later Ranger pulled to the curb. I was drenched, I had two blood-soaked tissues stuck up my nose, my eyes were swollen almost shut, and my clothes and arms were streaked with rain-washed bloodstains. Ranger got out of his black Cayenne, and I saw the set of his mouth go grim.

"Babe," he said.

"It's not as bad as it looks," I told him. "I just broke my nose."

We drove in silence to the emergency clinic. I had my head tipped back, trying to stanch the blood flow, and Lula was in the backseat, trying to fluff her Marilyn wig.

Ranger checked me in at the clinic and called for one of his men to take Lula back to her car. I got an incredibly painful shot of Novocaine, had my nose realigned and taped, had a dry bandage put on my broken finger, and was sent home with cold packs.

"So you did this to *yourself*?" Ranger asked.

"I shot off a monster gun, and it kicked back into my face."

"And the other guy?"

"I shot his ear off."

Ranger grinned.

"Unfortunately he got away."

Ranger took me home and walked me to my door. "The guy with one ear is probably going to come after you," he said. "Be careful."

I nodded. "Thanks."

I hadn't identified myself at the apartment, and with luck Antwan didn't know who I was or where to find me.

. . .

Morelli showed up at seven o'clock with Bob, a pizza box, a six-pack, and a bag from the drugstore. He looked at me and went pale.

"It's just a broken nose," I said, squinting at him through eyes that were reduced to slits in a face that looked like a Tequila Sunrise gone wrong.

"What happened?"

"Do you want the long version or the short version?"

"I want the long version."

I gave him the long version while we ate pizza and drank beer.

"At the risk of being insensitive . . . you're a disaster," Morelli said.

"No offense taken. You're right. I'm a disaster. I'm thinking about getting a different job."

Morelli set the pizza box out for the trash and got the ice cream from the freezer. "The world will be relieved to hear that." He got two bowls from the cupboard. "Do you have any good possibilities?"

"Possibilities? Yes. *Good* possibilities? No."

We ate ice cream in front of the television, and then Morelli watched a showing of *The Godfather,* and I sat next to him with cold packs over my eyes.

"I hope I look okay by tomorrow," I told him. "I have things to do."

"Cupcake, you're going to look like a train wreck tomorrow."

"We might not get to use all the items you got at the drugstore."

"No problem. They have an expiration date of 2023."

TWENTY-ONE

I COULDN'T BREATHE through my nose, and I didn't sleep well. Halfway through the night Morelli and Bob moved to the couch, and at six in the morning Morelli came in to check on me.

"I'm going to take Bob for a walk, and then I'm leaving for work," he said. "Can I do anything for you?"

"I'm beyond help."

He kissed me on the forehead. "You look better this morning. The swelling is down. Hardly any purple, and already you're turning green. Green is always a good sign."

"You should know."

"Yeah, I've been known to smash my nose into a fist from time to time."

I listened to the door click and lock behind him, and I went back to sleep. It was after nine by the time I finally dragged myself out of bed and stared into the bathroom mirror. Morelli was right about the swelling. My eyes weren't normal, but they were much better. Dark glasses and some concealer, and I wouldn't be too scary-looking. Not much I could do about the big adhesive bandage across my nose. That would have to stay in place for a while.

Truth is, I'd gotten off lucky. If Antwan had been two inches more to the right I might have killed an unarmed man. That's the sort of thing that can get you an orange prison jumpsuit. The bruising on my face would go away in days, but I could have been in the jumpsuit for *years*. And even beyond that I wouldn't have wanted Antwan's death on my hands. Bad enough I shot off his ear.

I did the best I could with makeup. I left my hair long and curly, letting it partially fall across my face. And I wore a scoop-necked red sweater, hoping to focus attention on my cleavage and not on my nose. I went to my living room window and looked out at the parking lot. The little black Honda CR-V was waiting for me. It had all its wheels and side mirrors. Ranger had obviously rescued it before the chop shop went to work.

First stop of the day was the office. Connie gasped when I walked in, and Lula leaned in for a closer look.

"I expected you to look a lot worse than this," Lula said. "Hard to tell with the bandage, but I'm guessing your nose isn't taking a right turn no more. And you look green under the makeup, which is much better than purple. Except you sort of got a zombie thing going on."

I went to the coffeemaker and poured myself a cup. "So I've been told."

"I checked the hospitals and emergency clinics," Connie said. "Antwan showed up at a clinic attached to Mercy Memorial. It sounds like you reconfigured most of his outer ear, and gave him a permanent part in his hair on the side of his head, but no further damage. His chart listed 'fall down stairs' as cause of injury."

"You think he gonna be playing basketball today?" Lula asked.

"I don't care if he's playing basketball today," I said. "I'm done. Antwan is someone else's problem."

"What do you mean, 'done'?" Lula asked.

"Done being a bounty hunter, fugitive apprehension agent, bail bond enforcer," I said. "Done, done, done."

"Oh boy," Connie said.

Vinnie stuck his head out of his office. "What do you mean, 'done'? Who's going to get Sunucchi?"

"You," I said to Vinnie. "You're up."

"I've got things to do here," he said. "I've got responsibilities."

"Is this about blowing off that idiot's ear?" Lula asked. "Because it was his fault anyways. And besides it was only an ear. Not to mention he ruined my Brakmin. And as far as your nose goes, it could happen to anyone with that gun. That gun's not normal."

Vinnie pointed at Lula. "I'm giving you a promotion. You're the new bounty hunter."

"Not me," Lula said. "I don't mind being the assistant bounty hunter, but I'm not taking over as bounty hunter. It's a terrible job. Everybody hates you and shoots at you. Look at Stephanie. She's a mess."

I pulled a folder with all my paperwork out of my messenger bag and handed it to Connie. "These are all the open cases."

"What are you gonna do?" Lula asked. "You got another job?"

"Maybe."

. . .

Randy Berger's deli was on the edge of the Burg. It had formerly been known as Schmidt's Meats, and Randy had changed the name to Berger's Bits. The place was primarily a butcher shop, but there were a few staples on shelves in the front of the store, plus there were racks of condiments. It was next to a store that sold cupcakes, and beyond the cupcake store was a dry cleaner and a pet groomer.

I parked in the small lot next to Berger's Bits and worked on my enthusiasm. This could be great, I told myself. It would be safe. I'd keep regular hours. And I'd learn something about meat. Morelli would like that. Meat was one of his favorite things.

I'd been in the store a couple times when I'd run errands for my mom, but not recently. Mostly she shopped at Giovichinni's, because it was closer. If Randy Berger gave her a discount she'd be shopping there. There were two large plate glass windows on either side of the door in the front of the store. They were papered with handwritten specials and ads for lottery tickets. The register was just inside the door. One register. One plump lady working the register. She was wearing a bright blue smock with "Berger's Bits" embroidered over her left breast. "Janice" was embroidered under "Berger's Bits."

I walked to the back of the store, where Randy Berger was waiting on an elderly woman. A second woman patiently stood in line. Randy saw me, and his face flushed even more scarlet than usual, but it was no match for my green and black bruising.

"I'll be with you in a minute," he said.

I attempted a smile. "No problem."

Immaculate glass cases lined three sides of the store. The poultry, lamb, beef, pork, and sausages were nicely displayed, considering it was all dead flesh. Cook it up and put some gravy on it and I'm happy. Anything precooking and I'm one step from gag. With the possible exception of bacon. Bacon comes shrink-wrapped in strips and has no relationship to anything other than bacon. I know there are rumors that bacon originates with Porky Pig, but I find that incomprehensible. If Randy gave me a job I hoped I'd get put in charge of the bacon. Sausage would be okay too.

The second woman whisked past me with her packet of

meat wrapped in butcher paper, and I returned to the back of the store, where Randy was wiping down a counter.

"What would you like?" he asked. "The lamb racks are nice today." He looked up from his cleaning, and his eyes glazed over as he took in my face.

"It's not as bad as it looks," I told him. "I had a gun kick back and smack me in the nose."

"Does that happen a lot?"

"No. It was partly because my broken finger made it hard to hold the gun." I held my finger up for him to see. "Anyway, I came in to see if the job was still open. I think I'm ready for a change."

"I thought you didn't like meat and poultry."

"That was yesterday. And I've always liked bacon."

"I could really use some help," Randy said. "When can you start?"

"Now."

"Are you sure you're okay with the broken nose and all?"

"Yep. I'm good. I can almost breathe through one side."

"I guess I could use you in the back room today if you don't mind doing mostly cleanup. It would help me out a lot. I have a big barbecue order to fill, I got a truck coming in with a side of beef, and I got a pig in the smoker out back."

"Gee, that sure sounds exciting."

"It's just the beginning. You're going to love this job. I'm going to start you off letting you watch the smoker for me. The pig's already in it and cooking. You just have to make sure the smoker stays on the right temperature."

I nodded. I thought I could manage that.

A woman stepped up to the counter and Randy sliced off a half pound of Virginia baked ham for her. The woman went to the register, and Randy turned back to me.

"For most of the day, there's a steady stream of customers coming in, and I can't wait on the customers and get anything else done, so I'm staying here until all hours doing butchering. With you here we should be able to split up the customers and the butchering and be home by nine."

"Nine at night?"

"Is that a problem? We stay open until seven and then it takes time to shut down and clean."

"No problem."

I hoped, while I was looking after the smoker, I didn't have access to sharp knives, because I was contemplating sticking one in my jugular.

"This is going to be great," Randy said. "Let me show you the back, we'll get you an apron, and we can peek in at the pig."

The back room reminded me of the embalming room at a funeral home. Stainless steel worktable, large stainless sink, buckets for blood and guts, big bottle of bleach. Randy had a walk-in refrigerator and freezer, a shrink-wrapping machine, a commercial stove, a massive chopping block, various slicers, a couple power saws, and some stainless steel rolling racks.

"Here's an apron for you," he said, handing me a black rubberized apron that would fit Sasquatch. "It's going to be a little big, but it's all I've got right now."

I put the apron on, and we went out to the parking lot behind the store to look at the pig. The smoker was a huge barrel on wheels with a wood-burning oven attached. Randy rolled the side door up on the smoker, and the whole pig was inside, head and tail and everything in between. Its mouth was open, it had aluminum foil wrapped around its ears, and its skin was singed black and crispy. I looked in at it, and it was goodnight Stephanie.

· · ·

Bells were clanging in my head, the world was whirling around, and my fingers were numb. I looked up, and Randy Berger swam into focus.

"What?" I said.

"You fainted. Lucky I caught you, or you would have cracked your head open like a muskmelon."

"The pig."

"I know just how you feel. I almost fainted the first time I cooked one, too. It's the smell of the gutted, fresh-killed pig roasting over the fire, dripping all its succulent oozy juices, its crispy skin charred mahogany and black." He smiled wide. "Life doesn't get much better than a roasted pig."

I heard someone whimper. I think it was me.

"It's overwhelming, right?" Randy said. "Like a religious experience. Sometimes I have dreams about pigs getting roasted."

I was on my back on the paved parking lot, staring up at Randy, who was at that moment looking very piglike, with his round little pig eyes glittering in his pink, sweaty face.

"The snout. The tail. The hooves," I said. "All there. Why?"

"Because it's all delicious," Randy said. "I have all I can do to keep from tearing into it."

My God, I was in the throes of a pig-corpse-induced nightmare. This wasn't real. This wasn't happening.

"I like my pigs big, too," Randy said. "If you're gonna roast a pig, I say get a big one."

He yanked me to my feet. "Up you go! Feeling better?"

I nodded. Get it together, I told myself. Don't show fear in front of the crazy pig man.

"Okay then, let me get you started," Randy said. "You see this gauge on the cooker?"

I did another nod.

"Just keep it right where it is." He stuffed some chunks of wood into the oven. "You got to keep feeding the fire to keep the temperature up."

"Feed the fire," I said.

"You got it. Follow me."

We went back into the workroom and he pointed to a stack of boxes.

"We just got these in," Randy said. "We need to check them off against the bill to make sure we got the right thing, and then they need to get put in the walk-in fridge. Some of the boxes are wings for the barbecue. They got to get put in the marinade.

Set them aside and come get me when you're done, and I'll show you how to marinade."

More nodding on my part.

Randy went back to waiting on customers, and I thought if anyone was capable of killing old ladies and throwing them in a Dumpster it had to be Randy Berger. They were probably lucky not to get roasted in the pig cooker. I carted the boxes into the fridge and looked around to make sure there were no pickled human body parts stacked up for late-night snacking.

I set the boxes of wings on the stainless table and went out to get Randy. I watched him slice roast beef, ham, and Swiss cheese, and weigh out a pound of ground round.

"Ready for the marinade," I said.

Randy got a large plastic container from a top shelf and poured a big jar of brown glop into it. "Put the wings in this and make sure they all get covered. There's another jar of sauce on the shelf if you need it. Cover the container and put it in the fridge. We'll cook them up in a couple hours. There's a box of disposable gloves by the sink."

I looked at the gloves, and I looked at my finger in the big metal splint. This was going to be like trying to get a condom on King Kong.

• • •

It was almost nine-thirty when I staggered into my apartment, got a cold beer from the fridge, and held it against my eyes.

"Have a tough day?" Morelli asked, strolling into the kitchen, followed by Bob.

"Unh."

I'd seen his car parked in the lot when I pulled in, so I wasn't surprised to find him in my apartment. He had a key. And even without the key he could get past a lock.

Bob sniffed me up and down and licked my shoe.

"You smell like bacon," Morelli said to me. "I think I'm getting turned on."

"It's roast pig. It's in my hair. I can't get away from it."

"What's Bob eating on your shoe?"

"Barbecue sauce."

"Did you just capture a cook?"

"No. I quit my job at the bonds office, and I took a job at Berger's Bits."

"The butcher shop?"

"You know how some men have wet dreams? Randy Berger has pig dreams."

Morelli burst out laughing. "What are you doing there?"

"I'm a butcher."

"Cupcake, you go green walking past the chicken parts in the supermarket."

"This is right up there for the worst day of my life."

"You've had some pretty bad days. Remember when you fell off the fire escape into the dog diarrhea?"

"This was worse."

"Wow."

I took the beer bottle off my eye and drank the beer. "I need a shower."

"Do you need help?"

"No. I need food. Something vegetarian."

"A salad?"

"A pizza. Hold the pepperoni and sausage."

. . .

I was working my way through my second beer and third piece of pizza, and I was beginning to feel human.

"How's your nose?" Morelli asked.

"It's good. I can breathe through it, and it doesn't hurt if I don't touch it."

"Are you going to keep the butcher job?"

"At least for a couple more days. Randy Berger has moved to the top of my list for murder suspects. He knew all the women. He's big enough and strong enough to pitch someone into a Dumpster. And he's scary."

"How is he scary?"

"He worships meat. His eyes get glittery and crazy when he talks about it."

"All meat?"

"Mostly pork."

"It's a guy thing," Morelli said. "Any normal, red-blooded guy is going to go a little gonzo talking about pig products. All the best food in the world comes from a pig. Hot dogs, bacon, ribs, pulled pork, pork roast, pork chops, ham, Taylor pork roll."

"He was roasting a whole pig. It was massive. And he had its ears wrapped in aluminum foil."

"That's so they don't burn."

"You know about this?"

"I can find my way around a smoker."

"So you don't think Randy Berger killed the women."

"I didn't say that. I said he's not crazy just because he gets a little sloppy over pork."

"What's your best guess for the killer?"

"I don't have a best guess," Morelli said. "What we believe is that he's local. And the women knew him. He's neat. Doesn't like a messy crime scene. Has some ego. Likes to leave a calling card. Feels safe. Maybe feels like he's above the law. Beyond that we don't know much."

"What about the bank accounts?"

"The bank accounts have for the most part been explained away. One account was moved to another bank. One account was cleaned out to buy a cruise ticket that was never used."

"Your profile doesn't entirely fit Randy Berger. He probably wouldn't choose a Venetian blind cord as his instrument of death. He wouldn't care about neat. He'd be more comfortable with a cleaver."

"And what about motive?" Morelli asked. "What's his motive?"

"Fun?"

"It sounds to me like you quit working for Vinnie but you're still working for Ranger," Morelli said.

"I can't bring myself to walk away from those women. And I think it's odd that four women have been killed and left in a Dumpster and no one saw anything. It's like the giraffe. There's a giraffe hanging out on Fifteenth Street and no one's reported it. What's with that?"

"It's a mystery," Morelli said, sliding his arm around me and leaning close. "You don't smell like barbecue anymore, but I like you anyway. Maybe we should take some of those items I bought at the drugstore for a test drive."

"If you touch my nose I'll make you incapable of fathering a child."

"Touching your nose wasn't in my game plan."

"Are you willing to chance it?"

"No," Morelli said.

TWENTY-TWO

I GOT TO the hardware store at seven-thirty in the morning and bought rubber boots. My credit card was declined, so I gave Victor my last five dollars and the promise of pork chops. I went from there to the butcher shop, where I pulled on my new boots and wrapped the Sasquatch-size apron around myself as best I could.

"This is a big day," Randy said, taking the first hit of the day from the peach schnapps bottle. "We just got blood sausage and tongue from a farm in Wisconsin, and we have to start butchering the side of beef. I thought after we fill the display cases, you could take care of the customers, so I can tackle the side of beef. You know how to work the slicer and the scale, and you can come get me if there's a problem. Just remember, the customer is always right."

235

I added rubber gloves to my ensemble and helped Randy set up the trays of sausages and steaks. He brought out the tongue, and I felt my gag reflex kick in. The tongue was big. In fact it was bigger than just big. It was monstrous. It was the biggest freaking tongue I'd ever seen. Good thing Morelli'd stayed over last night, because there wasn't going to be anything happening tonight after my seeing a tray full of cow tongue.

At eleven o'clock I was feeling pretty good about how things were going. I'd weighed out deli meats, steaks, and a roasting chicken, and I hadn't fainted or thrown up. I'd gagged a little when Mrs. Carlson came in and asked for chicken livers, but I don't think she noticed. Not that this was a career position for me. I thought I'd stick with it long enough to be sure Randy Berger wasn't the old lady killer, and then I'd try to get a job stuffing sanitary napkins into a box at the personal products plant.

The front door opened and I caught a glimpse of Joe's Grandma Bella scuttling past the register and heading for the meat counter. I ducked behind the display case and told myself not to panic.

"Who's here?" Bella shouted. "Who's working here?"

Randy stuck his head around the corner from the back room and looked down at me cringing behind the case.

"Dropped my pen," I said.

"Who's that?" Bella asked. "Who do I hear?"

I popped up. "Me. Can I help you?"

"You! What you doing here?"

"I'm working here," I said.

"Then I never shop here."

Randy rushed to the counter. "I have your special order," he said to Bella. "It just came in. I sliced into the blood sausage this morning, and it's the best I've ever seen. And the tongue is nice and fat."

"I like fat tongue," Bella said. "You give me good price?"

"Of course," Randy said. He reached into the case and pushed the tongues around until he found one he liked. He held it out for Bella to see. "It's a beauty," he said. "What do you think?"

"I've seen better tongue," Bella said. "But I guess this will have to do."

"You're a hard negotiator," Randy said to Bella.

"You give me good price or I give you the eye," Bella said. "And that one behind you I already give the eye. She going to hell."

Randy weighed and wrapped the tongue and weighed and wrapped Bella's sausage. "Anything else?"

"I get my discount?"

"It'll show up at the register," Randy said.

Bella left and I turned to Randy. "What discount?"

"The senior discount."

"Bella is in the wellness program?"

"She's a certified card-carrying participant. She comes in every other week for blood sausage and tongue."

I did an inadvertent shiver. God knows what she did with

the sausage and tongue. Probably ate it raw. Probably tossed it into her stewpot with beetle legs and rat tails and brewed up some evil concoction. Or she could be feeding it to Sunny.

"I thought you were almost engaged to her grandson," Randy said. "Why did she give you the eye?"

"Uncle Sunny failed to appear for his court date, and I was given the unpopular job of capturing him and bringing him in."

Randy nodded. "The Sunucchis and Morellis are a tight family."

Ten minutes later Lula swung into the store and marched back to the meat counter.

"I can't believe you abandoned us and now you're working here," she said. "I'm forced to be driving Vinnie around. My car's gonna have a grease spot on the headrest. How am I ever gonna get that out?" She looked down at the case with the sausages and organ meats. "Holy cannoli, is that a tongue? That's the biggest freaking tongue I ever saw. It's like it's all swelled up. I'm getting hot looking at it. Can you imagine what a tongue like that could do?"

"It's a cow tongue," I said.

"No wonder cows are so contented."

"Did you want something?" I asked Lula. "Lunch meat? Hot wings?"

"No. I just came in to see you, and see how you're doing."

"My nose feels a lot better."

"Are you going to Bingo tonight?"

"No. This job gets out late."

"It don't sound like such a good job to me," Lula said. "And that apron you're wearing is *yikes*. You need to go to the kitchen store and get yourself something with ruffles."

· · ·

Ranger called at noon. "What's with the butcher shop?"

"I quit the bonds office and took a job as a butcher."

"Babe," Ranger said. And he hung up.

By four o'clock Randy had hacked up half a cow and gone through a lot of peach schnapps. I saw no indication that the schnapps affected him, with the possible exception of increasing the ruddiness in his cheeks. Hard to tell if the ruddiness came from the schnapps or from taking a cleaver to Ferdinand the Bull.

"Do you live close to the store?" I asked him.

"I live a quarter mile away in an apartment over the laundromat. It's real convenient when I want to do laundry, only thing is my floor vibrates if all the dryers are going at once."

"Is that the laundromat on King Street?"

"Yeah."

"That's a nice laundromat. I use it sometimes. Maybe I'll use it tonight and come visit you."

"You mean you'd come in to my apartment?"

"Yeah."

"I don't get a lot of visitors."

"You could show me how to cook something," I told him. "A hamburger or a pork chop."

"I was planning on steak tonight."

"I'd *love* to learn how to cook steak. I won't even go home to get my laundry. We can go straight from the store."

"I guess that would be okay," Randy said. "Is it a date?"

"No. It's a cooking lesson."

"Maybe it could turn into a date someday."

"Sure. Anything's possible."

Okay, so I knew that wasn't possible, but it was a small fib for a good cause. I wanted to look around Randy's apartment to see if he had Venetian blind cord stashed somewhere.

I started cleaning up before the shop closed. By eight we were picking out steaks, and we were on the road by eight-thirty. I followed Randy and parked in the laundromat lot. I got out of the CR-V and looked up at the second-floor apartment. There were Venetian blinds on the windows. I cautioned myself not to get carried away. Lots of people had Venetian blinds on their windows, and most of those people weren't killers.

We trudged up the stairs, Randy unlocked his door, and we carted our dinner inside. Randy had a grocery bag with the steaks and a loaf of sourdough bread, and I had the half-empty bottle of schnapps.

He had a brown leather couch and a matching recliner positioned in front of a large flat-screen television in his living room. He had a floor lamp and a tray table by the recliner.

The floor was hardwood with a worn-out tan area rug under the furniture. No curtains.

The kitchen was almost as large as the living room. The appliances were old but obviously worked. The walls were lined with shelves holding cans of tomato paste, spices, oils, canisters of flour and sugar, steak sauce, garlic, apple juice, soy sauce, kidney beans, ketchup, and more. One section of shelving was given over to glasses and dishes. Another to pots and pans. There were two small cabinets over the counter on either side of the sink, and a small square wood table with four chairs was set into a corner of the kitchen. There were salt and pepper shakers in the middle of the table.

"This is nice," I said. "It's comfortable."

"It's okay. I don't spend much time here. The shop is open six days a week, and I get home late. I make dinner and then I watch television."

"What about Sundays?"

"I go to yard sales. I collect things."

I looked around. His apartment was bare-bones. "Where do you keep the things you collect?"

"In a garage behind the deli." He put a cast iron grill pan on the gas cooktop and turned the oven on. "Do you want a drink?"

"Sure."

He poured out two tumblers of schnapps. "All I've got is schnapps," he said. "I hope that's okay."

I took a sip of the schnapps and felt the burn all the way to my hoo-ha. I figured it was about a hundred proof.

"Boy, that's good stuff," I said, blinking back tears.

"I got started drinking it when I worked in the slaughter-house. It keeps you warm when you're working in the freezer all day carrying whole hogs around on your back."

"Good to know."

"Yeah, if you want to be a butcher, schnapps is the way to go."

He turned the burners on, then unwrapped the steaks and put them on the grill on top of the stove. He shook salt and pepper on them and added some hot sauce.

"I like my steaks good and salty, and then I give them some kick with the hot sauce," he said. "I start them out on the grill, so they get seared and marked, and then I turn them over. If you didn't know better you'd swear they got done outside on a grill."

I sipped some more schnapps and looked down at the steaks.

"Yep," I said. "They look grilled all right."

"We'll let these sit here and burn a little and then we'll finish them off in the oven. I'll set the table and you can put the bread on a bread board and get the butter out of the refrigerator."

The refrigerator contained a pound of butter, a quart of milk, and schnapps. No vegetables. No juice. Just bottles and bottles of schnapps.

"I guess you like your schnapps cold sometimes," I said to Randy.

"It's awesome cold. I keep some in the freezer too."

I looked in the freezer. It was packed wall-to-wall with

schnapps and vanilla ice cream. I was starting to like Randy. I didn't care if he killed old ladies, I was thinking he was okay. I looked at my glass and realized it was empty. Good deal. I could try some *frozen* schnapps.

I set the butter and the bread on the table and opened a bottle of the frozen schnapps. I filled our glasses, and we toasted the steaks.

"They're ready to go into the oven," Randy said. "All you do is pop them in, grill and all. You put them in, and I'll slice the bread."

"I don't see any potholders."

"Use a towel. There are kitchen towels by the sink."

I grabbed a towel and wrapped it around the end of the grill. I pulled the grill off the burner, slid the grill into the oven, closed the oven door, and then realized I'd caught the end of the towel in the open flame and the towel was on fire. I had a moment of panic before my schnapps-soaked brain thought to toss the towel into the sink. I tossed the towel, missed the sink, and set a roll of paper towels on fire. Randy grabbed the schnapps bottle, poured it over the flaming paper towels, hoping to douse the fire, and after that it was mayhem.

• • •

Two hours later I was in the street with Randy and a fire department investigator, explaining how the fire started. In the interest of transparency, I have to say it wasn't the first time I'd been in this position. Grandma and I had burned down a funeral home a while ago, and it had been much more spectacular.

"I guess I should have gone for the fire extinguisher instead of the schnapps," Randy said. "I just grabbed the first thing I saw that was liquid."

The glow from the schnapps was long gone, I was starving hungry, and I was finding it difficult to focus. I wanted to crawl into my bed and pretend the day had never happened. I'd called Morelli an hour ago, and he and Bob were close behind me, waiting to take me home.

The guy from the fire department closed his notebook, glanced at Morelli, and gave him one of those looks that said, *You poor bastard, how did you ever get involved with this idiot woman?*

"Really sorry about your apartment," I said to Randy. "Probably I'm not cut out to be a butcher, but at least I know how to cook a steak now."

Randy nodded, and Morelli maneuvered me across the street and into his SUV.

"Do you think he understands that I'm not going to show up for work tomorrow?" I asked Morelli.

"I don't think it matters," Morelli said. "The fire marshal found half a truckload of hijacked schnapps in Berger's apartment. He had cases of it stacked up like cordwood in his bedroom. There's a good chance Berger won't be showing up for work either."

• • •

Bob and Morelli and I trooped into my apartment and went straight to the kitchen. We made grilled cheese and ham sandwiches, and ate them with pickles and potato chips. Morelli had a beer, and I had a soda since I was sworn off alcohol for the rest of my life.

"I need to go back to Randy's apartment tomorrow and get Ranger's CR-V," I said to Morelli.

"The black one in the laundromat lot?"

"Yeah."

"I'm sure Ranger will just have it towed." Morelli fed the last half of his second sandwich to Bob. "You know it got totaled by a fire truck, right?"

"*What?*"

"I went over to talk to some of the guys while you were giving your report to the investigator. It looked like the truck rolled right over it."

I dialed Ranger on my cellphone.

"About your CR-V," I said.

"I know about the CR-V. This is almost as good as the time you totaled my Porsche with a garbage truck. Are you okay?"

"Yep. I'm peachy."

"Good to know," Ranger said, and he disconnected.

Morelli took a tub of ice cream out of the freezer and began spooning it into three bowls. "What's the word on Berger? Did you find Venetian blind cord stashed under his mattress?"

"I didn't look under his mattress. I burned his apartment down before I got to see the bedroom."

"More happy news."

"Your Grandma Bella showed up at the shop today."

"How'd that go?"

"Same old, same old. I've been cursed. Yada yada yada. I'm going to hell." I took a bowl of ice cream from Morelli. "You don't suppose the broken finger and nose and fire are from Bella, do you?"

"None of those things are from Bella. Let's face it, Cupcake, you're a klutz. And if you go to hell it will be your own doing and not Bella's."

Bob finished his ice cream in seconds and closely watched Morelli and me in case some ice cream should fall off a spoon and onto the floor.

"Bella bought blood sausage and tongue," I said to Morelli.

Morelli brightened at the news. "I bet she's going to make some up for the game."

"You eat that stuff?"

"It's great. You should learn how to make it. My mom and Bella cook it up with sauerkraut. The smell could peel wallpaper off a wall, but it tastes fantastic."

A chill ran down my spine. I had a flashback to the game party with the shrieking kids, and the dog poop, and crazy Bella. And now I find out there's cow tongue involved in the whole family thing.

"It's *cow tongue*," I said to him. "Have you ever seen one that wasn't in a stew?"

"I thought you liked tongue," Morelli said.

"Not *cow* tongue!"

Morelli grinned. "Guess it's an acquired taste. I have to go. Early meeting tomorrow."

I finished my ice cream, took two aspirin, and headed off to the bathroom. I washed my hair twice and stood under the water until the smell of burned steak was just a distant memory.

TWENTY-THREE

I HAD A terrible night. Weird dreams, a dull ache moving around inside my head, and night sweats. I gave up trying to sleep when the sun poured into my bedroom and the world turned into a big red fireball on the other side of my closed eyelids.

So here's a fast assessment of my situation. I was hungover, unemployed, had no money, no car, no food left in my fridge, and I owed Victor pork chops.

I dragged myself out of bed, dressed in my usual uniform of jeans, T-shirt, and sneakers, pulled my hair into a ponytail, and called Lula.

"I need a ride," I told her.

"Thank God," Lula said. "This better be a call telling me you're coming back, because I'm feeling overworked. The new issue of *Star* came out, and I haven't had a chance to read it. It's

248

'Lula, do this,' and 'Lula, do that.' Plus your pervert cousin is saying he's gonna hire Joyce Barnhardt, and you know how I feel about Joyce Barnhardt. I *hate* Joyce Barnhardt."

Joyce Barnhardt has double-D breast implants, a lot of dyed red hair, and a way with whips and paddles that Vinnie finds appealing. She's also a psycho sociopath and genuinely horrible person.

"First things first," I told Lula. "A fire truck totaled my loaner CR-V, and I don't see a replacement in my parking lot. I was hoping you'd give me a ride over to my parents' house so I could get the Buick."

"Get out! Are you shitting me? A fire truck totaled Ranger's car? That's almost as good as when the garbage truck totaled the megabucks Porsche he loaned you. That car was only one inch thick when they finally got the garbage truck off it. I can't wait to hear about this. My day is getting better already. I'll be there in a couple minutes."

I went through jacket pockets and four shelved handbags, and searched the bottom of my messenger bag for loose change. I found three tracking units from Ranger plus two dollars and seventy-five cents. I put it all in my messenger bag and took the stairs to the lobby.

I called Ranger while I waited for Lula.

"I cleaned out my closet, and I found three mini tracking units. I assume you want them back?"

"You can return them to me, or you can plant them on yourself. One of those units helped us find you on the bridge."

"True, but sometimes being tracked twenty-four hours a day feels creepy."

"Your call," Ranger said. "I'm guessing you need a car?"

"I'm waiting for Lula. She's going to take me to pick up Big Blue."

"I have a car coming in for you, but I won't have it until later today. I'll find you and swap Blue out for it when it arrives."

"How will you find me if I don't carry one of your trackers?"

"I'll call you on your cellphone."

I hung up and looked through my messenger bag one more time. I didn't believe for an instant that he wasn't tracking me somehow. Undoubtedly he had something stuck onto the Buick, but I knew in my gut there was something else.

I looked at the phone in my hand and dialed him back.

"Have you hacked my cellphone?" I asked him.

"Babe," Ranger said. And he disconnected.

Lula swung the Firebird into the lot to my building, stopped in front of the lobby door, and I jumped in.

"How'd you manage to get a fire truck to run over that cute little car Ranger gave you?" she asked me.

"I wanted to see if Randy Berger had any Venetian blind cord lying around, and while I was in his apartment I accidentally started a fire. And then the fire truck accidentally ran over Ranger's car."

"So I'm thinking you're not working as a butcher anymore."

"That would be good thinking."

"You got any other places you want to look for Venetian blind cord?"

"Randy stores things in a garage behind his deli. I wouldn't mind taking a look in the garage."

. . .

I had Lula drive past the front of Berger's Bits. Lights were on inside, and the OPEN sign was in the door. Either he hadn't been arrested, or else he was already out on bail. If he was released on bail he hadn't used Vinnie as his agent.

Lula parked behind the pet groomer two stores down from the deli, and we walked the short distance to the garage.

"Looks sturdy," Lula said.

Sturdy was an understatement. It was a bomb shelter. Big enough for a single car. Cinderblock construction. No windows. Metal roll-down door secured with a padlock.

"What's he keep in here?" Lula asked. "This is like Fort Knox. Maybe he's got gold in here."

"I don't suppose you have any bolt cutters with you?" I asked her.

"Darn," Lula said. "I left them in my other purse. You want me to shoot the lock off?"

"No! I don't want to attract attention."

"Well, I don't see how you're gonna get in here. I think we need another activity. Like we could go look for Kevin."

"Or you could drive me to the personal products plant and I could apply for a job there."

"No way. I'm not taking you there. That's a terrible idea. What kind of job you looking for?"

"The line. I could run the boxing machine for the sanitary napkins."

"You'll rip your arm off. You're not good with machines. You'll get your shirt caught in some moving part, and next thing you won't have one of your arms. And besides, you gotta come back to the bonds office so I don't have to work with Joyce Barnhardt. If I have to work with Barnhardt, I'll have to kill her, and then I might go to jail, and a orange jumpsuit isn't a good look for me."

"I need a job. I'm down to two dollars and seventy-five cents."

"That's enough for a value meal at Cluck-in-a-Bucket. You could get a Clucky Burger and a Coke for that. I bet you didn't have no breakfast, and that's why you got that pale desperate look to you."

"I have that pale desperate look because I have a hangover, and I'm broke, and unemployed."

"In that case you should add fries. Nothing gets rid of a hangover better than cheap-ass fries and a Coke. What were you drinking to get a hangover?"

"Peach schnapps."

"Girl, no one should ever drink peach schnapps."

We returned to Lula's car and drove to Cluck-in-a-Bucket. I got the value meal with fries, and Lula got everything else on the menu.

"How can you eat all that food?" I asked her. "It's not even a meal for you. It's a snack."

"I got a high metabolism. And I gotta keep my strength up in case we get into some dangerous situation. For instance, you need money, and one way you could get it is for us to snag Antwan and haul his butt back to jail. I wouldn't want to do that on a empty stomach."

"We didn't have a whole lot of success at snagging him last time."

"Yeah, but we got the advantage this time. We could sneak up on him, on account of he's probably not hearing so good since you blew his ear to kingdom come. And noon is coming up. He's probably at the basketball court. Even if he don't feel like playing with just one ear I bet he still goes there. If you're part of a group like that you gotta show up no matter what or they trash-talk you."

"I don't think men do that."

"Trash-talk don't have a gender. Whoever's missing gets talked about. It's a rule."

"So if I'm not at the bonds office, you and Connie talk about me?"

"Damn straight we do. Unless Vinnie isn't there. Then we talk about *him*."

"Do you have any idea how we're going to capture Antwan with all his gang around him?"

"I got it all worked out. We go to the office and get some stuff from the storeroom. You can't imagine what's back there. I'm saying we get loaded for bear. We go out there nuclear. There's rocket launchers and some really nasty-looking automatic weapons. There's stuff in that storeroom that makes an assault rifle look like a toy."

"We can't go onto a public basketball court with a rocket launcher."

"Sure we can. People do it all the time. Don't you look at the news?"

"Think of something else."

"Okay, but that was my best idea. You've gotten real picky since you became a butcher."

"I'm not a butcher. I was *never* a butcher."

"Well, you *worked* for a butcher."

"I say we go with the original plan of watching him and waiting for him to get separated from his posse."

"I guess we could do that, but it hasn't got much bling to it."

"I don't care about bling. I want to bring him in with as little violence and bloodshed as possible."

"If that's what you want, then that's what we'll do, but you're never gonna sell movie rights that way."

"This isn't a movie."

"You got that right. If this was a movie I'd have a rocket launcher."

• • •

We hung out at the basketball court until two o'clock, when the game broke up. Antwan had sat the game out, not saying much, not moving around. His ear was covered with a gigantic white bandage. He left with Bear, walking slowly, heading toward Bear's apartment.

"Antwan looks like he got a headache," Lula said. "He should have taken more drugs. I'm sure he got access to a lot."

We crept along in the Firebird, keeping them in sight, keeping as much distance as possible.

"I don't suppose you got any bullets in your gun yet," Lula said.

"I don't like shooting people."

"Yeah, but ironic how that works out."

Bear and Antwan stepped into a fast-food burger place, and we waited a block away. Ten minutes later they came out carrying bags of food and kept walking toward Bear's apartment.

"They're going in there and eat lunch and play videogames and take a nap," Lula said. "They aren't coming out for a long time, and I gotta go potty."

"You went to the ladies' room at Cluck-in-a-Bucket."

"Yeah, but I had the extra-large-size soda, and my body processes food real fast."

"No problem. I'll get out here and watch the apartment until you get back."

"Yeah, but you're not exactly inconspicuous standing here on the corner."

"I'm fine. I'm in jeans and a T-shirt. I have a broken nose and finger. I look like everyone else."

"You look like *no one else*. You're *white*."

"I could be Hispanic."

"Not on your best day," Lula said. "Besides, this is the wrong block for Hispanic. Hispanics get killed on this block."

"So what do you suggest?"

"I think we should go shopping. There's a shoe sale at Macy's. And I might put one of them Brahmin bags on layaway."

"This was *your* idea. Remember how I needed money, and you said we should go after Antwan Brown?"

"I temporarily forgot about that while I was thinking about how fine I'd look with my new handbag."

"Maybe it's not such a bad idea to go to the mall. It's just a couple miles away from the personal products plant. You could drop me off there and go shopping while I fill out an application."

"I got a better idea. You sit in the car, and I'll run across to the burger place to tinkle." She took her Glock out of her purse and gave it to me. "If anyone tries to steal my wheel covers you have to shoot them."

TWENTY-FOUR

LULA RETURNED TO the car with a bag of food.

"They had apple pies in there," she said. "I thought it would help us pass the time if we had apple pies."

We ate our apple pies and watched the apartment building. A little after three o'clock Bear came out and walked up the street. Antwan wasn't with him.

"You got your wish," Lula said. "It looks to me like Antwan is in there all by himself."

"We don't know that," I told her. "We just know Bear isn't with him."

"Yeah, but I got a feeling. I'm having one of those psychic aura moments. I'm like that sometimes. I'm one of those people that gets out-of-body messages."

"And you think this is a good time to strike?"

Lula closed her eyes. "I see him now. It's real clear. He's all by himself, and he's tired after eating a bunch of burgers. He might even have taken a pill for his ear, and he's all like *Where am I? What's going on?* Like he's fuzzy, you see what I'm saying?"

"Uh-huh."

"So I'm thinking we gotta go for it. Go get him now when he's fuzzy."

Deep inside my brain I knew this was a bad idea, but I needed the money. I wanted to get Antwan behind me, collect my capture fee, and move forward with my life.

"Okay," I said. "Let's do it."

I had cuffs tucked into my back pocket and my stun gun in hand. Lula had a second pair of cuffs, some defense spray, and her gun, which I insisted remain in her purse.

We crept up the stairs, marched to Antwan's door, and knocked. No answer.

"You see what's going on?" Lula said. "He's too fuzzy to answer the door."

I knocked again, louder. *BANG, BANG, BANG.*

The door was wrenched open, and Antwan stood there buck naked. His Mr. Happy was *very* happy, saluting the flag and wearing a raincoat.

"What the fuck?" he asked.

"Remember us?" Lula said. "We're the bounty hunters, and we came to capture you."

"What?" Antwan said. "Speak up!"

"Bounty hunters!" Lula yelled in the direction of his good ear.

A woman wearing five-inch red satin stilettos and nothing else stomped out of the bedroom. "What's going on here?"

"Where'd you come from?" Lula said. "You weren't supposed to be here."

The woman turned on Antwan. "I told you I don't put up with this kind of shit. You gonna bang these two, then you not gonna bang Shaneeka. I got my standards. I don't do no parties, and I don't put up with my man having some fat 'ho on the side."

"Excuse me," Lula said, pitched forward. "Did you just call my friend here a fat 'ho? Because that might be a hurtful statement."

Shaneeka narrowed her eyes at Lula. "I called *you* a fat 'ho."

"Better than being a skinny 'ho," Lula said.

Shaneeka leaned forward. "Are you implying something?"

"I'm implying nothing," Lula said. "I'm *calling* you a skinny 'ho."

"Listen up, you bitches," Antwan said. "I got a headache."

"First off, I'm not your bitch," Shaneeka said. "You're *my* bitch. And second, you're in big trouble. You've got some explaining to do, you little worm."

"Shaneeka, honey," Antwan said.

"Don't you 'honey' me neither," Shaneeka said. She whirled around and stomped back into the bedroom.

Antwan looked down at himself. Mr. Happy wasn't all that happy anymore, and the raincoat was wrinkled.

Lula clapped a cuff on him while he was considering the state of the raincoat. "Not that it's any of my business, but I think you could do better than her," Lula said to Antwan. "She's got a attitude, and I think she might be unstable."

Shaneeka marched out of the bedroom and she had a gun in her hand. "I heard that, and you better take your hands off my man. He isn't much, but he's *mine*."

"Don't get your panties in a bunch," Lula said. "You can have him after he gets out of jail in ten or twenty years."

Shaneeka squeezed off a shot and took out a lamp.

Everyone froze for a beat.

"Shit," Antwan said. "The bitch is gonna kill me. She can't shoot for snot."

Lula and I jumped to the door and took off down the stairs. We could hear Antwan and Shaneeka yelling at each other back in the apartment, and another gunshot, but we didn't stop running until we were in Lula's car.

Lula peeled away from the curb and raced to the corner.

"That didn't correspond to my vision," Lula said. "I must have been getting a vision ahead of time. Like it was a vision going on tomorrow." She stopped for a light and looked over at me. "Any more of those pies left in the bag?"

• • •

Lula parked at the corner of Fifteenth and Freeman, and we watched four boys who looked to be nine or ten years old tossing a football in the middle of the street halfway down the Freeman block.

"I'm going to ask them about Kevin," Lula said.

The kids stopped playing when we approached.

"I'm looking for a giraffe," Lula said. "I lost him, and I heard he was here in the neighborhood. Any of you kids see a giraffe?"

"What does he look like?" one of the kids asked.

"He looks like a giraffe," Lula said. "Have you seen him?"

"Maybe, but how do I know it's yours?"

"You're not supposed to be saying anything," a second kid said to the first. "I'm telling Mom on you."

"Where's your momma at?" Lula asked.

The kid pointed to one of the row houses. "Second floor."

I followed Lula into the house and to the second floor, and waited while she knocked.

A woman answered, with a toddler hanging on to her leg and another under her arm. "Yes?"

"I'm looking for my lost giraffe," Lula said. "I don't suppose you've seen him. He's about eighteen feet tall, and he's got spots on him."

"I don't know anything about that," the woman said. "And you should leave it alone. Go get a new giraffe."

"They don't have any more at the pet store," Lula said. "It's not like giraffes grow on trees."

The woman closed and locked the door.

"I think she knows something about Kevin," Lula said to me. "I think there's a conspiracy here."

"A conspiracy to hide a giraffe?"

"How else do you explain it? It's not normal to have a giraffe running around a neighborhood and nobody's seen it. I say these people are all conspiring to hide a giraffe."

TWENTY-FIVE

LULA'S PHONE RANG just as we reached the Firebird. It was Connie.

"She wants me to bring food," Lula said, plugging the key into the ignition. "It's been a real busy day and she couldn't get out to get lunch."

We stopped at Cluck-in-a-Bucket and got a super-sized Clucky Salad with Spicy Clucky Nuggets. There was a disclaimer on the box of nuggets saying they were processed in China.

"Isn't that special," Lula said. "These nuggets started out with a chicken in Maryland, went to China, and now here they are in Trenton. It's like a combination of the Travel Channel and the Food Network all in one."

Connie was waiting at the door when we rolled in.

"I'm so hungry I could gnaw my own arm off," she said.

"We got you the salad and the nuggets like you wanted," Lula said. "And they even gave us extra packets of sauces. There's soy sauce, and ranch dressing, and special sauce. I don't know what the special sauce is made of. The lettering's real small so it's hard to read. It might be antibiotic in case you get sick from the chicken."

"Where's Vinnie?" I asked Connie. "Is he still in hiding from Harry?"

"Vinnie had to go downtown to bond out Randy Berger. Turns out he was caught with a truckload of hijacked hooch."

Randy Berger was in jail! That meant his garage was unguarded. "When did Vinnie leave?"

"A couple minutes ago."

"Quick," I said to Lula. "Get bolt cutters."

Ten minutes later Lula and I were parked in the alley behind Berger's Bits, at work with the bolt cutters on the garage padlock. The lock snapped off and we rolled the door back enough to squeeze under.

"Holy crap!" Lula said. "Will you look at this! I feel faint."

I'd been hoping to find evidence that Randy was the old lady killer. What I found was more evidence that he was hijacking trucks. The garage was filled with boxes stacked floor to ceiling. A large percentage of the boxes contained computers. And there was a corner devoted to boxes stamped "Brahmin."

"I died and I'm in heaven," Lula said, caressing one of the Brahmin boxes. "I don't even know what bag's in here, and I love it already."

"This is all stolen merchandise," I told her. "You don't need a Brahmin bag this bad."

"It feels like I do."

We crawled back out, and I rolled the door down and secured it as best I could.

I ran across the alley and tried the deli's back door. It was locked, but I knew the four-digit thumb code to unlock it.

"What are we doing now?" Lula asked. "Are we going to look for Venetian blind cord in there?"

"No. I need pork chops."

"You're gonna rob a butcher shop of pork chops? Don't that sound like the pot calling the kettle black when you wouldn't let me take one of them handbags?"

"I worked two days and didn't get paid. I'm taking my paycheck in pork chops."

"I like your style. You got to admire a woman who takes her pay in pork chops."

I opened the door and the alarm went off.

"Jeez Louise," Lula said. "That's loud."

I rushed to the meat case, grabbed six pork chops, and stuffed them into a plastic bag. I dropped the pork chops into my messenger bag, and Lula and I ran out the back door and took off in the Firebird.

"Seems like you could have taken more than six," Lula said.

"I only need six. I owe them to Victor at the hardware store. It would be great if you could drive me over there."

We turned a corner and passed a cop car on its way to the deli.

"It's your friend Carl Costanza in that cop car," Lula said. "I bet by the time he leaves there's gonna be *no* pork chops left. And he'll probably help himself to a handbag, too."

When we got to Victory Hardware, Lula idled at the curb while I ran in and gave Victor his pork chops.

"I'll fry them up tonight," Victor said. "I might even share them with my lady."

. . .

Lula dropped me off at my parents' house.

"Are you sure you don't want to go out looking for Uncle Sunny one more time?" she asked me. "I got a feeling about it."

"I'm done with Uncle Sunny. I'm going to get the key to Big Blue, and I'm going to try to get to the personal products plant before the end of the day."

Lula motored off, and I went inside. I left my bag on the little table in the foyer and found my mother in the kitchen, ironing.

"Now what?" I asked her.

"It's your grandmother. Honestly, the woman is turning my hair gray. I went to the store to get soup meat, and when I got back she was gone. It's like she's fourteen years old." My mother pointed her finger at me. "It's like living with you all over again. You were impossible. Your sister was an angel, but you were always sneaking out, getting into trouble. And I blame it on Joe Morelli. He was the scourge of Trenton. He was a bad influence on you."

"He's better now," I said. "He's very responsible. He's got his own house, and a toaster."

And he eats tongue casserole, I thought. And he hoses down his nephew, and has a grandmother that makes mine look like chopped liver. True, he's still friggin' sexy. And I enjoy being with him. And I like his dog. But the whole big-Italian-family-cooking-tongue thing was giving me stomach cramps.

I went to the kitchen drawer where the extra keys were kept but couldn't find the key to the Buick.

"That's what I'm telling you," my mother said. "Your grandmother has the Buick."

"She doesn't have a license."

"She's a lunatic. She's going to get arrested and sent to jail. I'll have to visit her in prison. Do you have any idea what the neighbors will say? I won't be able to shop at Giovichinni's."

"Where did she go?"

"I don't know. She had a date. Big secret."

"With Gordon?"

"I don't think so. She said Gordon was a dud, and she had someone new on the hook. This morning there was a single sunflower on the doorstep, and it had your grandmother's name on it. You mark my words, she's fooling around with a married man. It's that Internet. She's on it all the time. I went upstairs and looked, and her laptop is missing from her room."

My heart did a painful contraction and a chill ripped through me.

"I'm sure she's fine," I said to my mom. "I'm going to use the bathroom, and I'll call someone for a ride."

I didn't need to use the bathroom. I needed to see my grandmother's room, and I didn't want to alarm my mother. She was already ironing. More bad news and she'd be chugging whiskey.

I went upstairs and looked through Grandma's bedroom. My mother was right about the computer. It was missing. Grandma had a small desk in her room. I rifled the drawers but found nothing. No names or addresses scribbled anywhere. She didn't have a cellphone. The single sunflower was in a bud vase on the desk. I looked through her dresser and under the bed. Nothing. I called Ranger and asked him to pick me up and track down the Buick.

"Who's picking you up?" my mother asked when I came back to the kitchen.

"Ranger."

My mother's eyes flicked to the cabinet where she kept the whiskey.

"What?" I asked. "Now what?"

"Morelli has turned into a nice boy, but now you have this Ranger. What kind of a person only wears black?"

"It's easy for him. Everything matches."

"I hear things about him. It's like he's Batman."

"He's not Batman. He's just a guy who owns a security agency."

"Why don't you call Joseph for a ride?"

"He's working."

I gave my mom a kiss on the cheek and promised I'd call if I heard from Grandma. I grabbed my messenger bag and went outside to wait for Ranger.

Five minutes later he rolled to a stop in his Porsche 911 Turbo. I slid in and thought there was some truth to what my mother had said. He was Batman without the rubber suit.

"What's up?" he asked.

"I'm worried about Grandma. I think she might be with the Dumpster killer."

• • •

The Buick had been left in a small parking lot attached to a 7-Eleven on Broad Street. Ranger and I got out of the Porsche and went to the car. It was unlocked. Empty inside. No bodies. No blood. No Venetian blind cord or cryptic messages.

"Where do we go from here?" I asked Ranger.

"Do you have suspects?"

"Randy Berger just got out of jail, and I helped burn down his apartment, so I think he's off the list. Hard to believe it could be Victor, but he did say he might have a lady friend in for pork chops."

"Then let's visit Victor."

"He owns Victory Hardware, but I have no idea where he lives."

Ranger made a phone call, and moments later he had an address.

"He lives over the store," he said. "He owns the building."

We were there in a matter of minutes. The store was still open, so we stopped in there first.

"Howdy," Snoot said to me, looking Ranger over. "I see you brought Batman with you."

"I'm looking for Victor."

"He's upstairs. He's got a big night planned."

"How do I get upstairs?" I asked Snoot.

"There's a door on the street, next to the store. There's a buzzer, but it don't always work."

We went outside and rang the buzzer. No response.

"Okay, Batman," I said to Ranger. "Do your thing."

Ranger took a slim jim from a pocket in his cargo pants and opened the door. We stepped inside and I yelled for Victor.

Victor appeared at the top of the stairs. "Did you come for pork chops?"

"No. I came to ask a question."

"Well, come on up. The missus and me are having a cocktail."

"You have a missus?"

"Don't everybody got a missus?"

We climbed the stairs and stepped into Victor's living room.

"This here's the missus," Victor said, arm around a woman who looked like Victor with a tan. She had a cigarette hanging out of her mouth and a martini in her hand.

"Was real nice of you to give Victor those chops," she said to me. "We got plenty if you want to join us with your fella."

"Thanks," I said, "but we have plans. I just wanted to stop by and say hello."

"Okay, then," Victor said. "Stop around anytime."

Ranger was smiling when we got to the sidewalk.

"What's with the smile?" I asked him. "I don't see you smile a lot."

"I liked them."

Here's the thing about the men in my life. They're smarter than I am, and they have a profound sense of humanity that I can only see from a distance. They work in the gutter, exposed to all the insanity and violence that human beings are capable of exhibiting, but they aren't destroyed or overwhelmed by it. They hunt down men who have done terrible things, but they see this as an aberration and not as the norm. And they recognize good people when they see them.

"Any more suspects?" Ranger asked. "Do we need to look at the man who took your grandmother to the viewing?"

"Gordon Krutch. My mom didn't think Grandma was with him, and I think he would need an accomplice, but he's definitely on the suspects list."

Ranger got the address and we drove across town to an apartment building by the DMV offices. We parked and took the elevator to the third floor. The building was very Practical Pig. Sturdy construction. Neatly maintained. Nothing fancy. We rang the bell to Krutch's apartment, and Krutch answered with his left arm in a plaster cast.

"What happened?" I asked him.

"I was picking Myra Flekman up to take her to her doctor's

visit this morning, and I tripped over the curb and broke my arm." He stared at my nose and grimaced. "What happened to *you*?"

"I fell down the stairs." It was easier than explaining how I'd hit myself in the nose with a gun barrel. "I was looking for Grandma, but I guess you haven't seen her today."

"No. I spent most of the day in the emergency room."

We returned to Ranger's car, and Ranger called his monitoring station.

"The Buick hasn't been moved," he told me. "It's still parked in the lot."

"Grandma left in the middle of the afternoon, so she's not going to Bingo, and she's not going to a funeral home viewing."

"What about her female friends? Have you called any of them?"

"My mom might have tried some close friends. I'll go back to the house and make some calls. I don't think there's any more you can do. Thanks for driving me around."

Ranger put the Porsche in gear and pulled into traffic. "I'll continue to monitor the Buick, and I'll have my men watch for your grandmother when they're on patrol. And I'll have your SUV dropped off at your parents' house."

TWENTY-SIX

MY FATHER WAS in his chair watching television when I walked in. My mother was setting the table for dinner. She set a place for Grandma even though Grandma wasn't there. And she set a place for me.

"Did you call any of Grandma's women friends?" I asked my mother.

"I called Betty Farnsworth and Loretta Best. She's been friendly with them lately. I didn't want to make a big deal of this and call half the Burg when for all I know your grandmother could be shopping at the mall."

I helped my mom get the food to the table, all of us trying to maintain some normalcy, trying to push aside the feeling that something was very wrong. My mom was aided in this effort by a large tumbler of whiskey. My dad took solace in gravy. I had nothing. On the outside I think I looked pretty good, but on the inside I was panicked.

I put my napkin on my lap and went through the motions of putting food on my plate. She's probably fine, I told myself, but in my gut I didn't believe it. My gut told me she was in danger, and it was partially my fault. I should have caught this guy by now. I should have been smarter and worked harder.

I was staring at my food, pushing it around, when my phone rang. I didn't recognize the number, but I recognized the voice. It was Grandma.

"Where are you?" Grandma asked. "Can you talk? I don't want your mother to know I'm talking to you."

"I'm at the dinner table."

"Well, I'm in a pickle. I need a ride."

I excused myself from the table and went to the kitchen.

"Are you okay?" I asked Grandma.

"Sure I'm okay. Why wouldn't I be okay?"

"There's a lunatic out there who's killing women and throwing them in Dumpsters. We were worried about you. We didn't know where you were."

"I'm at Sixteenth Street. I don't know the number, but there's a wine shop on the ground floor and I'm on the second floor."

"Are you alone?"

"I'm with Uncle Sunny. Only he's dead. Don't tell your mother. One minute he was singing 'My Way' and the next thing he was dead."

"Omigod, did someone kill him?"

"I guess you might say *I* killed him. He was sort of in the throes of passion when he keeled over."

I gave a gurgle of laughter, more out of horror than humor. "Did you dial 911?"

"Not yet. I was waiting for him to get normal, but I don't think it's going to happen."

"Normal?"

"Yeah, let's just say he was stiff way before rigor mortis set in."

"Are you sure he's . . . you know?"

"Got a boner?"

"No! Dead."

"Yep. He's dead all right."

"Don't move. I'll be right there."

"Grandma's fine," I said to my mother on my way through the dining room. "I'm going to pick her up."

"Take your father," my mother said.

"Not necessary. He hasn't finished eating."

My father picked his head up. "What? Did I miss something?"

I grabbed my messenger bag and ran out to the new loaner SUV that was parked at the curb.

I called Lula from the road. "I found Sunny," I said. "He's on Sixteenth Street. I might need help. Are you home?"

"Yeah. You want me to meet you?"

"I'll pick you up on my way across town."

Once a felon dies and is in the hands of the coroner, the paperwork is staggering, and it takes forever to get the bail bond released. If I could manage to get Sunny to the police station, claiming he died on the way, the whole process would be simplified.

Lula was waiting for me in front of her apartment house. "I see you got a new car," she said, buckling herself in. "It looks like another Rangeman car. You ever wonder where all these new cars come from?"

"I try not to think about it."

"How'd you come to find Uncle Sunny?"

"Grandma found him. And that's another thing I don't want to think about."

I parked in front of the wine shop, and Lula and I took the stairs to the second floor. Grandma had the door open when we reached the landing.

"I was looking out the window, and I saw you park," she said. "Snazzy new car. I bet it belongs to Ranger."

We stepped into the apartment and closed and locked the door behind us. Sunny was stretched out on the floor, covered by a white sheet.

"Is that what I think it is sticking up like a tent pole?" Lula asked.

"It won't go down," Grandma said. "I even tried bending it. I was gonna try smashing it with a fry pan, but it seemed disrespectful of the dead."

"Yeah, the dead don't like that," Lula said. "How'd he get in this condition?"

"Well, we started out at the movies," Grandma said, "and then we came here to his bachelor pad for some action."

Lula and I looked around the bachelor pad. Red velvet couch. White sheepskin rug. King-size bed with a red satin bedspread. Disco ball. A pole that wasn't intended to be used by firemen.

"I was stripped down to my new lavender thong, doing some real kinky things on the pole," Grandma said, "and he was singing Sinatra songs, and all of a sudden his eyes rolled back in his head, and *crash* he's dead."

"He had a bad heart," I told Grandma.

Grandma nodded. "I probably should have gone easy on him instead of using all my hot dance moves in the beginning."

"I know some working women who would kill for this setup," Lula said.

"He was a real swinger," Grandma said. "He even has champagne in the refrigerator."

"Too bad he had to croak on you," Lula said.

"Tell me about it. I finally think I've got a live one, and he turns out to be another dead one."

"How could you go out on a date with him?" I asked Grandma. "He was wanted for murder. And you knew I was after him."

"You gave up on being after him," Grandma said. "You quit being a bounty hunter. And it's not like he was ever *convicted* of murder."

"Granny's got a point," Lula said. "Everyone's innocent until proven guilty."

"I ran into him at the bakery yesterday," Grandma said, "and one thing led to another, and we emailed, and before I knew it I said I'd go to the movies with him. I didn't see any harm in going to a movie with him, but then our hormones took over, and now here he is dead as a doorknob."

"What about Rita?" Lula said. "Rita expected Sunny to marry her."

"He told me all about her," Grandma said. "He kept her around for appearances. He didn't really like her. And she wouldn't play Bingo with him. I brought my laptop so we could play Bingo if we wanted."

Lula looked down at Sunny. "What are we gonna do with him? We gonna drag his behind down the stairs, out to the car, and take him for a ride to the pokey so Vinnie gets his money back?"

"Yep," I said. "That's exactly what we're going to do."

Okay, maybe it was slightly unethical, but Sunny was dead. It didn't matter to him, but it would matter a lot to me. I'd be able to put gas in the car so I could go to the personal products plant to apply for a job.

I lifted the sheet and looked at him. He was fully dressed in a three-button knit shirt and slacks. This would make things a lot easier.

"I guess you were the only one in your undies," Lula said to Grandma.

"He was crooning, and I was stripping," Grandma said. "I would rather have had some disco, but I made do with Sinatra."

We pulled Sunny up and got him into a chair. He didn't look too bad. A little pale, but his eyes were open, and he looked sort of alert.

"We'll get him by the armpits," I said to Lula. "That way if someone sees us take him out it'll look like he's still sort of alive."

I looked down at his feet. He was wearing red socks but no shoes. "Where are his shoes?"

"He kicked them off over by the bed," Grandma said.

I went to the bed to get his shoes, and I almost stepped on a brand-new package of Venetian blind cord that was on the floor, next to the nightstand. I felt my eyes go wide, and my heart skipped a couple beats. "Holy shit."

"Now what?" Lula asked.

I held the package of cord up. "Venetian blind cord."

"He said that was in case we wanted to play *spanky spanky* or *bad boys and good girls,*" Grandma said.

"The Dumpster killer strangled all the women with Venetian blind cord," I told Grandma.

"I didn't know that," Grandma said. "They didn't say anything about that on television."

Lula looked over at Sunny. "Do you think he's the killer? It wouldn't be much of a stretch for him, being that he probably kills people all the time business-wise."

"Hard to believe," Grandma said. "He's so gallant. And look how cute he is in his red socks."

The bachelor pad was a floor-through efficiency consisting of one large loft-type room and bath. Windows looked out at the street and also at the alley. A shadow passed by an alley-side window.

"It's Kevin!" Lula said. "I bet he knows I'm here. I'll be right back."

And she ran out the rear door and down the rear stairs.

"Now what?" Grandma asked.

"Now we get Sunny to the car without her. I'm not waiting."

"Are you going to put his shoes on him?"

Dead people aren't on my favorite-things list. I could drag Sunny's body down the stairs if I really had to, but putting shoes on him was at a whole other creep level.

"Do you think it's necessary?" I asked Grandma.

"Maybe not. It's not like we have to worry about his feet getting cold."

The lock tumbled on the front door, the door opened, and Shorty and Moe stepped in.

"What the heck?" Moe said.

I was holding the Venetian blind cord in my hand, Sunny was looking a little droopy in the chair, and Grandma did a little finger wave to Moe.

"You aren't supposed to be here," Moe said to me.

It was starting to fall into place. I had a bad feeling Moe and Shorty were here to pick up Grandma's dead body and prepare it for a Dumpster burial.

"We were just leaving," I told Moe. "Grandma needed a ride home."

"Oh yeah? What have you got in your hand?"

I looked at the cord. "Sex toy?"

Moe slid a glance at Sunny. "What's wrong with Sunny? He doesn't look good."

"He's dead," Grandma said.

Shorty took a closer look. "Hey!" he yelled at Sunny. No reaction. Shorty poked him. Still no reaction. "Yep, he's dead all right," Shorty said.

Moe was looking disgusted. "Perfect. We come to do a simple cleanup, and we end up with this."

"Don't let us stop you," I said, grabbing Grandma's hand, yanking her toward the front door. "We'll be on our way."

"You'll be going nowhere," Moe said, pointing his gun at me. "You know too much. You've been trouble from the start. Always sticking your nose in where it don't belong. And nothing ever goes right with you. Everyone else dies when we drop them off the bridge, but not you. You have to have some hotshot Batman rescue you."

"I might have made it on my own," I said.

"You would have dropped like a rock to the bottom of the river without him," Moe said.

"What are we going to do with Sunny?" Shorty asked.

"Sunny can wait," Moe said. "We need to take care of these two first."

"Are you gonna pop them here?"

"No. It'll make a mess, and I don't feel like cleaning up a mess. I told Liz I'd be home to watch a movie tonight. She downloaded something with that DiCaprio weenie in it."

"He's pretty good."

"He wasn't in any of the *Godfather* movies."

"You got me on that one."

"We'll take them to the construction site," Moe said. "We already got a thing going there."

"A thing?" I asked.

"Yeah, we're having a party."

"I like parties," Grandma said.

I didn't think this sounded like a good party. And I wasn't excited about visiting a construction site. Lula was out there somewhere communing with Kevin. If I could get Lula's attention I would have help. She could call in the Marines, or at the very least she could shoot someone, which hopefully wouldn't be me or Grandma.

"Call Fitz," Moe said to Shorty. "He's working a late-night gig a couple blocks away. Tell him we need a short pour."

Moe walked Grandma and me down the backstairs and into the alley while Shorty called Fitz. The alley was deserted and in deep shadow. No sign of Lula.

"We're going to the building across from the social club," Moe said. "Sunny's been renovating it. Get walking."

"I don't think so," I said.

"Yeah, I don't want to go there either," Grandma said.

"You want me to shoot them?" Shorty asked.

"No. You don't know who's watching here. Remember the trouble Sunny got into because he was filmed running over some a-hole."

"Damn cellphone cameras," Shorty said. "There's no privacy anymore."

Moe poked Grandma with the barrel of his gun. "Move."

"Make me," Grandma said.

"All I want is to get home to watch a dopey movie with my wife," Moe said. "Could you try to cooperate?"

Grandma squinched her eyes together and opened her mouth to scream, and Shorty rushed at her and tagged her with his stun gun. Grandma squeaked and crumpled to the ground. I took a step toward Grandma, and Shorty pointed his stun gun at me.

"Stay," Shorty said.

"She's old and fragile," I said. "She could be hurt."

"First off, she doesn't look too fragile to me. And second, that's the least of her problems," Shorty said.

Moe waved his gun at me. "We're going two houses down to where the construction Dumpster is sitting. I don't want to make a scene out here, but I will if I have to. I can shoot you and drag you, or you can walk."

Shorty looked down at Grandma. "What about her?"

"You zapped her, so you get to drag her."

"I got a bad back. Why don't we get Bobby over here?"

"It'll take too long. Just suck it up and drag the old lady to the Dumpster."

Shorty got Grandma by the ankles. "I'm gonna remember this. I'm making a list. I'm tired of always being the one to drag people. I dragged Paul Mooney. And he wasn't no lightweight. I dragged him all the way to the river when we found out we didn't bring shovels to bury him."

Moe cracked a smile. "That was pretty funny."

Shorty smiled too. "We should write a book."

I watched Shorty drag Grandma down the alley, and I was so angry I could barely breathe. I didn't find any of this funny. I wanted to rip these two guys apart with my bare hands.

We got to the building that was under renovation, Moe tapped a security code into a door lock, and the door clicked open. Grandma was twitching and mumbling and trying to stand.

"Get her up and get her inside," Moe said to me.

I helped Grandma stand and maneuvered her inside. We were in a small back hall that was lit by a single overhead light. An open doorway led down to the basement.

"The party's downstairs," Moe said.

My rage was draining away, getting replaced by gut-clenching dread. The best-case scenario was that they'd lock us in the basement and Lula would have a chance to rescue us. I didn't want to think about the worst-case scenario.

The basement was dark and damp, lit by overhead bare bulbs dangling from sockets attached to wires. I carefully helped Grandma negotiate the construction-grade wood stairs. She was still wobbly, and I could feel her hand shaking in mine. A furnace and two water heaters were on a far wall. Rolls of fiberglass insulation were stacked by the water heaters. The floor was packed dirt, and the dirt smell was cloying. There was a door by the furnace. It was heavy wood with a large padlock attached.

"Over there," Moe said, motioning to the door.

I wanted this to be a closet or a storeroom, someplace where they would stash us until the time was more convenient for them to kill us. If I had enough time, someone would find me. Unfortunately it wouldn't be Ranger. The messenger bag, with my cellphone and Ranger's tracking gizmo, was back in Sunny's bachelor pad.

Moe opened the padlock and pushed Grandma and me into a room that was about ten by fourteen. The floor was poured concrete. The ceiling was unfinished, with exposed pipes and electrical wires running between wood beams. There was one small window high on the wall. It had been painted black.

"Fitz is here," Shorty said. "He just texted me."

"Okay, ladies," Moe said. "Make yourselves comfy. We have to help Fitz."

The door closed and locked, and we were in total darkness. Not a shred of light.

"I'm sort of scared," Grandma said. "And I think I wet myself when they electrocuted me."

I was scared too. I wanted to believe Lula was looking for us and had called in help, but I wasn't convinced. I could hear a truck rumbling in the alley. Men were talking. I thought I recognized Moe's voice. There were scraping sounds at the window, and the window opened. A shaft of light filtered in from the open window and drew my attention to something embedded in the cement floor. It was a tuft of platinum hair. Four feet away from the tuft of hair, like a small island in a sea of rock-hard cement, I found what I feared was the pointy toe to Rita Raguzzi's red patent-leather stilettos. I felt the chill originate at my heart and rush through me to all other parts.

A metal trough was shoved through the window, and wet cement began pouring into the room. I pulled Grandma against the far wall and tried to unscramble my thoughts and calm myself. The door was locked. I couldn't reach the window. I watched the cement creep toward us, and I wondered how long it would take for the cement to fill the room. We had some time, right? They'd need a lot of cement. They might even need to get a second truck.

The cement reached our feet and then the entire floor was covered. There was no longer any trace of Rita. The tuft of hair and the red shoes were covered in wet cement.

"This is a bitch," Grandma said. "I have one of them top-of-the-line caskets put on layaway at the funeral parlor. This is *not* the way I wanted to go out. Even if they find us and chip me out, it'll be closed casket, and you know how I hate that."

The cement was pouring in, and my heart was pounding in my chest. It was above my ankles, and then it was almost to my knees. And suddenly it stopped. The trough got pulled away, and Moe stuck his head into the open window and looked around.

"This is good," he said. "Tell Fitz he can get back to his job."

I heard engine sounds, heard the barrel of the cement mixer churning cement, and then I heard the truck leave.

Moe stuck his head through the window again. "This is what we call shooting fish in a barrel," he said.

He leaned in a little farther, with his gun in his hand, and before he could aim there was a scream from somewhere in the alley. The scream was followed by a gunshot that sounded like it came out of a cannon.

Moe yelped and pitched forward. I slogged across the room, grabbed his arm, and used my weight to pull him through the window. He fell on top of me into the wet cement, and we rolled around until Grandma got hold of the gun and fired off a shot.

I was head-to-toe cement, but I managed to get to my feet. Moe was still down, holding his leg, with Grandma training the gun on him. Her hand was shaking, but her eyes were narrowed and steady.

"I'm feeling mean as a snake," she said to Moe. "And I'd love to have an excuse to shoot you, so go ahead and make a move."

Lula looked in through the window. "Holy horse pucky," she said. "What the heck?"

Red lights were flashing in the alley. Men's voices. The rumble of a big truck. Blue strobes flashing with the red lights.

"What's going on out there?" Grandma asked.

"I saw Moe and Shorty standing there with the cement truck and I got worried, so I called everyone. We got police and a fire truck and EMTs and Ranger and half of Rangeman here."

There was scraping at the door and the door opened, oozing

cement onto the dirt floor. Morelli was the first one I saw. He grabbed me and pulled me out of the room. Cement was dropping off me in globs, but the cement on my legs was beginning to harden. He half dragged, half carried me up the stairs and out into the alley. A uniform followed with Grandma.

Morelli yelled for water, and an instant later Grandma and I were getting hosed down. Grandma went to the hospital to get checked out, but I refused. I shucked my clothes behind the fire truck and wrapped myself in a blanket. When I came out from behind the truck I saw that Moe had been hosed down and cuffed, and his leg was bandaged. Shorty was strapped to a backboard.

"What happened to Shorty?" I asked Lula.

"He got trampled," Lula said. "I guess the lights from the police cars scared Kevin out of his hidey-hole, and he came barreling down the alley and ran right over Shorty."

"Sunny is dead," I told Morelli. "Heart attack." I gave him the short version of the night and asked him to retrieve my messenger bag. I would have gotten it for myself, but I didn't think my legs could get me up the stairs. I felt like I was still encased in cement.

Morelli gave me a kiss on the forehead and handed me over to Ranger to take home.

"I need to stay and do my cop thing," Morelli said, "but I'll stop around when I'm done."

. . .

It was past midnight when Morelli let himself into my apartment.

"You did it, Sherlock," he said. "You solved the Dumpster murders."

I was on the couch, watching television, waiting for him. "It was an accident. Dumb luck."

"Better to be lucky than smart," Morelli said, slouching onto the couch next to me, handing me the messenger bag I'd left in Sunny's bachelor pad. "Shiller already questioned Moe and Shorty, and they blabbed everything. Turns out there were old ladies getting left in Dumpsters for the last ten years, over a three-state area. It was how Sunny got his kicks."

"Sick."

"Yeah. Big-time. There's a name for it. 'Granny grabbers.' They're like chubby chasers, but they like to do old ladies. Sunny added his own twist to it by killing them after."

"What was the connection? Was it Bingo? Was it the Senior Center?"

"There was no connection. They were all random encounters. Sunny was out and about, going to wakes, shopping in bakeries and grocery stores, meeting women in the casinos in Atlantic City. He was Mr. Charm, and after a couple phone calls there was a date."

"And a death."

"Yeah, and a death," Morelli said. "And a sunflower. We should have picked up on it. We should have made the Sunny and sunflower connection. Are you hungry?"

"Starved."

He went to the kitchen and came back with a bag of food and a six-pack. He gave me a beer, and he pulled Philly cheesesteaks out of the bag.

"Somehow Moe mysteriously got shot just before we arrived. I don't suppose you have any ideas on this?"

"Nope."

That was a fib. I only knew of one gun that made that much noise, and I suspect it was in Lula's purse. She was lucky she didn't have a broken nose.

"I've got more news for you," Morelli said. "Sunny was renovating the brownstone, hoping to turn it into an exclusive restaurant that served big game and endangered species. For an extra charge you could even kill the animal yourself. I don't exactly know how he was going to pull that one off. Take everyone out in the alley and give them an assault rifle, I guess. Anyway, the giraffe got delivered early and managed to escape. Eventually they gave up trying to catch it, since the restaurant wasn't done anyway."

"Why didn't anyone report the giraffe to the police or the Humane Society?"

"Sunny controlled those blocks. The giraffe cost him lots of money. He didn't want someone snatching it out from under him. Some of the people on those blocks hoped they'd get a job at the restaurant. They didn't want to jeopardize it."

"So what's going to happen to the giraffe now?"

"There's going to be a giraffe roundup tomorrow at noon.

Some people are coming in from one of the wildlife agencies. If they can get the giraffe unharmed, there's a zoo in Naples, Florida, that'll take it." Morelli tipped his head back and closed his eyes. "I'm beat. This was a long day. I'm so tired I don't even care about the bag from the drugstore."

"That's a first," I said. "I've never known you to be that tired."

Morelli grinned. "I could probably force myself to rise to the occasion if you were desperate for me."

TWENTY-SEVEN

LULA AND I stood behind a barricade at Fifteenth and Freeman that had been set up to keep people from encroaching on the giraffe roundup area. A bunch of residents of the Fifteenth and Sixteenth blocks were standing there with us. They'd been feeding and cleaning up after Kevin while he'd clip-clopped down the back alleys, evading capture by Sunny's henchmen.

"I'm happy Kevin's gonna get a good home in Florida," Lula said. "I might even visit him at the zoo. I talked to some of the giraffe wranglers, and they said they wouldn't have any problems catching Kevin. It turns out he was born in Philadelphia, and he's used to people, unless they chase him in a car and try to shoot him with a dart gun."

"Did they know how Sunny got Kevin?"

"He stole him. Hijacked his truck. The zoo in Philadelphia

had too many man giraffes, so they were already sending Kevin to that zoo in Florida. Kevin escaped when Sunny's idiots tried to get him out of his truck."

We could hear activity in the alley. It sounded like it was a block away. The wranglers had been working since early this morning, fencing off streets, shrinking the capture area. The goal was to get Kevin into his truck without sedation. One of the wranglers was tweeting and transmitting pictures, so we were all on our smartphones. A cheer went up from the alley, and a moment later the picture came through of Kevin in his truck.

"This here's a happy ending," Lula said. "It worked out for everyone. Kevin's going to a good home. Old ladies don't have to worry about getting choked and thrown into a Dumpster no more. It even worked out for Sunny on account of he died doing his favorite thing."

I looked at Lula. She'd gotten dressed up for Kevin's capture. She was wearing a tasteful beige suit and matching pumps. And she had a Brahmin handbag on her arm. It was a pretty bag with the classic Brahmin leather pattern and the little Brahmin gold tag.

"That's a real Brahmin, isn't it?" I asked her.

"You bet your ass," Lula said. "I bought this suit to go with it. I didn't want anyone getting the wrong idea about my character when I carry this bag. This here's a elegant bag, and I don't want to distract from it by someone trying to get a look up my hoo-ha 'cause my skirt might have rode up."

"You stole that Brahmin, didn't you? You went back to Randy Berger's garage and lifted a handbag."

"I didn't steal it," Lula said. "I rescued it. It was being held hostage there."

The giraffe truck slowly rolled down the street, and when it turned the corner we could see Kevin looking out at us. With its twenty-foot-high canvas roof, the truck looked like a horse trailer on steroids. Everyone waved at Kevin, and he disappeared from view, on his way to the Naples Zoo.

Lula and I returned to Ranger's loaner SUV, and just for the heck of it I drove past the basketball court. It was almost two o'clock and the court was deserted except for a lone figure sitting on a bench, looking into the court through the chain link fence. It was Antwan. He still had the big white bandage on his ear, and now he had an additional bandage on his foot. Crutches rested against the bench.

"I bet Shaneeka shot him in the foot," Lula said.

I idled on the side of the road, and we watched Antwan for a couple minutes.

"He looks depressed," Lula said. "You think we should go cheer him up?"

"We're supposed to be trying to arrest him."

"Yeah, but that was back when you were a bounty hunter. Of course, if you wanted to be a bounty hunter again then we could slap some cuffs on him. We don't have to worry about him running away from us. And we don't have to worry about him hearing us creep up on him. And he probably don't even have a gun, since I still have his gun."

"Kind of takes all the fun out of it," I said.

Lula nodded. "I see what you're saying."

We watched him for another minute.

"Oh hell," I said. "Let's take him down."

"Freakin' A!" Lula said. "My girl's back in the saddle."

Don't miss the explosive new FOX AND O'HARE series from #1 *New York Times* bestselling author

JANET EVANOVICH
and LEE GOLDBERG!

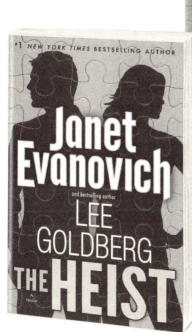

THE HEIST
In hardcover, eBook, and audio
Coming in paperback 2/25/14

THE CHASE
In hardcover and eBook 2/25/14

Turn the page to start reading THE HEIST . . .

KATE O'HARE'S FAVORITE outfit was her blue windbreaker with the letters FBI written in yellow on the back, worn over a basic black T-shirt and matching black Kevlar vest. The ensemble went well with everything, particularly when paired with jeans and accessorized with a Glock. Thirty-three-year-old Special Agent O'Hare didn't like feeling exposed and unarmed, especially on the job. That all but ruled her out for undercover work. Fine by her. She preferred a hard-charging style of law enforcement, which was exactly what she was practicing on that 96 degree winter afternoon in Las Vegas when she marched into the St. Cosmas Medical Center in her favorite outfit with a dozen similarly dressed agents behind her.

While the other agents fanned out to seal every exit in the building, Kate pushed past the security guards in the lobby and made her way like a guided missile to the first-floor office of Rufus Stott, the chief administrator of the hospital. She blew past Stott's stunned assistant without even acknowledging her existence and burst into Stott's office. The startled Stott yelped and nearly toppled out of his chrome-and-mesh ergonomic chair. He was a chubby, bottom-heavy little guy who looked like a turnip that some bored wizard had tapped with a magic wand and turned into a fifty-five-year-old bureaucrat. He had a spray tan, tortoiseshell glasses, and crotch wrinkles in his tan slacks. His hand was over his heart, and he was gasping for air.

"Don't shoot," he finally managed.

"I'm not going to shoot," Kate said. "I don't even have my gun drawn. Do you need water, or something? Are you okay?"

"No, I'm not okay," Stott said. "You just scared the bejeezus out of me. Who are you? What do you want?"

"I'm Special Agent Kate O'Hare, FBI." She slapped a piece of paper down on his desk. "This is a warrant giving us full access to your concierge wing."

"We don't have a concierge wing," Stott said.

Kate leaned in close, locking her intense blue eyes on him. "Six obscenely wealthy and desperate patients flew in today from all over the country. They were picked up from McCarran airport by limos and brought here. Upon arrival at your private concierge wing, they each wired one million dollars to St. Cosmas's offshore bank account and immediately jumped to the top of an organ waiting list."

"You can't be serious," Stott said. "We don't have any offshore bank accounts and we certainly can't afford to rent limos. We're teetering on bankruptcy."

"That's why you're conducting off-the-books transplant surgeries using illegally acquired organs that you bought on the black market. We know those patients are here and being prepped for surgery right now. We will lock this building down and search every single room and broom closet if we have to."

"Be my guest," Stott said, and handed the warrant back to her. "We aren't doing any transplant surgeries, and we don't have a concierge wing. We don't even have a gift shop."

Stott no longer looked scared, and he didn't look like he was lying. Not good signs, Kate thought. He should be in a cold sweat by now. He should be phoning his lawyer.

Eighteen hours earlier, Kate had been at her desk in L.A., tracking scattered intel on known associates of a wanted felon, when she'd stumbled on chatter about a certain financially strapped Las Vegas hospital offering organ transplants to the highest bidder. She dug deeper and discovered that the patients were already en route to Vegas for their surgeries, so she dropped everything and organized a rush operation.

"Take a look at this," she said, showing Stott a photo on her iPhone.

It was a medium close-up of a man about her age wearing

a loose-fitting polo shirt, soft and faded from years of use. His brown hair was windblown. His face was alight with a boyish grin that brought out the laugh lines at the corners of his brown eyes.

"Do you know this man?" she asked.

"Sure I do," Stott replied. "That's Cliff Clavin, the engineer handling the asbestos removal from our old building."

Kate felt a dull ache in her stomach, and it wasn't from the Jack in the Box sausage-and-egg sandwich she'd had for break-fast. Her gut, flat and toned despite her terrible eating habits, was where her anxieties and her instincts resided and liked to communicate with her in a language of cramps, pains, queasi-ness, and general malaise.

"Cliff Clavin is a character on the television show *Cheers*," she said.

"Yeah, crazy coincidence, right?"

"What old building?" she asked him.

He turned to the window and pointed at a five-story building on the other side of the parking lot. "That one."

The building was an architectural artifact from the swinging '60s with its lava rock accents, big tinted windows, and a lobby portico topped with white gravel.

"That was the original hospital," Stott said. "We moved out of there a year ago. We built this new one to handle the demand for beds that we wrongly anticipated would come from . . ."

Kate wasn't listening. She was already running out the door. The instant she saw the other building, she knew exactly how she and those six wealthy patients had been duped. The man in the photo on her iPhone wasn't Cliff Clavin, and he wasn't an engineer. He was Nicolas Fox, the man she'd been pursuing when she'd stumbled on the organ transplant scheme.

Fox was an international con man and thief, known for the sheer audacity of his high-risk swindles and heists and for the obvious joy he took in pulling them off. No matter how big his scores were, and he'd had some huge ones, he kept going back for more.

Kate had made it her mission at the FBI to nail him. She'd

come close two years ago, when she'd discovered Nick's plot to plunder a venture capitalist's twentieth-story Chicago penthouse of all his cash and jewels at the same time that the self-proclaimed "King of Hostile Takeovers" was getting married in the living room.

It was a ballsy move, and pure Nick Fox. To pull it off, he somehow got himself hired as the wedding planner and brought in a motley crew of thieves as the caterers. When Kate crashed the wedding with a strike team, Nick's crew scattered like cockroaches when the lights go on, and Nick parachuted off the top of the building.

Choppers were called in, streets were closed, roadblocks were set up, and buildings were searched, but Nick slipped away. When Kate finally straggled into her hotel room at dawn, there was a bottle of champagne and a bouquet of roses waiting for her. All from Nick. And charged to her room, of course. The whole time she'd been hunting for Nick, he'd been relaxing in her room, watching pay-per-view movies, ordering room service, and helping himself to the Toblerones in her minibar. He'd even stolen the towels on his way out.

The bastard is having way too much fun at my expense, Kate thought as she bolted through the hospital lobby, out the door past two surprised agents, and charged across the parking lot.

When she reached the cyclone fence around the old hospital building, she was sweating and her heart was pounding so hard she could almost hear it. She drew her gun and slowly approached the entrance to the lobby. As she got closer, she saw a red carpet and a sign that had been obscured in the shadows of the alcove under the portico. The sign read:

Welcome to the St. Cosmas Concierge Medical Center.
Please excuse our dust as we remodel to give you more
privacy, luxury, and state-of-the art care.

Hugging the lava rock walls she made her way to the door, yanked it open, and spun into the open space in a firing stance. But there was no one to aim at. Kate faced an elegantly furnished lobby decked out with contemporary leather furniture, travertine floors, and lush plants. On the wall behind the empty reception desk were photos of the surgical staff. She looked at the photos and immediately recognized two of the faces. One of them belonged to Nick Fox, a stethoscope around his neck, exuding doctorly strength and confidence. The other one was her, with a dopey, drunken smile on her face. Her picture had been lifted, cropped, and photoshopped from the bridal party pictures taken years ago that were now on her sister Megan's Facebook page. "Dr. William Scholl" was written in bronze letters under Nick's photo, "Dr. Eunice Huffnagle" under hers.

Okay, so where was the "surgical staff" now? she asked herself. And what about the six rich patients who'd come from far and wide for organ transplants?

Kate headed for the double doors that were located to one side of the reception desk. She pushed them open and stepped into a foyer, ready to fire. But once again, there was no one there. Directly in front of her were three more sets of double doors. One was marked "Operating Room #1," the second "Post-Op #1," and the third "Pre-Op." An elevator was to her left. A stairwell door was to her right.

She eased open the door to the operating room and found a fully decked out surgical suite that took its design cues from an Apple Store. Everything was sleek and white. All the equipment gleamed like new cars on a showroom floor.

She closed the door and peeked into the post-op room. There was the standard hospital bed, the IV stand, and the usual monitoring devices, but the similarities to any other hospital room ended there. The room was luxuriously appointed with fancy French furniture, ornate shelves filled with leather-bound books, a flat-screen TV, and a wet bar stocked with assorted spirits.

He's smart, she thought. Posing as an asbestos removal company was the perfect cover for Nick's scam. It ensured that everyone at the hospital kept their distance from the old building while Nick and his crew were actually creating an elaborate set and staging their con.

Finally, she went to the pre-op room. The door opened onto a long ward with an abandoned nurses station and several curtained-off areas behind it. She stepped inside and cautiously slid open the first curtain. An unconscious middle-aged man in a hospital gown was stretched out on a gurney and hooked up to an IV drip. Kate checked his pulse. It was strong.

She made her way through the ward, yanking open curtains as she passed. All six of the men who'd come in that day from the airport were there, each of them sound asleep and, she assumed, a million dollars poorer.

The windows in the building vibrated, and she heard the unmistakable *thwap-thwap-thwap* of helicopter blades above her. Nick Fox was on the roof, she thought. *Again!*

She ran out of the room and to the stairwell, climbing the four flights as fast as she could, which was remarkably speedy for a woman whose most frequent dinner companions were Colonel Sanders, Long John Silver, Ronald McDonald, and the Five Guys.

Kate burst onto the roof ready to fire and saw a blue Las Vegas Aerial Tours chopper on the helipad, its side door open, several "doctors" and "nurses" inside.

Nick Fox was not among them. He stood casually midway between her and the helicopter with his hands in his pockets, the wind created by the chopper blades whipping at his hair and flaring his white lab coat like a superhero's cape.

Kate had created the man of her dreams when she was twelve, and she'd hung on to the image. The dream man had soft brown hair, intelligent brown eyes, and a boyish grin. He was six feet tall with a slim agile body. He was smart and sexy and playful. So it was with terrible irony that over the course of the last couple years it dawned on Kate that Nick Fox was the living embodiment of her dream man.

"Dr. Scholl?" Kate yelled over the chopper noise. "Really?"

"It's a very respected name in medicine," Nick yelled back. "Glad to see you're wearing sensible shoes."

Nick knew she always wore Dr. Scholl's gels in her black Nikes. It was one of the many things he'd learned about her over the last couple years. Most of what he'd learned intrigued him. Some of it was downright scary. The scary part was offset by a physical attraction to her that he couldn't explain.

Her brown hair was pulled back in a ponytail, and her flawless skin had a slight sheen from her dash across the parking lot and up the stairs. Sexy, but he suspected the fantasy the sheen inspired was better than the reality. She was the job. Probably wore Kevlar to bed. End of story. Still, he did enjoy playing with her. He liked her big blue eyes, cute little nose, slim athletic body, and her earnest dedication to making the world a more law-abiding place. It made his dedication to crime much more interesting.

"You're under arrest," she shouted.

"How do you figure that?"

"Because I've got my gun on you, and I'm a great shot." She took a step toward him.

He took a step back. "I'm sure you are, but you're not going to shoot me."

"Frankly, I'm surprised I haven't shot you already." She took another step toward him.

"Still upset about those Toblerones?" He took another step back.

"Take one more step, and I'll put you down."

"You can't," he said.

"I can shoot the testicles off an eagle from a hundred yards."

"Eagles don't have testicles."

"I may suck when it comes to metaphors, but my aim is excellent."

"You can't shoot me because I am unarmed and not presenting any threat of physical harm."

"I can shoot the helicopter."

305

"And risk it crashing into a hospital full of children? I don't think so."

"The hospital isn't full of children."

"You're missing the point." He stole a glance down at the parking lot to see scores of FBI agents rushing toward the building and then looked back at her to see she'd advanced two steps closer. "It was really good seeing you again, Kate."

"It's Special Agent O'Hare to you," she said. "And you're not going anywhere."

He smiled and bolted for the chopper.

"Damn!" She holstered her gun and charged after him.

Even after racing up four flights of stairs she was still faster than he was, and she took a lot of pleasure in that. She was quickly closing the distance between them, and she was pretty certain that she'd get her hands on him before he could climb inside the chopper.

Apparently the pilot and Nick's crew shared her optimism, because the chopper suddenly lifted up and out over the edge of the building, leaving their ringleader behind. Nick picked up speed and kept running as if the rooftop extended another hundred yards instead of just a few more feet.

With mounting horror, Kate realized what he intended to do. He was going to jump. And this time, he didn't have a parachute.

"Don't!" she yelled, launching herself at him, hoping to take him down with a flying tackle before he could make a suicidal mistake. Too late. She missed him by inches, and hit the concrete hard just as Nick leapt off the building toward the hovering chopper. Her heart stopped for a couple beats while he was in midair, and resumed beating when he latched on to the helicopter's landing skid. He held on with one hand, blew her a kiss, and the chopper veered off toward the Las Vegas Strip.

Within seconds of his escape, Kate was on the radio, trying to get a police chopper into the air and patrol cars on the ground to chase Nick's helicopter. Kate knew it was a waste of time and effort, but she went through the motions anyway.

There were half a dozen identical Las Vegas Aerial Tours choppers in the airspace above the Strip, and even though only one of them had a man hanging from a landing skid, by the time she got the word out Nick's helicopter had disappeared. It didn't help that in all the excitement, she'd failed to note the chopper's tail number and had nothing to give to air traffic controllers so they could track its transponder. Not that it would have mattered. The helicopter wasn't actually part of the tour company's fleet. It had just been painted to appear as if it was.

Kate sped straight from the hospital back to the room she'd booked at Circus Circus, the least expensive hotel on the Strip. She approached her door quietly, one hand on her holstered gun. She slipped her key card into the lock and slowly eased open the door, hoping Nick Fox had been arrogant enough to pull the same stunt twice, hoping to catch him in the act.

No such luck. The room was empty and smelled like a freshly chlorinated swimming pool. She sat down on the edge of the bed and sighed. Not her best day. And she knew she'd catch a lot of crap for letting Nick get away instead of finding an excuse to shoot him. She certainly had plenty of them, the latest one being the picture of "Dr. Eunice Huffnagle" that she'd managed to snatch off the wall before anyone noticed it.

Kate stared glumly at her reflection in the mirror and started to take off her Kevlar vest. And that's when she noticed it. She didn't believe it at first, and had to look over her shoulder to confirm it, but there it was: a Toblerone bar on her pillow.

ABOUT THE AUTHOR

JANET EVANOVICH is the #1 *New York Times* bestselling author of the Stephanie Plum series, the Fox and O'Hare series, the Lizzy and Diesel series, twelve romance novels, the Alexandra Barnaby novels and Trouble Maker graphic novel, and *How I Write: Secrets of a Bestselling Author.*

Visit Janet Evanovich's website at
www.evanovich.com
Facebook/JanetEvanovich
or write her at
PO Box 2829
Naples, FL 34106

ABOUT THE TYPE

This book was set in Minion, a 1990 Adobe Originals typeface by Robert Slimbach (b. 1956). Minion is inspired by classical, old-style typefaces of the late Renaissance, a period of elegant, beautiful, and highly readable type designs. Created primarily for text setting, Minion combines the aesthetic and functional qualities that make text type highly readable with the versatility of digital technology.